To Hunter,
All my Best!

Also by Susanne L. Lambdin

A Dead Hearts Novel Series:
Morbid Hearts
Forsaken Hearts
Vengeful Hearts

Coming soon:
Defiant Hearts
Immortals Hearts

FORSAKEN HEARTS

FORSAKEN HEARTS

A DEAD HEARTS NOVEL

by

Susanne L. Lambdin

WYVERN'S PEAK PUBLISHING
An imprint of The McGannon Group, Ltd. Co.

Published by Wyvern's Peak Publishing
An imprint of The McGannon Group, Ltd. Co., 2014

Forsaken Hearts
by Suzanne L. Lambdin

Copyright © Suzanne L. Lambdin, 2014

Forsaken Hearts / by Suzanne L. Lambdin – 1st ed.

Summary: Cadence and her team struggle to build a new camp, and a new life, at Seven Falls. As the Kaiser's threatening presence draws near, they begin to question each other, and what it means to be human.

1 2 3 4 5 6 7 8 9

ISBN-13: 978-0-9861458-1-0

All rights reserved. No part of this publication may be reproduced, distributed, or transmitted in any form or by any means, including photocopying, recording, or other electronic or mechanical methods, without the prior written permission of the publisher, except in the case of brief quotations embodied in critical reviews and certain other noncommercial uses permitted by copyright law.

This book is a work of fiction. Names, characters, places, and incidents are either the product of the authors' imagination or are used fictitiously, and any resemblance to actual persons, living or dead, business establishments, events, or locales is entirely coincidental.

Except in the United States of America, this book is sold subject to the condition that is shall not, by way of trade or otherwise, be lent, re-sold, hired out, or otherwise circulated without the publisher's prior consent in any form of binding or cover other than that in which it is published and without a similar condition including this condition being imposed on the subsequent purchaser.

www.DeadHeartsNovel.com

www.WyvernsPeak.com

Dedicated to my loving parents.

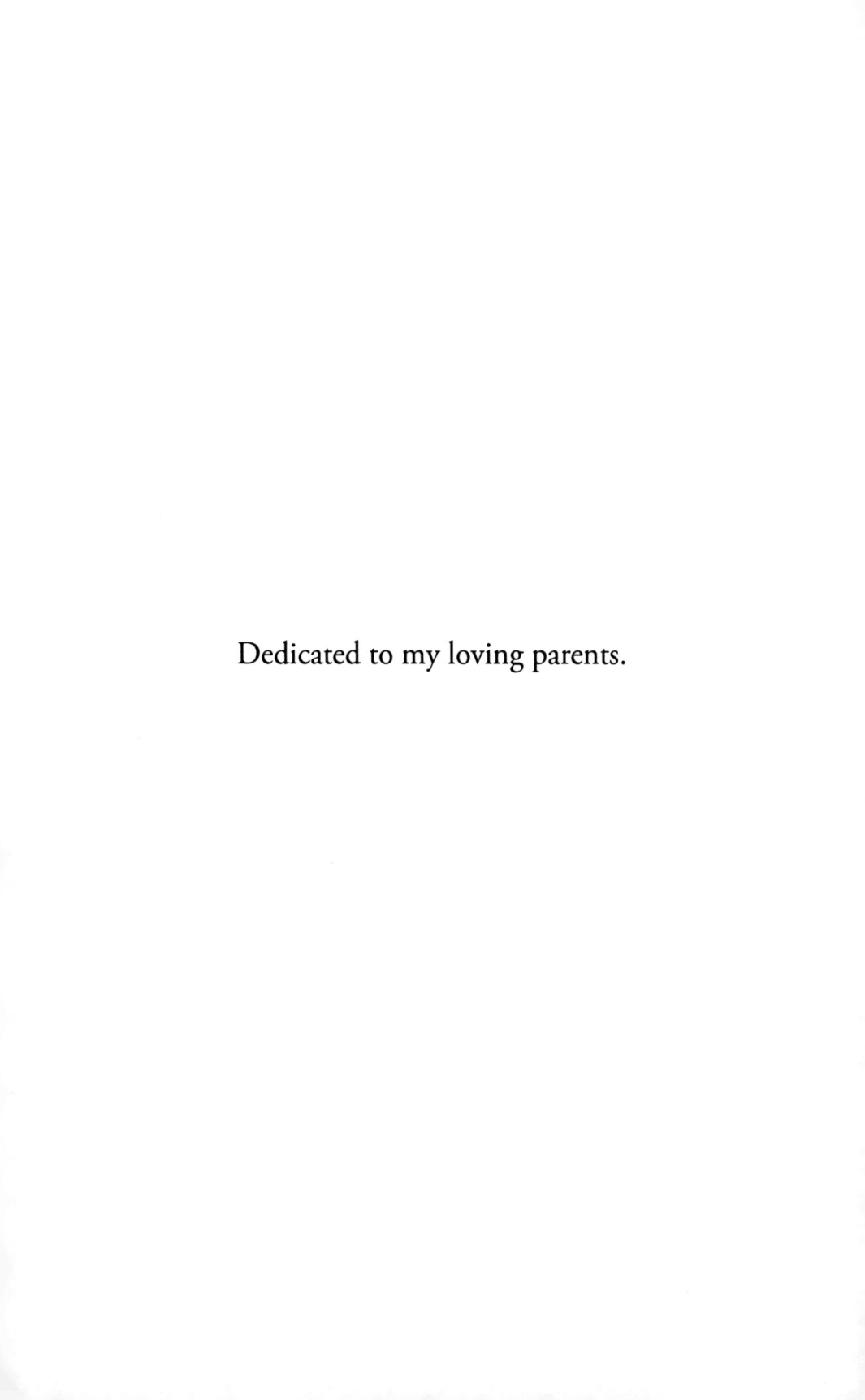

Chapter One

Sunlight gave new life to gray clouds, illuminating the ruins of Colorado Springs. Abandoned by the living, houses stood vacant. Fractured storefronts had long surrendered to the elements, while grocery stores and pharmacies were ravaged by survivors and street-wise entrepreneurs. The living dead lingered on playgrounds and at emergency room entrances, ambling with hungry faces and desperate intentions.

ATVs hauling the Fighting Tigers sped through an obstacle course of rusting cars and debris, while a Jeep outfitted with a spiked grill and steel-caged rear was in friendly pursuit. Leading the mission, Thor demonstrated the precision of a professional stunt driver.

"Those nuts are getting too far ahead," shouted Thor, frowning.

"Not many dead heads on the road," said Dragon from the passenger seat, eyes peeled for wandering zombies. Two swords in his grip, he was always ready. "Turn left at the next corner. We're meeting Rafe near the radio station. I'm anxious to see what's going on at the Academy. From what the Dark Angels are saying, it's not good."

"The city reeks of death," said Whisper. Wrapped in his dirty blue parka, the team sniper huddled in the back of the Jeep, clutching his rifle.

Freeborn sat next to Whisper as the team rolled into historic Colorado Springs. The Tigers went too far, missing the turn. Thor navigated the remains of battle that littered the road. He was so busy staring at rotting bodies that he narrowly missed an enormous blast hole in the asphalt. He jerked the wheel hard right.

"Watch out!" shouted Freeborn.

Unable to compensate in time, Thor caught the tail end of an abandoned vehicle, spinning the Jeep full circle, jarring Freeborn and Whisper. A loud pop brought them to a sudden halt. The front tire whined with the rapid loss of air. Furious at his own stupidity, Thor jumped out to survey the damage. Twisted metal extended from the hissing tire.

"Everyone out," shouted Thor. "Dragon, get the others back here. It's going to take me a few minutes to change the tire."

Thor wasted no time removing the spare and saw Freeborn had already detached the jack and lug wrench. Whisper kept a lookout for zombies.

"Need a hand?" said Freeborn.

"I've got it," Thor muttered. "When Dragon gets back, fan out and search for Rafe. This is a reconnaissance mission. We're not waiting."

Freeborn lifted her shotgun. "Make it fast," she said. "I don't like the look of this place. It's too quiet."

Dragon ran back toward the Jeep. Moments later, three ATVs zipped around the corner and pulled next to him. Blaze climbed off, looking like a tribal warrior with her purple hair and piercings. She reached for her crossbow and joined Smack and Dodger, laughing at Thor. Thor tossed the flat to the side and slid the spare into place.

"Can we shop while we wait for Rafe?" asked Smack. At twelve, she was more mascot than soldier, though her skills as a marksman were reputable.

Thor grumbled. "No."

"Let's get to work," Freeborn said. "You three cover the road. Dragon and I will take the sidewalk. Rafe's got ten minutes. We made too much noise coming into town. No doubt we've attracted zombies."

"Hold up," said Dragon, catching Freeborn by the arm. "I know you're anxious to get out of here, but we go by the book on this one. Stay with Thor and Whisper. I'll go with Blaze."

The teams split up and moved out.

"Look, a stray dog," said Smack, pausing to point at a dried corpse. "Know why we never see any dogs in town? They all get eaten by zombies. I'd give anything to have a puppy."

A snort came from Dodger. "We can't take a puppy back. You don't want to wake up one morning and find a zombie dog eating your face. Stop staring at it. It's disgusting."

"You're disgusting." Smack popped an angry pink bubble.

As Thor began to tighten the first lug nut, the street erupted with heavy gunfire. Dragon and Blaze fired against a group of walkers, while Whisper started dropping targets. With sweat stinging his eyes, Thor focused on the last three lugs.

"Hurry up, Thor," shouted Freeborn. Her shotgun boomed at a limping corpse.

Snarling, groaning zombies filed out of vacant buildings and around every corner. A mass of skeletal faces dragging blackened innards crept closer, while others moved slower with missing or crippled limbs. Open cavities raging with rot and maggots lurched for the taste of flesh. One by one, mangled bodies dropped as Whisper and Freeborn provided a steady barrage of gunfire.

"Finished!" shouted Thor. He tossed the jack and wrench in the back and grabbed his Glock from the dashboard, leveling three headshots against approaching monsters.

Blaze didn't flinch to drop a child zombie as Dragon appeared near a tank, holding goo-dripping swords. Blaze and Freeborn cut through a group of zombies tumbling out from a pharmacy storefront.

Thor slid behind the wheel and punched the accelerator, crushing a female zombie as he spun the Jeep around and looked for the others. He found Dragon in the middle of the street, spinning and slicing heads like it was a dance. Whisper offered support, but advancing ghouls replaced the fallen at an alarming rate.

Fifty yards out, Dodger and Smack ran out of a store, followed by too many zombies to count. Dodger's coat was splattered in blood, while Smack sported a new backpack. Thor wanted to throttle both of them. Dangerous and irresponsible, they had been scavenging amidst the fighting.

Thor sped to them, and Blaze, Dodger, and Smack scrambled over the cage and took defensive positions. Freeborn continued to advance toward Dragon, blasting shots into the oncoming horde.

"Dragon! Freeborn!" Thor shouted, honking at them.

Dragon took a final swipe and they ran toward the vehicle. Freeborn waited until he was in before climbing into the back. As she swung a leg over the side of the cage, an engorged zombie shambled up and caught her leg. He dragged her, screaming, toward the hungry crowd. Thor put a bullet in the zombie's head.

"Get in!" shouted the Viking.

Freeborn scrambled back to the Jeep, jumped in and landed hard on her back. Bodies fell beneath the wheels as the vehicle accelerated through the throng. Everyone fired on the grim assembly, clearing a path as they drove.

"Fire trucks are blocking the road ahead," shouted Dodger, sticking his head between the two front seats. "We're surrounded by dead heads!"

Dragon pushed him back. There was no way around the blockade and turning around was not an option. Dragon leaned toward Thor, pointing upward. A figure in a long coat ran along the rooftops.

"It's not Rafe," said Dragon, firm. "Don't stop!"

"Do something," Smack screamed. "We're going to crash!"

Thor eyed a way out and took a sharp turn through a cluttered alley, accelerating and ramming his way through.

"Turn left here," said Dragon. "I know a shortcut to the Academy."

He peered over his shoulder and surveyed the group, eyes lingering on Freeborn. "Is everyone okay? No injuries?"

"We're fine," she answered for her teammates.

Dragon glanced at Thor. "We're in good shape, buddy, ease up. Zombies don't run."

Thor felt his pulse slow as he drove onto Interstate 25. Abandoned vehicles were missing from the far right lane, indicating the Dark Angels had been busy. A few zombies reached for them as they sped past. Ammunition was precious, so they spared the creatures.

"Rafe is dead meat," Blaze shouted into the wind. "I'm going to pull his fangs out with pliers when he shows up! He's undependable and worthless, as always."

"As always," chimed Smack.

"That was too close," said Thor. "Was that guy on the roof Shadowguard?"

Dragon nodded. "Had to be. Moved too fast to be a human. Tandor said there might be Shadowguard in town." He glanced at Thor, a lopsided grin on his face. "I know you don't like vamps, but Tandor and Picasso are all right. I'm glad to have the Dark Angels on our side. If they're right and the Kaiser means to stay here, we need to find out his intent."

"Why pick the Air Force Academy?" Smack chomped on her gum. "I thought it fell first when the Scourge broke out? Can't be much left. I'd have gone to the Hilton."

Blaze leaned forward. "Military resources, dummy. Speaking of, I still don't think Highbrow's dad is coming."

"I'm not ready to give up on the armed forces yet," said Dragon. "I have to believe help is still coming. We just have to hold on until they get here."

Blaze pointed to a section of the interstate damaged in battle. Exploded tanks were pulled off of to the side, along with overturned Army transports and light-duty trucks. The mangled remains of a jet were jutting from a crater in the ground.

Thor shook his head. "I don't trust the Dark Angels. For all we know, they could be working for the Kaiser. Who is this guy anyway? Where did he come from? Of all the places a guy could pick, why come here? There's nothing special about Colorado, apart from mountains."

"Only a half dozen bases and airports," Dragon explained. "That adds up to transportation and supplies. A lot of natural resources, too. That Shadowguard could have killed us, but he didn't. My guess is the Kaiser is assessing our strengths and weaknesses. Turn in about a quarter mile. Still got gas?"

Thor nodded. "Half a tank. We're okay."

Thor exited the interstate, following the marked road to the Air Force Academy. Gutted buildings lined the street, and the evidence of a battle between academy cadets and National Guard against the zombies remained from a year ago. Locals flocked to the Academy hoping to escape the Scourge on transport planes, never making it. Those who heeded the radio moved to Pike's Peak, dug in, and fought back.

"There's activity ahead," said Dragon. "Pull off at the next road and park behind one of those buildings. We need to get a closer look."

Thor drove behind the ruins of an apartment complex. The team climbed out and entered, taking the stairs to the top floor. A fire had gutted the building and charred bodies filled the stairwell. Thor reached a door, leading the team onto the roof. Everyone crouched, staring at the new Citadel while Freeborn guarded. Whisper peered through his scope at vampires in the main courtyard.

"Okay, maybe the Dark Angels were right," said Thor, squinting through his binoculars. "The Kaiser is here to stay. There are trucks and uniformed vamps unloading supplies. Maybe three hundred soldiers in the yard. Most of the buildings have windows covered with plastic, and it looks like they're renovating. I see furniture being unloaded, which means they're moving in, and I think that's a Black Hawk."

Dragon took the binoculars, turning grim. "I see prisoners." He handed the binoculars to Blaze. "I thought about coming here to school, but didn't have the grades to make the cut. Rafe was on the football team, and lived in one of those burned-out buildings. It would have been helpful if he'd joined us, since he knows his way around the campus." He paused. "Did anyone bring a camera?"

"Yep," said Blaze, passing the binoculars back to Thor. "Smack's got it."

Smack reached into her new backpack and revealed a digital camera still in its box, along with sealed batteries. She handed it to Blaze, who tore it open, loaded the camera, and started clicking. Smack and Dodger exchanged a high five.

"The Dark Angels know the Kaiser." Dragon watched vehicles driving the main road. "They met up with him in Denver months ago. Tandor said the Kaiser started rounding up survivors and turning them. Tandor and Picasso didn't like what was going on so they left with Rose and the others. If the Kaiser is moving this fast, he has help. We need to get back."

The team kept an eye on the Citadel as they drove back to the interstate. Thor knew everyone was relieved they made it in and out without incident. Scouting the Citadel without Rafe was risky but the new information made it worthwhile.

They had known for some time they were no longer alone, but this confirmed the Kaiser was up to something. Whatever it was, it was big.

Chapter Two

Once inside the gate to camp, Whisper hopped out and started walking toward the cabins. He liked walking back to camp. It gave him time to clear his thoughts.

Blaze shouldered her crossbow and hurried after Whisper. It was only a mile, and Blaze figured a walk would do them both good.

Tall green pines, cedars, aspens and spruce trees flanked their path. Whisper pressed on, oblivious to the surrounding beauty. Blaze, however, loved autumn and how the leaves of every tree emulated fire and clay. She caught up with Whisper at the Pillars of Hercules. The two large rock formations rose over a thousand feet, casting a shadow over the road where it narrowed.

"It's so pretty and peaceful here," Blaze said. "Such a contrast from the city and the Citadel. I wonder how long we have before the Shadowguard come for us."

Blaze looked up as an eagle cried overhead. She watched the enormous bird circle, bumping into Whisper. He grabbed her arm and pulled her aside, as Freeborn sped by in a golf cart, leaving a cloud of dust.

"Freeborn just has to be the first one to tell Cadence what we found," said Blaze. "I already know how Cadence is going to react. We'll be on patrol, no time for fun. She'll probably make us move camp since it's not safe here anymore. I guess it never really was. We've been fooling ourselves thinking we could create a normal life."

Thor raced by on a motorcycle, and Dragon followed in another golf cart with Smack and Dodger in the backseat. Dodger waved at Blaze as Star drove past them in the next cart.

"Aren't you worried, Whisper?" she continued. "There are only thirty Dark Angels. It doesn't make any sense for them to be at the Broadmoor instead of here. Vampires are stronger and faster. You've seen what Rafe can do. He said he'd meet us, and then doesn't show up. I don't like the guy, but I'm worried about him."

Whisper remained silent as usual. Blaze fell into step beside him and refrained from talking further until they arrived at camp. RVs bordered either side of the road, merging with several older buildings. The tourist office served as a barracks by the officers and adults in the Freedom Army. She watched the soldiers drilling in the courtyard, under the supervision of Destry. He had been a lieutenant under the former captain, but was demoted by Cadence, being ineffective in his duties. In his forties, Destry was ancient, and a total idiot as far as Blaze was concerned.

Camp rules changed significantly when Cadence took command. Everyone in camp served as a member of the Freedom Army, no matter their age. Those under twelve weren't allowed to carry guns, but they were treated with respect. Micah, one of the Dark Angels, found a warehouse full of blue berets and brought them to camp and gave one to each person. Most of the patrols continued wearing their old caps with team patches, but it was a nice gesture.

The RVs and campers that were brought in by the Dark Angels weeks earlier improved living conditions. The Kaiser had restored electricity, not only in Colorado Springs, but in Denver and other areas where vampires were living, so life had a few more comforts than the months previous. Since Rafe introduced the Dark Angels to the camp, the vampires brought in supplies, helped build the barricade and guard towers, and turned a storage building into an infirmary.

In what was likely a political move to make friends with the Freedom Army, the Dark Angels elected Rafe as their new leader. Rose assumed second-in-command, though was still regarded as the true leader of the Dark Angels. She stepped into the role of camp doctor and set up a small lab in the infirmary. It was primitive but she began working toward creating a cure for the virus.

Seven Falls had been a huge tourist attraction at one time. The tourist cabin served as headquarters, with a store and mess hall. Music blared from inside and Blaze heard laughter. The Dark Angels found some pinball machines and pool tables in a storage shed and brought them in. Most people hung out at the mess hall in their spare time, but Blaze knew all that was about to change.

She caught Whisper's arm. "Let's not go in. Everyone knows we were on patrol today, and they'll start asking questions. Come back to the RV. I'll make you a sandwich."

Whisper turned toward her. His warm, honey-brown eyes held her gaze and Blaze felt her heart skip a beat. "Why would you do that?"

She blushed and tugged at a strand of her purple-tipped hair. "I don't know," she said, shuffling her feet. "I thought it might be nice to hang out together." She paused and took a deep breath. "Don't you think?"

She was nervous waiting for his response. Her reputation around camp was not the best, but Blaze wanted to put her past behind her. She wanted to know what it felt like to have a real relationship with someone before she died. Whisper brought out a softness in her, and she felt unsure of herself around him. That scared her, but she wanted a closer connection.

"What kind of sandwich?" inquired Whisper.

"Venison. And we have barbeque sauce."

"Fine."

Blaze smiled all the way back to the Tiger's RV. Their new home nestled by the creek, under the shade of tall oak trees. A cement table with two benches sat alongside the big trailer, and ATVs were parked outside. Whisper sat down and lit up a cigarette, offering one to Blaze. She declined.

"I'll go fix lunch," said Blaze. "We have fresh tomatoes, thanks to our vampire friends. Did you hear Betsy is trying to get another garden growing? She has a greenhouse now, thanks to Micah. That's one vamp with a green thumb."

"You talk a lot when you get nervous," said Whisper. "So talk."

Blaze bit her bottom lip. Whisper focused on her.

"Things sucked before the Scourge," he continued, surprising her. He took a long drag, and tossed the cigarette aside. "Now the Kaiser is here, things really suck. Don't take it personally that I don't talk very much. It's my way. I do like you, Blaze. Always have."

Blaze shivered when he got up and took a step toward her. "We're Tigers. I'm on your team," she said, butterflies launching a full-scale assault in her stomach. "Why wouldn't you like me? I've saved your life a dozen times."

"Wrong." Whisper chuckled. "I've saved your life a dozen times. But I think we both know what I'm talking about. When I say I like you, I mean more."

She met his eyes, her voice tiny. "You do?"

"You're a cool chick, Blaze. You've got great style." Whisper put his hands on her shoulders, drawing in a deep breath. And then he revealed more than she ever thought he noticed. "You've got five silver rings in your right eyebrow. The sixth one fell out a week ago when we were patrolling up at Midnight Falls. Seven silver hoops in your left ear, and seven gold circlets on the right. Even your belly button is pierced." He grinned and then pointed at her neckline. "You've never taken off the bear claw necklace Freeborn made for our team."

"You never take yours off either."

Whisper stepped closer. "Your ink is the best in camp. I really like the peacock on your right hip and the kitty cat on your left foot. You have angel wings across your shoulders, but all that's only skin deep."

He slid his hand down her shoulders and took hold of her hands. "You dress like you do to be different. Getting close to people isn't your style, but you look after Smack like she's your kid sister. You hate being told to calm down, and you hate country music. You read romance novels when you think no one is watching, and you snore. It's cute." He pressed his nose against hers. "I always liked you, Blaze. You never noticed, so I kept it to myself. Guess I never thought anyone like you would ever go for someone like me."

Blaze's heart beat faster with every word. It was the most she'd ever heard Whisper speak in a single day. "Are you kidding? I thought I wasn't good enough. I keep up a wall to avoid pain. The bad temper is just an act."

"No, it's not." Whisper leaned forward and kissed her. "Sometimes love happens at the worst times."

Her violet eyes twinkled. "Don't you think I'm a little fickle, unable to make up my mind up, always playing a game? Sure you want to get involved with someone like that?"

Whisper looked at her for a long moment. Pulling one hand free from her grasp, he reached up to slide a stray hair behind her ear. "You're my girl now. I can deal."

When he kissed her again, Blaze kept her eyes open to make sure she wasn't dreaming. It was all she could do to keep from crying. He was not her first, but it was the first time she'd ever been in love.

Dragon stared at his reflection in the mirror. Having stripped off his blood soaked leather coat, his padded shirt came next. The majority of black goo was in his hair. Lifting his arms over his head, he twisted his torso from side to side. Both his arms were covered with tattoos. A green dragon snaked up his left arm, resting its spiked head on his shoulder, mouth open in a snarl. His right arm featured a red dragon with a black tongue licking across the back of his hand and curled around his index finger. He found no sign of any cuts, scratches, or bites.

"Dragon?"

He spun around to find Star entering the RV. The slender girl placed her gun belt and katana on the kitchen counter, the screen door swinging closed behind her. Dragon leveled a disapproving look her way.

"What? I live here too, you know." Star pulled her hair out of a ponytail and smoothed it out with her fingers. "Lotus is looking for you. The girls are at the mess hall and want to hear about your big adventure. Since when did you and Lotus become so chummy? Does Freeborn know Lotus has a crush on you?"

"Freeborn has more reason to be jealous of you than Lotus," Dragon said. "Give me a break. I live with five girls. Lotus is like a sister, you know that."

Star glanced in disgust at Dragon's clothes lying in a pile on the floor. "You better wear rubber gloves when you clean that black blood up, and no, you don't have any bite marks. God, you do this every time you get back from a mission."

"Then why act so surprised I made a mess?" asked Dragon, fishing in a drawer for a sweater. "Freeborn was supposed to meet me here. Have you seen her? She took off without waiting for me. I think she got spooked."

Star went into the kitchen and poured herself a glass of tea. "Am I that ugly? Be honest." He shook his head. "Then explain why no matter what, Thor treats me like I have a wart on the end of my nose. He couldn't even say hello. I waited all morning at the gate for you guys to get back." She took her tea to the couch. "I was worried."

Dragon finished dressing. "Rafe didn't show up and we barely got out of town. The place is crawling with zombies. It gets worse. The Dark Angels never said how many vampires were at the Citadel, but the Kaiser has moved in with an army. They've turned the place into a fortress and they have all the supplies they need. I wouldn't believe it if I hadn't seen it with my own eyes. I don't see how this camp can hold out much longer. We need to move up into the mountains while we still can."

Star sat forward, shocked. "What do you mean? How can that many vampires exist when there are only four Makers and Rafe is on our side?"

"While we've been hiding here, apparently the Kaiser has been busy. Everyone assumes there are only four Makers and they all live here. That isn't true. If we could get in touch with Senator Powers, maybe we could find out what's really going on."

"I saw Smack crying when she came in. I figured it was bad news."

Star set her glass on a table and went back to the kitchen. She returned with a trash bag, rubber gloves, and sanitizing spray. It didn't take her long to clean up. She tossed the bag and gloves outside and came back in, returning to her spot on the couch.

"You could say thank you."

"Thanks." Dragon said as he collapsed next to her. He took a sip from her glass. "We were followed by a member of the Shadowguard in town. I suppose the Kaiser knows we were spying on his camp. They've got helicopters and the air strip is in use."

Dragon laid his head on her shoulder, thinking about his old life. Star had saved him from his own mother. On the same day Dragon had witnessed his best friend, Hank, ripped apart by a mob of zombies, he stumbled home to find his mother had eaten their dog on the front lawn. It was hard to see the woman that had taught him everything he knew about life and martial arts reduced to a mindless monster. Star rescued him from having to make a heartbreaking decision. From that day, the girl had become his best friend.

Snapping out of it he said, "I see why you like Thor and I approve. He's a pretty amazing guy." Dragon laughed at Star's surprised look. "Thor got us out of the city with our skin on. He's a good team leader.

I'd be honored to go on any mission he leads. Give me a minute and we'll go over to HQ. I need to clean *Hebi* and *Lóng* first. I'll be quick."

"Only you would name your swords. Go on. I'll get you something to drink so you'll leave my tea alone."

Dragon laid a towel on the table before laying his swords out, taking great care in cleaning both blades. Star pulled a cold bottle of *sake* out of the fridge and placed it on the end of the table.

"I wish you'd wear gloves when you clean your swords," she said, picking up her glass. "You could cut yourself and get infected."

"I'm always careful," said Dragon. He finished polishing his weapons before he reached for the bottle of sake. "What are you waiting for? I thought you'd at least brush your hair, since Thor will be there."

Star perked up, ran to her bedroom and returned with her hair brushed and a coat of fresh lipstick. Dragon always felt Star was one of the prettiest girls in camp.

"Come on, goofy," said Dragon, leaving his swords on the table. "Maybe Thor will be in a better mood. You never know, you might get lucky tonight, China Star."

Chapter Three

Rose showered, slipped into a black leather jumpsuit, and laced up a pair of boots. Her light blue eyes were bright and alert, accentuated by her pale blonde ponytail and no makeup. She fastened a utility belt around her narrow waist, and sheathed a hunting knife in the side of her boot. With a large bag containing medical supplies in hand, she opened her door and found Lachlan waiting.

The Irishman stood over six feet and was a mass of solid muscle, crowned with red hair and a ready smile. A green and orange kilt, boots, and a dark-green wool sweater served to punctuate his statuesque physique. He never parted with the galloglass that was strapped to his back since the dark day the Scourge broke out while visiting his brother in Denver.

"Did you stand guard all day or are you coming to get me?" questioned Rose.

"Call came in on the radio. Captain Highbrow is asking for the fence to be brought in from the old camp at the Peak. He also asked where you were," Lachlan said in a lilting Irish accent. "I can't say you look like a doctor with that blade in your boot."

"I try to be prepared," said Rose, sidestepping his pry for information.

A strong smell of dust and mildew permeated the hallway of the hotel where the Dark Angels were staying. There were leaks in the roof, and many windows in the rooms were covered with boards. Dampness set thick and the entire hotel stunk.

"I wouldn't mind heading over early myself. Cadence is a very attractive young lady, and if she wasn't already taken . . ." Lachlan grinned.

The elevator door opened and Lachlan stepped aside for Rose to enter. He entered and hit the lobby button, while elevator music serenaded them. Picasso had considered turning it off, but it served everyone's amusement and broke the tension from time to time.

"Did Highbrow say Rafe took the team to the Citadel?"

Lachlan shook his head. "He just said they're still waiting for Thor's team to return. It concerns me we have not heard from him since he set up the meeting. Rafe's selection as the new leader of the Dark Angels might not have been a good idea, but I know why you put it to a vote. He's chummy with Cadence. I like it, actually. Very sly. But Rafe and Highbrow hate each other because of her. She attracts males like bees to honey."

"I guess that makes you a very big bee." Rose smiled. "Maybe I should have told Cadence and Highbrow the truth about the Kaiser. I thought it would be easier for them to hear it from Rafe. Cadence trusts Rafe, and when he volunteered to take a team to the Citadel, I let him at it. As far as those kids know, vampires only came into existence a few weeks ago. They don't know the Kaiser has been around a lot longer than we have. They need to see the extent of his growing empire."

Lachlan smiled. "I think you didn't tell Cadence and Highbrow because you were afraid they'd blame you for bringing the Shadowguard here."

The elevator groaned and rocked like a plane in turbulence as it descended.

Lachlan hit the nail on the head, of course. Rose sent Rafe to be the bearer of bad news. She knew what they would discover at the Citadel.

The Kaiser was there to stay. It would be hard for the humans to understand things were changing quickly, and not for the better.

Survivors were taken to be turned into vampires or consumed as food. She had not wanted to tell Cadence and Highbrow that bit of information either. Rafe didn't care if he was liked or not, and had no problem telling the humans what they were up against.

The elevator doors opened. Picasso and Tandor stood in the lobby.

"Good afternoon," said Picasso, adjusting his purple tie.

"Is this really necessary?" asked Rose, stepping out to meet her bodyguards. "I was planning to drive over by myself. I don't need you two going everywhere I go."

Lachlan swept past Rose and approached the two female guards standing adjacent to the glass front door. "Is everything secure out here, ladies?" asked Lachlan. "You're looking rather lax when you should be worrying about those zombies approaching. Did you not notice?"

"We're escorting you, like it or not Rose," said Tandor, walking outside. "Pallaton hasn't returned my calls."

Captain Pallaton of the Shadowguard lived a precarious life, serving the Kaiser while informing the Dark Angels. Rose trusted Pallaton. He had arranged for their escape from Denver and without his help, they would all be dead or prisoners of the Kaiser.

"I'll contact him," said Lachlan. "Micah and Ginger will come to the camp later. Don't look for me before midnight, but I'll be there when I can." He disappeared around the corner.

Rose exited the front doors with Picasso and Tandor. Several Dark Angels stood guard in the parking lot, on the hotel roof, and in room windows, waiting for the team to reach the vehicle.

"It's your turn to drive, Tandor." Picasso tossed his buddy a set of keys.

Tandor caught them and unlocked the doors with the remote. He moved fast, opening the back door for Rose. She made herself comfortable as Tandor took the wheel. Picasso entered the passenger side as zombies approached the vehicle. Rooftop snipers eliminated the festering problems.

"I love German cars," said Tandor. "It's like driving a tank, but in style."

"Rafe was a no show, commander," said Thor in a firm voice. "We went to the Citadel anyway. The Dark Angels were smart to send us. From what we saw, the Kaiser is setting up permanent camp. It's a big production. We're heavily outnumbered and under-supplied."

Thor stood in front of Cadence's desk as her eyes narrowed to study the digital photos. Cadence was dressed in civilian clothes, hair down, relaxed. Her hair was long again, hanging past her shoulders. It had grown rapidly in the past month, though she couldn't explain why. Highbrow stood beside her, uniformed and disciplined.

Thor noticed Highbrow's gear was no longer in Cadence's cabin, having heard he had moved into the barracks. He and Cadence were not getting along, but he saw no change in their behavior. They both held themselves as professional and focused, like career officers. They shared the difficulties of command and put the camp before their relationship.

"I had hoped it wasn't true." Cadence passed the camera to Highbrow. "We've got a war on our hands. The Kaiser didn't come here to make friends. All this time we've operated like we were the only survivors in the world, but that's not the case. He's turning everyone into vampires, and we're next."

"Not if we tighten security," said Highbrow. "Our patrols are good, but we need the Dark Angels to fight against the Shadowguard. It's a good thing they arrived in advance of the enemy." He scanned through a few more photos and set the camera on the desk. "I know you don't want to hear it, but Rafe may be working for the Kaiser."

Cadence glared at him, eyes firm. "Rafe isn't working for the Kaiser.

He'll show up. For now get more people to the gate, Highbrow. If the Kaiser is serious about taking over Colorado Springs, we'll have every zombie in the state at our doorstep. The Kaiser is smart. He'll have us expend our ammo and manpower killing zombies, so he doesn't have to. I'd do the same thing if I was in his shoes."

"We're sitting ducks, that's what we are," said Thor. "If that barricade doesn't hold, we'll be overrun. If it does hold, the Kaiser will just think of something else."

Highbrow threw his hands into the air. "I don't think we need to move quite yet, people. Where would we go that's safe? The Kaiser would only follow. We've spent this much time fortifying the camp, and I don't want to leave. This is our home. I say we stay here and fight back with everything we've got."

"This is the information we need, Thor." Cadence avoided Highbrow's argument. "You kept your head and completed the mission."

"My dad will come," said Highbrow. "He'll bring the Armed Forces and wipe these no good blood-suckers out of existence. I believe he'll come, now more than ever. People did survive, and if we could get word to my dad, I know he'd be here soon."

Cadence shook her head. "Sending even one Dark Angel to Florida to look for your dad isn't prudent. I need every Dark Angel here to protect this camp. They've promised protection. Let them prove it. Vampires aren't only in Colorado Springs, Highbrow. Send Picasso to Fort Carson to bring in more weapons and ammunition. I wouldn't mind having a few tanks and a helicopter of our own. In the meantime, I'll ask Luna and the werepumas to patrol the upper trails."

A voice came from a radio on Cadence's desk. *"Captain Highbrow. It's Lieutenant Sterling."*

Highbrow picked up the device and walked outside to talk in private. Thor found it odd that Highbrow wouldn't speak directly to a lower-ranking officer in the commander's presence. She didn't comment, and he seized the opportunity to lodge a complaint.

"Commander, I think you should know I didn't take the Hummer. Logan refused to give me the keys. Nomad offered a battle truck, but we're low on fuel and I didn't want to be stranded on the road. I took a Jeep and three Tigers rode ATVs." Thor continued. "We lost the ATVs in the ambush. The cage worked, but I wouldn't take the Jeep back into the city."

"Logan told me he gave you the keys. You were smart not to mention it to Highbrow. He'd toss Logan out of camp. I'd let him, but Rose says Logan has been helpful with her research. She's been testing to see if anyone here, other than me, is immune to the virus."

"I think there's a little more going on between those two."

"Don't mention that either."

Thor nodded and the door opened. Highbrow walked back in with a worried look and set the radio on the desk.

"It's just like we thought," said Highbrow. "Sterling says there are a lot of zombies gathering at the barricade. I'm going up there. I'll send Destry later to fix your shortwave radio. Rose should get here soon."

Cadence leaned over and slid the radio into Highbrow's coat pocket. She had several more mounted on the back wall. "Keep it. I want an update when you get up there. As of this moment, we're at Code 3. Send soldiers to Midnight Falls. I want patrol teams at the infirmary and Lookout Point. Coordinate the team's time schedules, and have Betsy take the kids to the tunnel. Provide her with one of the better patrols. We have to be ready for anything."

"I'll have Lieutenant Kahn coordinate the teams," said Highbrow. "The Bandits can help Betsy. Nomad and Sturgis have built a few more battle tanks out of those old armored bank cars. I'll get teams to drive along the road. The fence isn't up on the ridge yet, but we'll be able to keep it lit tonight."

Cadence nodded. "I want the Dark Angels on patrol tonight as well. Let me know the moment Rose gets here. I need to talk to her."

"Sunday sermons? Good idea or not?" Highbrow walked to the

door and picked up his rifle. "Betsy thinks the younger kids need to hear something positive to keep their spirits up. Your call, commander."

"Sounds good." Cadence offered him a rigid smile. "You've got a lot on your plate. I wish we had time to catch up. I'll be at the infirmary, if you need me. Ask Micah to build us a lab similar to what they have at the hotel and bring everything over. Tell him to bring some more RVs, too, and set up behind the infirmary. I want the Dark Angels here permanently."

"Add that to the growing list," said Highbrow, grinning. "Get something to eat, Thor. I want the Vikings standing guard at the waterfall. We're vulnerable at Midnight Falls." He saluted Cadence and hurried out the door, leaving it wide open.

A cool breeze blew through the cabin. Thor looked toward the door.

"Am I dismissed, commander?"

Cadence didn't answer. She lowered her face into her hands, her shoulders slumped, and it looked as though the fight had just left her. Thor wasn't sure, but he thought Cadence was crying. He walked over and pushed the door closed.

"You okay, Cadence?" Thor sat on an old leather couch that faced the desk. "I know it's none of my business, but is everything okay between you and Highbrow? I know he hasn't been sleeping here. He's got a lot on his mind."

"It's not Highbrow," said Cadence, lifting her head. Her eyes were bloodshot, but she wasn't crying. "We're drifting apart, but that's to be expected when running a camp this size. That's not the problem, Thor." She looked at the table. "One of the Tigers was bitten today."

"What? Who?" Thor felt his heart leap into his throat.

Cadence's voice quivered. "Freeborn."

"But she never said a thing. Does Dragon know?"

"No one knows," she said, blinking back tears. Her voice betrayed guilt. "Not even Highbrow. Freeborn made me promise I wouldn't say anything. She knows Rose has been working on an antidote, so she is waiting for her . . ." She tried to continue, but her voice cracked.

"I'm sure Rose will get here in time," Thor said, offering an empty promise.

Swearing softly, Cadence gazed up at the ceiling. "Of all people, I can't lose her. Highbrow is a huge help, but Freeborn's strength gets me through the day. What am I going to do without her?"

"No wonder I sensed tension between you two. I'm trying to think when it could've happened. We got back here about an hour ago. It doesn't take long to turn, Cadence."

"We need Rafe. He's a Maker. He saved me. I'd rather Freeborn be a vampire than a zombie. But if he doesn't get here and soon—"

The door opened. Dragon, Star, Blaze, and Whisper entered the cabin. No one looked more upset than Dragon.

"Why didn't you tell me?" demanded Dragon.

"Because Freeborn didn't want you, or anyone else, to know," said Thor, speaking on Cadence's behalf. "If you heard us talking, then you know Freeborn is at the infirmary. You better get over there, Dragon. Rose is on her way."

"There isn't a cure," shouted Dragon. "If the Kaiser had one, wouldn't he already be using it? Vampires can't feed on zombies. What's wrong with you people?" He spun and stormed out.

"Should one of us go after him?" suggested Blaze, knitting her brows together.

Whisper shook his head. "Let him be." He took her by the hand. "Come on. Smack and Dodger need to hear this from us, not someone else."

Whisper and Blaze shut the door behind them, and Thor glanced at Star. The girl looked devastated. Without thinking, he slid his arm around her shoulders.

"Come sit down. You're pale as a ghost." Thor walked Star to the couch, taking a seat next to her. She threw her arms around his neck. "Hey! It's going to be okay. Rose is coming."

"Not fast enough," said Cadence. She grabbed a pistol from her desk and marched to the door. "I'm going after Highbrow. This is something I need to say in person, not on a radio. Stay here and wait for Destry. He's supposed to fix the radio."

The moment she walked outside she began shouting, the door neglecting its duty to muffle her voice.

"What the hell are guys doing out here? This camp is on Code 3. Everyone is on guard duty. Get your guns and take your posts. Loki, I see you over there. Go get the rest of your team and come back here. The Vikings are to stand guard at the waterfall. I'll send Raven to you when I can. Move it, people!"

Thor gazed at Star. Her hazel eyes were gorgeous, and her perfume smelled like a garden of flowers and citrus. He had known for some time that she liked him. Everyone said she did. Star never talked to him, but he caught her watching him many times. He didn't resist his instinct and kissed her. Her lips were soft and warm. It would take a few minutes for Loki to get back with the remaining Vikings.

They had time.

Chapter Four

Blaze stood outside of the RV, unable to go inside and spill the news to Dodger and Smack. Whisper stood with her, finishing a cigarette.

"I can't go in there and tell them," said Blaze. "This will hit them too hard. Searching the store and finding that camera was a great idea, but they weren't following orders. Smack will blame herself, and Dodger will go into one of his silent moods. I'd rather stay out here with you and pretend it didn't happen. Is that so wrong?"

"They're probably not inside. Dodger likes to hang with the Razorbacks and play cards. Smack fishes with the Amazons. Maybe they already know."

"You don't want to face them either." Blaze felt a little better when he hugged her. "This is the worst thing that could have happened."

"No," he said, tossing his cigarette. "Don't be a chicken. If they're here, we'll pretend everything is okay."

"Okay." She nodded, resolved. "We'll play it cool until I get the nerve to tell them."

They found the RV empty. Whisper took a moment to scrub up in the kitchen, while Blaze went to the room to scour herself with baby wipes and change. When she came back out, she found Dodger and Smack seated on the couch. Whisper was in the kitchen pouring drinks.

"I told them," said Whisper. "Couldn't help it."

"Yeah," Dodger said, wiping his eyes. "Of all the times you start talking, it had to be about Freeborn. It's our fault. If we hadn't run into that store . . . she should have climbed into the Jeep."

"Poor Freeborn." Smack had already cried enough for one day. She buried her face in a pillow to muffle her shouts. "Why did anyone else have to be bitten? Why not Rafe? I hate him!"

Blaze sat between the two young Tigers. "The Dark Angels are working on a cure. When Rose gets here, she'll give it to Freeborn. She's going to be back with the team in no time." She sniffed the air. "Is that popcorn?"

"Yep," said Whisper. He set a bowl filled with hot popcorn on the table and flipped on the TV. A banner scrolled across the lower edge of the screen.

Stay tuned for the Halloween Night Death Games. Aries of Athens will be competing for the world title against a new opponent. Find out more here as details are available, only on Vampire TV! Brought to you by the Kaiser.

The banner scrolled continuous, bringing more frustration.

"Is this for real?" Blaze snapped. "This guy has to be a joke. What are the Death Games anyway?"

"It's got to be bad," whimpered Smack.

Dodger looked around for the remote. "Couldn't the Kaiser at least give us some world news? Tell us how many people are still alive? The guy is crazy."

"Let's not talk about the Kaiser." Blaze loaded a DVD in the player. She turned around, hands on her hips. "We can have popcorn and pretend fast food joints will reopen. I'd give anything for some fries."

"Move," shouted Smack, Dodger, and Whisper.

The movie started and Blaze shooed the kids off of the couch. "I want to sit next to Whisper. We're a thing now. Besides, you're both dirty."

"Yes, mom," said Dodger, muttering under his breath. He bunkered down beside Smack, who had gathered all the pillows in the room.

Blaze cuddled against Whisper, popcorn between them. The Tigers always lifted each other's spirits, warding off the misery of the world in the way only a family could.

Barging into the infirmary, Dragon spotted Logan and Raven tying Freeborn to the surgery table. Freeborn noticed him at the door and looked away, crying. Dragon's face wrenched when he heard her sob. He had never seen Freeborn cry.

Logan was nothing more than an arrogant scavenger in Dragon's opinion. He tried to hide his distaste when Logan snapped at him.

"What are you doing here? I thought the Blue Devils were guarding the door? Why did they let you in?"

Raven mimed a zipper across her lips. "Boyfriend, remember?" She glared at Logan, crossing to the fridge. The shelves were filled with assorted medicines brought in by the Dark Angels. She found what she needed and walked back to Freeborn.

"I need a break," Logan said, walking to the door. "Try not to administer the wrong pain medicine, Raven. You don't want to kill your friend." Laughing, Logan let the door slam shut behind him. The tension left the room with him.

Dragon stepped beside Freeborn, hands in his pockets.

"Hey, babe," said Dragon. "Trying to face this alone? You don't always have to act so tough. That's for me to do."

"You're not doing a very good job," Raven said, filling a syringe with the contents of a vial.

Freeborn's arms and legs were strapped tight. A large bite mark glowed an angry red on her right hand, lined with dried, black blood. Dragon didn't want to think about tomorrow or the next day. No matter what happened, he would stay with her until the end.

"I didn't want you to see me like this," cried Freeborn. "Cadence promised she wouldn't tell anyone, especially you. Now everyone will be afraid of me."

Raven let out a snort. "Duh," she said.

"You're not going to end up a zombie, so both of you knock it off," said Dragon, fighting off panic.

Freeborn wasn't fooled. She knew her chances were slim and she gave him a sad smile. Dragon regretted taking the time to clean his swords. He should have been here with her.

"I am not just anyone. I'm the guy who loves you, remember?"

Pulling up a chair, Dragon sat beside Freeborn. He leaned over and placed a hand on her arm.

"Be strong. Fight it, babe."

Freeborn turned her head, gazing at him with eyes that remained her normal shade of brown. *For now*, he thought. Needing her to know he wasn't afraid, he rose to kiss her, then sat back down.

"I love you too," said Freeborn. "I'm sorry."

"I wish you had told me when it happened. I can't imagine how hard this is on you. I'm sure Rose will get here soon. She's working on that cure. Isn't that right, Raven?"

"That's right." Raven for once pretended to be optimistic.

"We wouldn't have gone to the Citadel if I had told you. It was important we found out what's going on." Freeborn blinked rapidly. Tears escaped and Dragon brushed them away. "Did we get good pictures?"

"Yeah," he whispered. "Cadence and Highbrow have reviewed them. They're taking things extra serious now that we have an idea of what we're up against."

"I'm going to turn." Freeborn looked away. "You know it's true."

Raven held up the syringe. For a second, Dragon thought Raven would administer the cure herself.

"It's not what you think it is," Raven said. "I'm going to give Freeborn a shot of morphine. Maybe I'm not the one to make that decision, but I'm doing it anyway. It takes a while to turn, and it's painful. I don't want her to suffer needlessly." She pushed Freeborn's sleeve up and cleaned a small spot in the bed of her elbow.

Dragon gave Raven a worried look. She slid the needle into Freeborn's vein and pushed down on the applicator. Freeborn took a deep breath and let it out slow. Raven tossed the syringe into a waste can and returned with a bandage.

"Don't worry," said Raven. "I know what I'm doing. I was a hospital volunteer in high school. My dad became the first doctor in our family. He would have me and my sister work at the clinic, and we'd help with his patients."

Freeborn lifted her head. "Thanks. My hand isn't stinging anymore."

"I'll clean it and wrap it back up." Raven reached into the pocket of her lab coat and handed Dragon a small bottle of pills. "Go to the sink, get a cup of water, and take one. It's valium. This is my personal supply. Works like a charm."

Raven cleaned Freeborn's wound. The morphine worked fast, and Freeborn started to doze. Dragon scooted closer, wanting to be near her as long as possible. Raven stepped back and Dragon placed his hand on Freeborn's arm, feeling a lump in his throat when he noticed her skin blotching.

Raven stepped back in to take Freeborn's pulse. With two fingers to Freeborn's wrist, she kept her eyes on the clock.

"How's she doing?" inquired Dragon.

"She's fine" said Raven, as she put away the supplies. "Go take the pill like I told you to, Dragon. You don't have to pretend with me. I can tell you're ready to climb the walls." She walked to the door and looked out. "I wonder what's keeping Rose. She should be here by now. I bet they ran into trouble getting here."

"Zombies or Shadowguard?"

"Both. Logan has been talking about the Shadowguard all afternoon. I'm a bit concerned. Rose tells him everything about herself, but he shares nothing from his past." She lowered her voice. "Logan said Rose used to conduct experiments on prisoners." Dragon's eyes widened. "You look surprised, but don't tell anyone. I think Rose is ashamed of what she did before coming here."

Dragon didn't care what Rose had done before coming to Seven Falls. She had been brave enough to steal the prototype cure from the Kaiser and bring it to Cadence. Now, he was counting on Rose to save Freeborn's life.

Chapter Five

Rose spotted three cars following at a distance before the bulletproof window popped from an incoming bullet. Several more pops ricocheted and the glass began to crackle. Two more cars pulled out from a side street and gave pursuit. The Shadowguard never attempted to overtake Rose's vehicle. Instead, they pulled close and shot off a few rounds, always managing to appear at the end of whatever road Tandor took. The game continued for what seemed an eternity, ending when Tandor found the interstate.

The Shadowguard had orchestrated a full-scale zombie attack, and a well-timed distraction. As the creatures lumbered toward Seven Falls, Rose could not remember the last time she had seen such a horde. The limo crept through the bodies until they were forced to come to a stop. The zombies were thick, shoulder to shoulder. Tandor opened the moonroof, and Picasso peered out. Vampires didn't emit the same odor as humans, but the ghouls still enjoyed eating their flesh. Zombies closest to them noticed Picasso and began climbing toward him. He sat down and closed the window as a half-faced monster snarled through the glass.

Tandor grimaced. "There's no way I can drive through this mob. We'll have to arrive on foot."

Zombies swarmed the limo, slamming their skulls against the windows. Some smashed their own skulls in, slinking to the ground and smearing gore across the sides of the vehicle. More pressed against the vehicle, but despite their efforts, the limo remained stationary.

"I can get Rose to the camp without you," said Picasso, turning toward the driver. "You should go back to the hotel. If the Kaiser has Rafe, we need to plan a way to free him. You're the best one to get the job done."

"Why didn't you say so before?" said Tandor, placing his hand on the horn. "Once you're both on the roof, I'll give it a few taps to draw their attention and then you'll have to play leap frog. One slip and those things will be all over you."

Picasso bristled. "I'm not going to slip."

The moonroof opened again. Picasso climbed out and Rose scrambled after him. The vampires' scent excited their grisly cousins. The walkers reached toward the pair, vying for their legs. Taking a step back, Picasso sailed over the heads of the zombies and landed on top of a nearby truck, Rose beside him in seconds. Tandor revved the engine and started honking, backing into the crowd. Bodies fell beneath the wheels as zombies followed the limo. Picasso and Rose hopped across stranded hoods toward the gate.

Picasso took to the rooftops, and Rose followed. She felt a rush of exhilaration as they raced across the shingles. While she remained under constant watch and protection most of the time, Rose did not get many chances to exercise her vampiric speed or strength.

Standing on the peak of the last roof, Rose caught Picasso's arm, pulling him back. An easy hundred yards stretched between the house and the camp barricade. Two tall guard towers flanked a chain link gate, with a twenty-foot high electric fence stretching from the gate to the canyon walls. A horde of monsters piled at the main gate, funneling into a mass of infected, hungry death. Armed patrols manned the guard towers, firing at the zombies. Rose noted the soldiers watching from the new observation deck.

"With our speed, no one will notice," said Picasso. "You ready?"

Rose watched a zombie touch the fence. The offending creature fried with a grizzly screech. The patrols fell silent as the zombies grew more agitated.

With the aroma of burnt flesh filling the air, Picasso held out his hand and Rose latched on. Together they timed a running leap and soared across the mob of wailing zombies, landing atop an SUV and springing upward before anyone spotted them. They cleared the barricade, landing silent on the unfinished roof of the observation deck. Dropping through an opening in the roof, they found Lieutenant Sterling with five other startled soldiers.

"Take it easy, soldier," said a steel-toned Picasso. "Highbrow sent for us."

"It's about time! I need your help. Damned things followed the Tigers back to camp." Sterling did not sound happy. "Go ahead, Dr. Rose, you're expected. Highbrow is on the ridge with Micah."

Gunfire from the guard towers grew frantic. Rose left Picasso with the lieutenant and raced the winding road to the infirmary. She entered, reached for her lab coat, and smoothed her hair before meeting Logan and Raven beside a surgery table. Surgical lights illuminated the scene as Dragon sat to the side, head buried in his hands.

"Rose! Thank God you're here," said Raven.

Rose gave an empathetic smile. "I came as soon as I could." She had developed a great respect for Raven and her skills as a lab assistant.

"Don't tell me zombies gave you trouble getting here?" said Logan. "Freeborn has been here an hour. We expected you thirty minutes ago."

Rose had not sought romance with Logan, but he'd been so persuasive. They began working together and spending the majority of their free time together. Without a doubt, he was the most attractive, yet annoying man who had ever entered her life.

"We were chased by Shadowguard out of the city, and there's a swell of zombies at the front gate," she answered. "Picasso and I had to get here on foot. I've got a bad feeling Rafe has been captured. He hasn't shown up here, has he?"

"Nope," said Logan. "I was worried about you, not Rafe."

Raven was one of a few who knew they were seeing each other. While she did not like Logan or any of the scavengers living in camp, she liked Rose and decided to keep quiet.

"Let's have an update," said Rose.

Freeborn was covered to her chin with a sheet. Logan pulled it back and Rose smelled a rancid stench coming from her. Dark circles swam thick under the girl's eyes. Her skin was graying and her breathing labored. Under purple eyelids, her eyes darted frantic.

"Freeborn is a fighter," Logan said. "Must be her Cherokee blood. She should have turned by now. It's a deep bite and it's up to you to produce a miracle, Doc."

Rose put on a pair of rubber gloves. "How is Dragon?" She knew the young man was suffering, blaming himself for the accident.

"He's fine," said Logan. "Raven gave him a sedative."

"This is your fault." Raven glared at Logan with narrowed eyes. "If you had let Thor take the Hummer, this wouldn't have happened. It should be you lying on the table, not Freeborn."

Rose grasped Logan's arm. "Why must you be so difficult? When you're asked to help, no matter what it is, you should do it with a smile on your face."

"And a song in my heart." Logan smirked, his arrogance bristling. "No one drives my Hummer but me, babe. I'll try to be more helpful in the future, but look at the bright side of things. You have a test subject."

Rose examined the reddening mark on her hand. The wound was festering. "Where is Cadence? I need to give Freeborn the antidote now. We can't wait any longer."

Checking Freeborn's forehead, Rose felt an intense heat coming from the girl's body. The disease was aggressive, attacking her system. The cure had never produced effective results in the Kaiser's lab. Curing zombies wasn't the Kaiser's top priority. She had worked with qualified doctors and scientists, however the Kaiser preferred his medical staff to find new and twisted ways to create better fighters for the arena.

"Cadence came in to check on Freeborn," said Logan, "then went back out again. Our lovely savior has taken every precaution against the Kaiser. Is there a difference between a Code 3 and 4?"

"A Code 3 means everyone has a weapon and stands guard," said Raven, glaring at Logan. "Code 4 means everyone shoots strangers first and asks questions later. In your case, it's always a Code 4." She walked over to Freeborn. "I cleaned the wound with an antiseptic Doc, but I think it only made it worse. All this black crap started oozing out."

Logan let out a snort. "Well their blood is toxic, Raven. It tends to react that way when you smear a bunch of antiseptic on it. I thought you'd treated infected patients before? When they brought her in here, you should have cut off her hand."

Rose scrutinized Logan's attire. Raven wore a lab coat and rubber gloves, but Logan didn't. "You're careless, Logan. Carelessness can get you killed." She produced an extra pair of gloves from her pocket and gave them to him. "Put these on. Even the smallest cut around a nail bed can allow the infection to enter your blood stream."

"So, Thor went to the Citadel and discovered a nest of blood suckers." Logan fumbled with his gloves. "You knew the Kaiser set up camp permanently, Doc, but you failed to tell Cadence the part about the Kaiser bringing along an army. Were you saving that for later?"

"If you know so much, Logan, why didn't you tell her?" snapped Rose, resisting the urge to toss him out of the cabin.

Cadence slammed through the door, donned a lab coat, and snapped on a pair of gloves. Dragon looked up.

"Sorry," said Cadence. "I got tied up. How is Freeborn? Are we ready to give her the antidote?"

"Not good." Rose gestured for Raven to pull supplies from the refrigerator. "You should have sent for me the moment you knew about this, Cadence. Precious time has been wasted."

"We did, Rose. Let's get to it."

Raven stepped to the refrigerator and took out a tray containing a syringe and vials of the Kaiser's cure. A groan escaped from the unconscious girl, and Logan strapped Freeborn's head, buckling it at the bottom of the table. Raven hurried with the metal tray and presented it to Rose. The vampire picked up the syringe, filling it with a greenish liquid, and tapped it free of air.

Rose slid the long needle into a vein in Freeborn's neck, administering the antidote.

An immediate jerk lifted Freeborn's head to press against the strap, followed by a violent, systemic shudder. Rose placed her hand on Freeborn's forehead, using her vampire senses to check the girl's racing pulse. Freeborn's eyes opened red and wide, pupils enlarged, and her mouth stretched open to reveal a black tongue and gums. Her jaw shifted, popping cartilage. Freeborn wanted to speak, but only a groan escaped. With another jerk, she coughed up reddish-black mucus.

"Is it working?" asked Dragon, appearing beside Cadence.

Rose kept her hand on the girl's forehead, feeling her temperature decreasing. Another jerk and Freeborn grew still.

Rose counted to ten.

When her eyes reopened they were glazed with a gray film. Black dripped from the corners of her mouth. She thrashed against the straps, snarling and trying to bite Rose. Black splatter landed on Rose's gloves.

"We have to put Freeborn in the cage," said Rose. "This should have worked. I'll take a blood sample and run some tests. When Rafe arrives we can give her a shot of his blood. She's turning."

"You know this is useless, Rose," Logan whispered. "She needs a bullet."

Rose pushed Logan back, furious with his cavalier attitude. She cleaned her gloves before sitting at her computer. Raven took a blood sample before she and Logan rolled the surgery table to the cage. Cadence opened the door, and they pushed the table inside.

"Let me handle this," said Rose. "Everyone get back. She's dangerous."

Moving faster than human eyes could comprehend, Rose unfastened the straps, tossed Freeborn onto a cot, and exited the cage with the table, slamming the door shut. Freeborn charged the door, testing it and let out a frustrated scream. She reached a hand through the bars. Dragon grasped his gun and staggered to the cage.

"We have to do something," he groaned, lifting his aim toward Freeborn.

Rose moved fast, disarming the grieving young soldier. "I am." She turned the safety on and tossed the gun to Cadence. "You need to calm down, Dragon. I know this is hard, but it's far from over. The decomposition of a zombie depends greatly on the strength and health of the human prior to being bitten. Fat deposits increase the speed of decay. If a person is in top physical shape when they're bitten, like Freeborn was, it takes longer to turn. I know you want immediate results. I still think the cure may work, but we have to wait and see."

"Go get Highbrow on the radio," said Cadence, pulling Dragon aside. "Find out if Rafe has been located."

Dragon picked up the handheld and stumbled outside.

Rose was limited in her makeshift lab, but she was still able to test blood samples and continue her research.

"While we wait, I'd like to resume my work. Mind giving a little more blood?" she asked Cadence. "I've used up everything you donated earlier, and I'd like to check Freeborn's blood against yours. I can't understand why the antidote isn't working."

Cadence looked apprehensive, but she nodded. "Take what you need."

Logan returned the surgical table to its former location, removed the sheets, and locked the wheels. Cadence climbed onto the table, pushing up the sleeve of her sweater, and Raven began drawing her blood. After a few minutes, Rose spoke up from her computer station.

"That's enough, Raven. Logan, bring me those vials of blood. I also need the vials labeled A through G in the fridge. Quickly! Cadence needs rest and an IV, hurry up."

Dragon returned, nodding to Cadence as he set the radio on the table. "Rafe is still missing." His voice was raspy.

The sound of glass breaking drew Rose's attention away from the computer. Raven had dropped the tray and stood looking at the blood and broken pieces. Dragon walked over, shaking his head, and bent down to clean up the mess. He cut his finger and let out a yelp. Out of instinct he stuck his finger in his mouth to clean the blood away. Rose was out of her seat and standing next to Dragon in the blink of an eye.

"Are you crazy?" The vampire grabbed Dragon's arm and yanked his hand away from his face. "Properly clean Dragon's cut, Raven. Why would you lick your finger? Show some common sense. This place isn't sanitary." She waved a hand at Freeborn. "Do I have to remind you of the dangers here?" Frustrated, Rose shook her head and walked away. "The lack of a sterilized environment is why I can't progress with my research."

"That's next on the list," said Cadence.

Rose pointed to a broom in the corner and Logan retrieved it, along with a dust pan. Seeing Raven in tears, she felt bad about raising her voice. She knew belaboring the point further wouldn't help anything and sat back down at her computer.

"Logan, Raven, back to work. Try to think before breaking things."

"I'm sorry, doctor," Raven said, voice quivering. She cleaned and bandaged Dragon's wound.

Dragon held up his bandaged finger. "Look. Good as new."

Rose continued to command. "All contaminated items in the red box when you're done. Don't leave anything to chance."

"I know what I'm doing, Doc," Logan, sounding amused, as he bleached and wiped the area clean.

"Everyone stay out of this area," Rose warned. She became a blur, too fast for their human eyes to follow.

Freeborn groaned and stuffed her mouth full of the blanket and cot stuffing she was shredding. Seeing the girl in this deplorable condition was hard on the humans, but it motivated Rose. All she needed was to isolate the missing element to the cure in Cadence's blood. From the moment she heard about Cadence's miraculous recovery, she knew her blood held the key.

She needed to understand that miracle, and replicate it.

Chapter Six

Still dark outside, Thor woke up yawning. He lay beside Star on the couch, with his arm draped over her slender body. There was only one cot in Cadence's cabin, and her gear was stacked beneath it, along with supplies that she had been stockpiling. A short wave radio sat on a small table behind the desk, and a CD player with a stack of music was tucked under her cot. Curious about her taste in music, Thor rose to take a look.

"Wow. She likes some cool stuff," said Thor, picking up the top disc. He heard a crackle from a radio charging on the wall and returned the disc to its stack.

Thor turned up the volume on the receiver, and heard an unfamiliar voice. He adjusted the dial and held it to his ear, trying to listen.

"*I'm in position*," said a man, with a thick, guttural accent. "*Any problems?*"

After a pause and the crackle of static, another voice answered. "*No problem. It's clear up here. Stars are bright overhead. Ready when you are.*"

Figuring it was chatter between guards at Midnight Falls and the front gate, Thor turned it off. Star woke up and found two bottled sodas in the cabin's economy fridge.

"Aren't you supposed to be on guard duty?" asked Star, nursing a long drink. "I haven't told China Six about Freeborn."

Thor gave her a kiss and took a swig. "They probably know already and are on guard duty." Thor pointed at the radios. "You can try to reach Lotus."

"We should contact our teams." proposed Star. "The Vikings should be at the waterfall. We might see them through the window."

She pulled the curtain aside, and confirmed Loki, Baldor, Heimdall and Odin were standing at the stairs.

"The guys are, but Raven's missing. She must still be with Freeborn. I'd like to go see how she's doing. Want to come with me?"

"Nah. I'd rather stay here with you for a while. We have the place to ourselves. Why leave?" Thor placed his arms around her waist, pulling her close. "I can play some music. Cadence has good taste. Our teams have things covered. They don't need constant supervision."

"Are you suggesting something inappropriate, sergeant?" Star slapped his arm. He took her bottle from her hand and set it on the desk. "I must tell you something first, though. It might change your mind about us."

"Us? I kinda like that," said Thor, nuzzling his face against her neck. She smelled like orchids, and it drove him wild. "What is it?"

Star took a deep breath. "I'm in love with you. I have been for a long time."

"Huh?"

Star hugged him tight. "I've never felt like this. You don't know how happy I was when you broke up with Raven."

"Do we have to talk about this now?" He didn't mind listening to someone else talk about their emotions, but didn't feel comfortable expressing himself.

Tears appeared in Star's eyes. "Life is so short. If anything happened to you, I'd never get over it. Never. You're an amazing man, and when I'm around you, I feel safe. "

Thor was taken aback by her unexpected show of feelings. "I'm seventeen, like you," he said, carefully choosing his words. "Are you ready for anything serious? I mean, I do shave, Star, but . . ." He laughed. She didn't.

"I trust you with my life," she said. "Can I trust you with my heart?"

Thor was not quick to respond. He had to think about what to say.

"I don't know what I've done to deserve you, but I'm not running away this time." Thor cracked a toothy smile. "Give me a little time, I'm not used to being so honest. I do care about you. How about some music, huh?"

Star slid her arms around his neck and stood on tiptoe. The top of her head reached his shoulders. "It's okay if you can't say it now. You'll tell me one day. I know you will."

Wanting to end the conversation, Thor kissed her. It worked, this time.

Dragon sat beside Cadence. His attention was divided between making Cadence drink water and trying to keep up with Rose. The inhuman doctor moved around the room so fast that he only saw her when she paused to jot notes down at the work table. Logan and Raven were sifting through a basket of flowers, analyzing them through a microscope, and placing them into labeled jars. Dragon glanced at his girlfriend. Freeborn was chewing on her fingernails, making the tips bleed.

"I wish you wouldn't do that," said Dragon. Freeborn snarled in response.

"She can't help it, Dragon." Cadence leaned back against the wall. "My head hurts so bad."

She finished a bottle of water and dropped it to the floor, as an IV continued to feed nutrients to her body.

"Mine too." Dragon rubbed his temple with clammy hands. "Sorry I'm complaining. You look worse than I feel. You really do."

"I've been leeched." Cadence smiled, stretching out her legs. "Freeborn is in good hands. Rose worked at a cancer research center before the Scourge. Picasso said they found her and a few technicians in the center outside of Denver. I'd love to get a peek inside the Kaiser's lab. I'm sure he has one at the Academy."

"I'm sure it's pretty much like Frankenstein's lair. His lab team would love having you on a table. You're not like anyone else." Dragon reached out to touch the two sets of scars on Cadence's neck. One scar, a discolored square, was from the zombie. Rafe's two small puncture wounds lined up above the other. He pulled back. "Sorry. I'm just trying to work things out in my head."

"Like why Rafe became a vampire Maker?"

"Yeah. Those kids he saved, Cinder and Cerberus, along with the Kaiser . . . There are far too many vampires for only four Makers, and Rafe didn't turn anyone else."

Cadence tried to sit up. "You want to know how Makers were created. Rose could probably tell us. With Rafe and the kids, they weren't bit but ingested the infection on the same day. The virus had mutated in that moment. It never happened again."

"Why them?" Dragon wondered. "If Rose or Tandor bit a human, they'd make a zombie. Makers can infect animals, but regular vamps can't. If the infected animal bites a human, they become a therianthrope."

"And, likely, still a carrier of the infection," said Cadence. "Luna and the pride haven't turned anyone, but I assume they could if they wanted to."

"Do you think Luna's blood could cure Freeborn?"

"I don't think so," Cadence contemplated. "I'm immune to any form of the virus, but I'm not a Maker."

"Could Rafe turn her? It's been five hours."

A sad grin appeared on Cadence's face. "You want to rescue him."

He nodded.

"Even after what happened today? Rafe may not be at the Citadel. He might have decided to leave town. He's not the bravest guy."

"I can't sit here and do nothing," Dragon moaned. "The Dark Angels are our best hope of finding him. I know Tandor will help me look for him."

"Highbrow would never allow it. While I'm stuck here, he's basically taken over running things."

"You're still the commander. If you give the order, Highbrow has to go along with you. Picasso is here. He could take me to the Broadmoor so I can join the Dark Angels to search for Rafe. After we locate Rafe, we can bring him back here. Rose doesn't have a cure. I don't want to spend the rest of my life without Freeborn. If I don't go, Cadence, Freeborn is going to remain a zombie."

Dragon glanced at Rose. Logan was standing behind her, and both were taking turns looking through a microscope. They were excited about something. He didn't know where Logan had learned so much about medicine, but the guy was helpful. Maybe they had found a possible flower candidate and could commence work on creating a cure.

"My mother and I were once in a serious car wreck," said Dragon. "I wasn't injured, but she was thrown through the windshield and required a massive amount of stitches. She lost so much blood that she needed a transfusion. We shared the same rare type, so I was the one to give her my blood. If I hadn't been there, she would have died. It was my blood that saved her."

"Wouldn't it be ironic if my blood can cure zombies?" Cadence wondered.

"Would it hurt to give her some of your blood?" Dragon shrugged. "I want to cover all of our options. But I still want to go after Rafe."

"With that logic, I can hardly refuse." Cadence sat up slow, swaying to the side. "I'm ordering you to get a team together and go after Rafe.

I suggest you take China Six, but tell Highbrow before you head out. You'll have trouble getting out of camp, but he may have a few ideas."

Dragon stood. "You have no idea how much this means to me."

"Rose, come here," Cadence called out, her voice weak.

"I'm here," said Rose. She stood in front of Cadence in an instant. "What is it?"

Cadence explained what she wanted Rose to do while Dragon listened. Too much of Cadence's blood had been taken to give Freeborn a full transfusion, so Rose used the blood samples to fill syringes. It was agreed that Freeborn would be given shots at intervals.

"I'm not promising anything," said Rose, pointing at Dragon. "Logan, come and help me."

Logan grinned. "My pleasure, Doc."

Anxious, Dragon watched as Rose and Logan approached the cage. Logan wore thick leather gauntlets and opened the door, allowing Rose to slip inside. In the blink of an eye, the vampire had Freeborn pinned to the floor, her hands and legs secured with ropes. Rose straddled Freeborn, holding her firm with one hand to her chest as Freeborn fought without success.

"Come in, Logan," said Rose. "Give her the first shot."

Logan lifted the syringe, tapped it, and knelt. A loud, miserable moan came from Freeborn and she snapped her teeth. Rose pushed Freeborn's head aside while Logan slid the needle into her neck. She tried biting them again.

"Get out of the cage," said Raven. She reached in for Logan and pulled him. "Do you want to get bitten?"

"Gee, I didn't think you cared," Logan said. He laughed when Raven walked off. After a while, Freeborn stopped struggling and became still. Rose used her stethoscope to listen for a heartbeat.

"Is she alive?" Dragon's voice held a note of hope.

Rose nodded. "Her pulse is steady. That's a good sign." She took out a small flashlight and opened one of Freeborn's eyes, shining the light into her pupil. "Pupils are dilated. Her temperature remains a few degrees lower than a vampire. Let's give it a little more time." She removed a syringe from her pocket and injected Freeborn. "I'm giving her more painkillers. When she wakes up, I want her calm." The doctor vanished from sight as she untied Freeborn and closed the cage door behind her. She glanced at her watch. "I'll give her another shot in an hour."

Dragon wasn't waiting. He took one more look at Freeborn before turning to leave, and noticed her foot twitch. He ran to the cage and Freeborn opened her eyes. The gray had faded. Excited, he grabbed hold of the bars and pressed his face against the cold iron.

"She's awake," Dragon shouted. "She's looking at me, Doc. Come here!"

The vampire was at Dragon's side before he finished his sentence. She put a restraining hand on his shoulder. "She's still infectious. You have to stay back. If Freeborn bites you, you'll be in the cage with her. Why don't you go outside and get some fresh air?"

"I have a better idea." Dragon saluted the commander. "Wish me luck."

Rose intercepted Dragon at the door. "If you could just give it a little more time . . ." she began.

"I'm going, Doc. I've waited long enough. If it works, contact the Dark Angels, but I'm bringing Rafe home, no matter what."

Logan approached. "This time I'm coming with you. Bring along that sniper kid. Whisper. We need the best." He opened the door. "Well? What are you waiting for? Go get your team ready. I'll meet you at the front gate."

Dragon nodded and took off. Gazing up at the crescent-shaped moon, he silently prayed for Freeborn, asking her spirit guides to be with him. It was Freeborn's custom to ask her ancestors for protection before she went on a mission. Seemed like a good idea.

He heard a lone wolf howl in the distance, sending a shiver down his spine. Good omen or bad, he was going after Rafe.

Chapter Seven

Hidden in a cluster of pine trees, Rose stood with Logan, lost in his dark brown eyes. His grasp tightened over her hands. She sensed his anxiety to leave, but something else troubled him. Logan had so many layers, it was impossible to peel them all back at once. In the past, she avoided complicated men.

"I want to understand," said Rose. "Being part of this camp isn't easy for you. You were the leader of your own band of survivors and brought them here. I know what they say behind your back. Once a scavenger, always a scavenger. Maybe I'm naïve, but I don't see you that way. What you've done for Nomad, Betsy and the others, in my opinion, puts you right up there with Cadence and Highbrow."

Logan cracked a smile. "High praise coming from you, Doc," he said in a husky whisper. "I'm not sure putting me on a pedestal is a good idea. When I fall back to earth, I'm going to fall hard. I have many flaws. Comparing me to Captain Pallaton would make more sense and also keep you from having grand illusions."

"Pallaton saved the Dark Angels. He's the only reason we got out of Denver." Rose felt her thoughts jumble when Logan pulled her close. His lips glided across her cheek and down her neck. "I trust Pallaton with my life. He told us to come here and it was the right decision."

"Now you're just making me jealous," said Logan. He took hold of her chin and kissed her. "This isn't about leaving you to do all the dirty work, Doc. I'm a man of action. Picking flowers is about as slow as you can get. Dragon won't be able to lead a mission like this at night without help."

"I thought all of that talk about you being in the F.B.I. was meant to impress me." Rose slid her arms around his body. "You don't need to. The fact that you saved the lives of many people tells me what type of man you are, Logan. What happened at Pike's Peak wasn't entirely your fault. The Captain could have let you in without a fight. Maybe Highbrow and some of the others think you still have something to prove, but I know Cadence believes in you. I do, too."

Logan released her. "Then you understand why I have to leave with Dragon? I do have something to prove. These kids don't trust me. If I can help bring Rafe back to camp, I might earn their trust. I have to do this, Rose. It's important."

"More important than finding a cure for Freeborn?"

"I knew you didn't think Rafe could help Freeborn," Logan said, zipping up his coat. "I don't either, but that's not why I'm going. I'd like to think I'll make a difference. I may even keep those kids alive. They have no idea what they're dealing with. The Kaiser isn't some storybook villain. You and I both know why he came here and what he plans to do with this camp. Right now we need everyone that can help fight the Shadowguard. Rafe may be a jerk, but he's good in a fight, when he fights."

"Fine," said Rose. "Then go, but be careful. You don't know the Kaiser like I do, Logan."

A glint of anger flashed in Logan's eyes and he turned away from her. Rose wasn't sure whether he was upset with her, or the situation. He walked to an ATV parked near the mess hall and glanced back at her. Rose felt a tug on her heart. She cared for Logan more than she wanted to admit. She watched him start up the four-wheeler and drive off.

Feeling her cheek damp, Rose brushed aside a bloody tear. The dark smear was plain to see on her glove. She slipped back inside the building and straight to the bathroom. Her reflection caused her to gasp. Streaks of blood stained her pale cheeks. She removed her gloves and washed her face.

A light rap on the door revealed Raven standing outside. The girl gave off a strong scent of fear.

"Cadence doesn't look so good," said Raven. "I'm worried. I've replenished her fluids like you told me too, but she has a rash on her neck. What can that mean? You think she's turning back into a zombie?"

"Calm down," said Rose, firm. "Don't jump to conclusions. Having a positive attitude is the only reason I've managed to survive this long."

"I'll work on it. You better check on her all the same."

Rose checked on Cadence, and she opened her eyes, smiling, when Rose leaned down. Rose examined the rash spreading from her neck upward to her cheeks.

Cadence sniffled. "I have hay fever. I'm probably allergic to those flowers. In fact, I'm allergic to just about everything that grows, Doc. It's no big deal."

"I'm not worried." Rose turned to Raven. "Give Cadence some allergy meds and open the windows. It smells like a mortuary in here."

Rose moved to follow up with Freeborn and found her fast asleep. "How is our patient doing? Rest is the best thing for you, my dear."

"I like you, Doc. You're good at what you do." Raven sat, pulling a basket of flowers between her feet. "Maybe it's not my business, but I don't think Logan is good enough for you. When you're not around, Logan is always snooping through your files. He thinks I don't notice, but he's not that clever."

"You're right," said Rose. "It's none of your business."

"So it's okay for him to read your files?"

"I've nothing to hide. If Logan wants to see what I've been working on, he's more than welcome to go through my files, Raven. You can as well. They're not locked up."

The girl gave a shrug. "I think you should keep your files locked up, but then, I'm a pessimist. I see the worst in people, and I believe that's why I've survived as long as I have."

Returning to her desk, Rose tried to ignore Raven's implications about Logan. She felt he was as concerned as anyone else about finding a cure.

"Raven, I know this is boring work, but what we're doing is important. I do appreciate your concern for my welfare. Logan rubs a lot of people the wrong way, but I still need you both to help me."

"Yeah, well, Logan's not here, is he? Some help he is."

Rose couldn't argue. Logan had picked a fine time to get an adrenalin rush. She didn't think Dragon or Tandor needed his help finding Rafe, but then again, he had acted like he knew more about Rafe's disappearance than he let on.

Blaze was curled up beside Whisper watching another video. He hadn't said much all evening, but he was holding her hand, and she was content with that. A knock on the door pulled them apart.

Crunching spilled popcorn under her feet, Blaze tiptoed to the door and opened it. Dragon ducked inside the RV, letting in the chill of the night air. He was dressed from head to toe in black. His long hair was pulled into a ponytail and he carried a large box that he placed in front of Whisper.

Blaze let the door scream shut, shivering from the cold air. "We've been worried sick about Freeborn," she said, giving Dragon a hug. "I hope you're bringing us good news inside of that box."

"I'm going to find Rafe. I need Whisper."

With the tip of his boot, Dragon nudged the box to Whisper. Whisper stared at it as if it contained something alive. Blaze threw the top back and showed a stack of folded, black clothing. Whisper pulled out a black leather coat.

"I have my own gear, and I'm not a ninja. Sniper. Remember?"

"You need to wear black, not your parka," said Dragon. "It's Lotus' second outfit. Should fit you just fine. The cure didn't work and Dr. Rose hasn't come up with anything else. She did try giving Freeborn an injection of Cadence's blood. It might work, but without a real lab, Rose is limited to what she can do. We need Rafe."

"Rafe?" asked Blaze. "You're going after Rafe. Where is he?"

"I don't know. I'm going to the Broadmoor to meet up with the Dark Angels. Cadence cleared it and instructed me to take a team. Get your rifle and whatever weapons you want, and suit up."

The voices from the television seemed louder than ever. Blaze paused the program.

"Do I get to go?" When no one responded, she threw her hands into the air. "Come on! I want to go. Tigers travel in a pack. Or at least in pairs."

Dragon shook his head. "Sorry, Blaze. I need stealth, not steam."

Chuckling under his breath, Whisper stripped off his green sweater and undershirt. Small, round, puckered scars marred his chest, filling Blaze with curiosity. Whisper started to remove his pants and Blaze took a seat to watch. Her whistle caught him by surprise.

"Knock it off." Whisper sounded embarrassed.

"If I can't come with you, I'll make sure you have everything you need. The silencers are in your pack." Blaze feigned a pout. "Be careful, you dope."

Whisper finished dressing and ducked outside. Blaze watched him leave and shut the door. The bedroom door opened, and Dodger emerged with Smack. Both were dressed in black with their hair tucked into stocking caps.

Smack held up Blaze's crossbow. "Well, are we staying here or shall we go vampire hunting?"

"You want to go after them?" Blaze was shocked.

"We heard everything," said Dodger, grinning. "Fighting Tigers always travel in a pack or in pairs, like you said. We have to hurry if we're going to catch them."

Blaze nodded, the spark returning to her eyes. "Then let's catch a bloodsucker."

Chapter Eight

Dragon and Whisper drove through the towering granite walls of the canyon. Lotus, Kirin, Monkey, and Cricket rode in the back, or on the sideboard, of the golf cart. Dragon had located a stash of katana at a surplus store in downtown Manitou Springs months ago, so each girl wore one strapped to her back. The swords were a gift from Dragon to the girls for completing their training.

Lotus was the guard for China Six, and in many ways the female version of Dragon. Outfitted with two revolvers, and two daggers sheathed in her boots, her weapons of choice for close combat against zombies were the dual hunting knives strapped across her lower back.

Kirin and Monkey were identical twins. Kirin served as the team's scout and was so-named for the mythical Japanese creature after saving a young boy from choking. Monkey was the team sniper and fancied her scoped rifle, and was a frequent training partner to Whisper. The two were a fierce site with Kirin's cobalt blue, shoulder-length hair, and Monkey's crimson short-layered, angled bob.

Cricket was the youngest member of the team. At five-feet-one, she had no problem introducing you to her steel-tipped and heeled boots to be sure you knew she was to be taken serious. She wore her hair in braids tied with a red leather cord, and preferred fighting with two extendable batons that she kept in the sleeves of her coat.

As Dragon and his team approached the barricade, gunfire mingled with groans and snarls echoed through the canyon. Dragon parked fifty yards from the blockade.

"Told you we had a problem," Lotus said. "Highbrow isn't going to let us drive out, Dragon, and you know it."

Whisper lit up a cigarette. "What's your plan, Master Dragon?"

"Cheyenne Road links up with 25," said Dragon. "No doubt it's packed with zombies, so we'll have to take Evans Avenue over to Mesa. Nomad and Sturgis outfitted Logan's Hummer with a snow plow and flame throwers. It has a full tank of gas, too. Here are the keys. It's in the garage." He tossed the keys to Lotus. "I stole them from Logan. The jerk never even noticed."

"Rose noticed," said Lotus, jumping out of the cart. "Vampires notice everything. Stop smoking, Whisper. You're going to stink."

Kirin peered toward the gate. "We need to be shadows out there. Unseen and unheard." She patted her twin on the head. "That means no talking, chatterbox."

Dragon headed to the observation deck where he found Highbrow, Sterling, and Logan inside watching the mob in the streets.

"Ah, Dragon," said Highbrow. "It's about time you showed up. The Bull Dogs said you were on your way."

"Then you know why I'm here."

"Logan told me, but I can't let you drive out of camp." Highbrow turned toward the street. "We're under siege. The Kaiser has delivered the zombies to our doorstep. The Freedom Army and Picasso are bringing up heavy artillery and we'll clear this road in a few hours."

The Panthers were stationed in the north tower, supported by the Buccaneers in the south tower. Snipers were picking their targets. The violence of gunfire was loud under the tower's metal roofs.

"No one is going anywhere tonight," said Sterling. "There are a thousand hungry bastards attacking the fence. Sending anyone out in this would be a mistake."

"I'm aware of that, lieutenant," said Highbrow, annoyed.

Dragon spoke up. "Commander Cadence ordered me to go, and this time I'm taking a battle-ready vehicle. Lotus is bringing up the Hummer."

"Oh, so we're back to that again," said Logan, crossing his arms. "Who the hell stole my keys? Nevermind, let's get to the real problem here. The Kaiser has you pinned down. He's bringing zombies in from all over the area and dropping them at your doorstep. It's a clever battle tactic. While your forces are preoccupied at the front gate, the rest of your camp is vulnerable to attack. They're called Shadowguard for a reason."

"The War Gods, Vikings, and Blue Devils are guarding our back door," said Highbrow. "Every team is out, and more Dark Angels are coming. We'll fight back with everything we've got. The Kaiser isn't getting in here."

Logan leveled a cool glance at Highbrow. "The thing is, Captain High Hat, your opponent isn't a novice. The Kaiser wouldn't be in charge if he didn't have brains. Your fence might keep zombies out, but not vamps. Not the Shadowguard. You think you've got a zombie problem? It's nothing compared to what the Kaiser has in store for this camp."

The sound of the Hummer's engine rumbled near. Dragon wondered how Logan knew so much, unless he was just guessing.

"Permission to speak, sir?" asked the lieutenant. "Sending them out the gate isn't an option. Commander Cadence isn't up here. She doesn't understand what we're up against."

Highbrow nodded. "I've already talked with Picasso and we came up with something." He put his hand on Dragon's shoulder. "The teams in both towers will provide a diversion while you and your team repel the south tower. There's a Blazer on the other side. Keys are in the ignition. Nomad put a lot of effort into making it battle-worthy, so try to bring it back in one piece . . . with your team."

Dragon bowed. "I will. I swear it."

Lieutenant Sterling wore a look of displeasure. "Sir, can I have a word with you?"

Highbrow glanced at the man. "Not right now."

"What about me?" asked Logan. "If you want to help Freeborn, let me go with the team."

"Permission denied," said Highbrow. When Logan protested, Highbrow squared up with him. "I said no, and that is final." Turning back to Dragon, he gave him instructions. "Once you reach the Blazer, take Colorado Avenue to Fillmore and go west. If Picasso can get word to him, you'll find Tandor waiting at a gas station at the corner of Chestnut Street. He'll lead you to Rafe. Think you can find it?"

"I know the place," said Dragon. "Sonderman Park is nearby, my old haunt."

"Then get going," said Highbrow.

Dragon descended the stairs as an argument erupted between Highbrow and Logan.

"What is this about?" shouted Logan. "Are you really buried this deep in your own delusion? Want to throw your weight around? Do it with someone else. We're at war here, and you don't have a clue what you're doing!"

Dragon found his team waiting and they slipped under the spotlights through the safe zone.

"Hold up a second," Dragon said, stopping Lotus. "I want you to promise me something. If I don't make it, swear to me you'll bring Rafe back."

"I will," Lotus said, uncomfortable with the tone of the conversation. "Anything else?"

"Tell Freeborn that I . . ." Dragon paused. "Tell her I did my best, and that I'll see her later. She'll know what I mean."

Lotus flinched as a zombie slammed into the electric fence and sizzled. She looked back at Dragon. "You just make sure you get us all back. Together."

They continued through a maze covered with limbs and canvas held down by rocks on all sides. The rest of the team waited at the door to the south tower, bright lights overhead revealing hundreds of zombies lurking on the other side.

"You first," said Whisper, opening the door.

Dragon scaled the stairs and emerged through a trap door. The Buccaneer's leader, Black Beard, welcomed Dragon and his team.

The Buccaneers were firing into the crowd from the tower. There were so many zombies pressing forward, the dead were trampled and covered the moment they dropped.

"These gut-chewers just keep coming," announced Black Beard. "You must have somewhere important to go. Why isn't Star leading the team?"

"I couldn't find her in time. Just keep them off of us," said Dragon. "Which one is our ride?" The Buccaneer pointed at a black Blazer parked ten yards from the fence. "Think you can create a big enough diversion for us to reach it without being devoured?"

"Buccaneers love to play with fire and things that go boom," laughed Black Beard. He patted the railing. "We're ready when you are, Dragon."

"Give us ten seconds before you climb down, then run like hell," said Black Beard. "Things are going to get interesting real fast."

Whisper and Lotus tied ropes to the wooden posts on either side of the tower. Dragon surveyed the street below. The zombies were crammed together in a tight mass, surrounding the Blazer. Near the vehicle, stood a tall zombie in a red bath robe, sniffing the air. The ghoul spotted Dragon, and emitted a guttural moan. Heeding the zombie's signal, a wave of zombies charged the fence. The fence hummed and sparked, growling like an animal, as the bodies spasmed in a grotesque dance of grilled flesh.

"Buccaneers, on my mark," shouted Black Beard. He pulled the pin and lobbed a grenade into the horde. An explosion sent a shower of bodies, partial bodies, and gore flying through the air.

Flame throwers rained streams of fire from each tower, engulfing the front lines. The fire spread through the ranks as they tried to escape. Zombies lit up like torches.

With the zombies in retreat, Dragon motioned to Whisper. The pair repelled the tower, and ran for the Blazer. Dragon jumped in the driver's seat as the remainder of the team packed in.

"Move it!" shouted Lotus, slamming the door.

The zombies moved to block their path as another blast of flames swept the crowd, clearing the road. The team completed the first phase of the trip, disappearing into the dark.

"This sucks," said Blaze, pissed off. "What do we do now?"

Blaze, Smack, and Dodger lifted up their heads from the back seat of the Hummer, upset. Making certain the coast was clear, Blaze opened the back hatch and the three climbed out.

"They just had to switch vehicles!" Dodger complained.

"Let's grab a golf cart and go back to the RV," said Smack. "I didn't want to go anyway. Creeping around in the city after dark is not my idea of a good time. That's how you end up like Freeborn."

Dodger put his arm around Smack. "That's my brave, little girl."

"I'm not a little girl!"

Hearing the pair squabble was a daily experience. Blaze shouldered her crossbow and stomped to a golf cart. She drove Smack and Dodger to the mess hall, parked, and started walking toward the RV. Across the road, she noticed a tall figure watching from the shadows. She marched on, until she saw the same figure ahead of her, standing beside the Blue Devils' RV.

She didn't recognize him, and turned to look for her teammates. Dodger and Smack were still at a vending machine, arguing. She readied her crossbow and turned back toward the stranger, but he had vanished.

The hairs on her neck prickled, and someone tapped her on the shoulder. "Looking for me?"

She spun and triggered an arrow. The dark stranger caught the arrow and snapped it in half. Gasping, Blaze ran for the Blue Devils' trailer, but the figure intercepted her. Face to face with Blaze, the man exposed his fangs and hissed. *Shadowguard*, Blaze thought. She threw the crossbow at the vamp and ran, yelling for Smack and Dodger. They spun and sprinted toward Blaze, but the vampire materialized ahead of Blaze again, and she turned through a gap between the campers. Cutting her off, she dove for cover and felt a sharp pain in her throat. She swatted at the sting, knocking a tranquilizer dart from her neck.

She attempted to cry out, but a gurgle escaped her swelling throat instead. The drug acted fast. She was paralyzed in seconds.

Blaze remained conscious, face down and unable to move. Someone turned her over. Blaze gawked at the stars overhead, as a pale face came into view. Eyes burning amber pierced her vision as his cold breath rested on her cheek. Her mind begged to scream and fight as the stranger tossed her over his shoulder.

"My name is Aldarik." A German accent tinged his sinister voice. "I wanted to introduce myself before I present you to the Kaiser, who is anxious to meet you. He's looking for a few new fighters to compete in the Death Games."

Hope ran cold as Blaze lost consciousness. The effect of the tranquilizer was sudden and deep.

Chapter Nine

Thor and Star faced the waterfall. She had tried to call her team but couldn't reach them. It was a chance to stay with Thor, if only for a little longer. His arms wrapped around her body and he rested his chin on top of her head, enjoying the gentle fragrance of her hair.

The Vikings, on his orders, reported to the infirmary. They were to stay with Raven until she reported for guard duty. The War Gods went to Midnight Falls to check on Uther, while the Blue Devils returned to their RV for some rest. Thor thought himself brilliant. He had Star to himself at the most romantic spot in the camp. Star raised her lips for a kiss and Thor spotted someone standing on the staircase. He assumed it was a member of one of the patrols.

"Some idiot is spying on us," Thor said, amused.

"If people want to stare, let them. I've never been happier."

Laughing, Thor met her lips for a kiss. A moment later he looked up again, but the figure was no longer there.

"Let's go back inside. It's cold."

"I'm on guard duty," said Thor. "Loki is bringing me a gun and a heavier coat. I'll let you wear it, okay?"

They heard two voices calling out in the darkness, and spotted Dodger and Smack running toward HQ. Thor pulled away from Star, and met the Tigers as they came up the stairs. Smack was carrying Blaze's crossbow, both distraught.

"What's wrong?" asked Thor.

"Didn't you hear us?" Dodger shouted. "They took Blaze!"

Thor put his hand on Smack's shoulder to calm her trembling. "What's Dodger babbling about? Who took Blaze? What the hell is going on?"

"Blaze was kidnapped," said Smack, shaking. "Some guy appeared out of nowhere and snatched her." She held up Blaze's crossbow. "We found this between the RVs."

Dodger wiped his damp cheeks. "It was a Shadowguard," he huffed. "Had to be. She was gone so fast. What are we going to do?"

"Get Cadence. She's at the barricade." Thor took off running, then turned expecting to see Star behind him. "Where did Star go? She was just here."

"I don't know. Maybe she was captured too!" said Smack, looking toward the staircase. "I don't hear any shooting. Where are the patrols?"

Thor hurried back to where he had been standing with Star. He found her silver China Six necklace lying on the ground, clasp broken. He picked it up, shouting her name. Everyone within earshot came running.

"What's this about?" asked Logan, concerned. "Did zombies get through the barricade? It wasn't vampires. Not this soon."

Thor had a lump in his throat. "Star has been taken. Blaze, too. Dodger and Smack saw Shadowguard right before Blaze was abducted. We need to go after them. We might be able to catch up if we move now."

"Vampires move fast," said Xena, gazing up at the cliffs. "They'll be long gone by the time we get up to the ridge."

"The A-Team and the Elite are at Midnight Falls," said Smack. "We can start there. They might have seen something."

"Hold on, kiddo," said Logan, trying to calm everyone down. "You're positive you saw Shadowguard?"

"I'm sure it was a Shadowguard."

"I'm taking the Vikings and going after them," Thor said, pocketing Star's necklace. "Smack, wait here for Dodger and Cadence. There may be more Shadowguard in camp. Spread the word! Everyone needs to wake up and be ready. We're under attack!"

"We'll wake anyone who is not on duty." said Xena, hurrying away with Phoenix.

Thor felt a tap on his arm. He turned to find Smack offering him Blaze's crossbow. He slung it over his shoulder and blocked Smack when she started for the staircase.

"I need you to wait for Dodger. When he gets back, bring backup." Thor turned to a ready group of patrols, all waiting for direction. He gave orders to gather and distribute weapons, then patrol the street.

"What about you?" asked Aurora.

Thor looked to Midnight Falls. "I'm going hunting."

"I'm going with you," said Logan. "Vampires move fast. They won't be at Midnight Falls. I doubt the patrols saw them, but I can track them."

Thor nodded and pointed at the leader of the Valkyries. "Hey, Aurora, take over here. Make sure everyone stays diligent. Anyone got a radio I can use?"

"I do." Logan held one up. "Let's go, big guy."

Thor raced up the stairs. He made it half way before Logan caught his arm and pointed down. Cadence stood beside Smack and Dodger, flanked by the patrols.

"Bring them back, sergeant!" Cadence shouted, waving.

Thor waved back and kept running. The rest of the Vikings were waiting at the top. Thor assumed the forward position as he addressed his group.

"It's going to be dark on the path. Stay in tight formation. Be sure you know what you're shooting at, Star and Blaze may have escaped and hid in the trees. Play it cool." He lowered his rifle at the sound of bodies crashing through the woods.

The War Gods ran toward the Vikings. Lieutenant Kahn walked beside a soldier with a cut across his cheek.

"Don't go down that path," said Kahn, shaken.

"Where are the A-Team and Elite?" asked Thor.

"Up ahead somewhere. Uther spotted people on the path and took both teams with him. It got dark fast. When we heard gunfire, we came back. Are you going after them? Want us to join you?"

"No, I've got this. The commander is at the bottom," said Thor. "Send one man back to report to Cadence. Hold formation at the stairs, Kahn. You're to hold Midnight Falls, so stay put."

Smack and Dodger caught up with the group, carrying rifles and flashlights. Logan shook his head as the War Gods raced toward the falls.

"Great," said Logan, disgusted. "We could have used the War Gods, but instead we get two kids. I feel better already. I'm sure they'll come in handy if we find what you're all so eager to encounter."

"No one asked you to come, scavenger," said Raven, letting out a hiss. "Go back if you're afraid. We don't need you. Rose might, though, so scurry off to her."

"Let's move out," said Thor, ignoring Logan. "Keep a look out for Uther. If anyone can kill a vamp, it's the Elite."

Standing beside Freeborn's cage, Rose studied the girl. The Bull Dogs and Cadence went to the barricade to help Highbrow, but had not returned. She knew other teams were outside, but worried over the uproar at the waterfall. Raven was on guard duty, and Rose expected Logan to return with an excuse to stay in the lab with her. The door opened behind her. She smiled and turned around, but no one was there.

"Okay," she said. "Logan? Is that you? It's not funny."

Rose heard a sound and spotted a scalpel on the floor. She caught a whiff of cheap aftershave before spotting two Shadowguard sneaking up on her. Reaching behind her, she unlocked the cage. The vampires rushed her and grabbed her by the throat, fangs flashing before she was thrown across the room. She hit the wall at the far side of the lab as one of the undead stepped in front of her, holding a knife.

"Dr. Rose, I presume," said the vampire. "I have orders to bring you in or kill you. Which would you prefer?"

"Freeborn! Help!" shouted Rose.

With a vicious snarl, Freeborn ripped through her cage door, destroying the lock, and charged the nearest Shadowguard. Apprehending him with ease, she sank her teeth into his throat. Rose took the opportunity to run, looking for a weapon as Freeborn pulled the vampire into her cage. She rounded her work table when the second Shadowguard blocked her path. Rose reached into her coat pocket and felt a syringe. The vampire charged her, and with unearthly reflexes, she dodged and stabbed him in the neck. The Shadowguard stumbled, gasping, and fell dead.

"Holy hell," exclaimed Rose, her eyes growing wide.

Minutes earlier, she had given Freeborn the last dose of Cadence's blood before placing the used syringe in her pocket. Not once since she had been testing Cadence's blood had she considered it to be lethal to vampires. If the mere residual of her blood could kill a vampire, what would it do to a zombie? What had it done to the two teenagers in her care? Dragon had certainly been exposed to Cadence's blood while cleaning the spill earlier. As for Freeborn, she'd administered several doses of Cadence's blood into her veins.

"What have I done?" Rose looked at Freeborn, horrified.

"Any more? He was delicious!" The girl dropped the remains of the vampire's heart onto the floor. Blood covered her face and hands. "It's hot in here. Mind if I go outside and get some fresh air, Doc?" She started to exit the cage and found Rose blocking the door.

"You just ate a vampire. How do you think you should feel?"

"Full," said Freeborn. "But I want more."

"Freeborn, you're . . . a zombie. Well, that's until . . . I'm not sure what you are. If you promise not to eat me, I'd like you to come to the table and sit down."

Freeborn laughed. "I'm not going to eat a friend. You're safe, Doc."

Guarded, Rose led Freeborn to the surgery table. The girl hopped up, and Rose turned the overhead light on. A morsel of vampire flesh hung from Freeborn's chin. She noticed Rose staring and brushed her hand across her face, popping the last bite into her mouth. Rose choked down a gag.

"I want to run a few tests, Freeborn. Is that okay?"

"Sure, Doc, but shouldn't you tell Cadence about the dead vamps?"

"It can wait." Rose held a light to Freeborn's pupils. "Your eyes are clear. No redness. No glaze." She held a finger to Freeborn's throat. "Heart rate is steady, but temperature has elevated." Lifting Freeborn's injured hand she cleaned the blood off and checked the bite wound. "Your flesh has regenerated. Cadence's blood has reversed the decomposition."

"So, I'm cured?" said Freeborn, wiggling to leave the table.

"Yes . . . no. Would you mind if I took a blood sample? I want to see if it's similar to Cadence's. You've ingested a vampire. Though eating one shouldn't have any effect, I still need to be sure."

The girl held up her arm. "Take what you want, Doc."

"Hold on." Rose walked to a cabinet and removed a hand mirror. Returning, she held the mirror to Freeborn's face. "You might as well look," she said. "It's shocking, so be prepared."

Freeborn studied her reflection, fascinated. In the past few minutes, Freeborn's skin had returned to its normal shade. Her hair and nails had grown, and despite the blood smeared across her mouth, she looked healthier than she ever had before. While she gazed in the mirror, Rose helped herself to several vials of her blood. Another alteration was the color of blood. Human blood was red. Zombies produced a black ooze, but Freeborn's blood was maroon.

While Rose studied the blood samples, Freeborn slid off the table and dragged the remains of the Shadowguard outside.

"At least you're not a zombie."

Rose heard footsteps running toward the lab. She looked up as Highbrow appeared in the door with the Bull Dogs.

"You okay in here?" Highbrow narrowed his eyes. "Shadowguard have been sighted, and two people were kidnapped." He looked around the infirmary. "I guess you saw a little action too."

Rose stood. "You'll find two dead Shadowguard outside. I killed one and Freeborn killed the other. Who was taken? Did you send a team after them?"

"Freeborn?" Highbrow frowned.

The Tiger guard walked back in, still splattered with blood. Highbrow's face flushed and several of the Bull Dogs flinched, raising their weapons.

"Easy!" shouted Rose. "Put your guns down!"

"Did she bite someone?" Highbrow asked, still looking at the splatter on her hands and face.

Freeborn smiled, revealing flesh still in her teeth. "Hello, Highbrow."

"She killed one of the Shadowguard," Rose explained.

"She's a zombie," whispered Highbrow. He took a step closer to Rose.

"Not quite."

Rose, Highbrow, and the Bull Dogs watched as Freeborn picked up the crashed door of her cell and righted it, sitting down on her cot.

Highbrow shook his head, snapping out of his stupor, and turned to the Bull Dogs. "Not a word to anyone, you all understand? Clean up this mess. I need to have a conversation with the doctor." He pulled Rose aside as the patrol team began mopping up the blood and picking up broken instruments. "How is this possible? You used Cadence's blood, didn't you?"

"Yes."

"It makes sense. But that means Freeborn is still infected. Cadence, too." Highbrow's eyes grew grave. "Cadence is a carrier, isn't she, Rose?"

Rose didn't like the tone of his voice. "Let's not jump to conclusions. Listen, something amazing has happened. I killed one of the Shadowguard by stabbing him in the neck with a used syringe. It had been filled with Cadence's blood. I've been giving Freeborn direct injections of Cadence's blood, thinking she might be a type of Maker. I didn't expect her blood to be toxic to vampires, and yet it saved Freeborn"

Highbrow shook his head in frustration. "So Rafe wasn't needed. I wish I hadn't let Dragon leave. Everything we do here is being monitored by the Kaiser."

"Captain, you can't second guess yourself every time something goes wrong. Freeborn's health is improving, but I do think Cadence needs to be your number one concern. Make sure she is guarded around the clock. If the Kaiser gets his hands on her, things are going to go south, fast."

"Keep this under wraps, Rose." Highbrow glanced at Freeborn. "I don't want this getting out to anyone. Find out what Cadence's blood would do to an uninfected person. Come to me, not Cadence, when you find out. That's an order." He smiled. "Need anything else?"

Rose studied Highbrow. His reaction to the news had her worried. Ordering her to report to him and not the commander was against protocol. "No," she said, apprehensive. "Not at the moment."

Echo burst into the room. "Captain! Blaze and China Star have both been taken! According to Thor, Shadowguard were seen just before they disappeared."

Highbrow cursed. "Echo, you and the Blue Devils stay with Rose. They attacked here as well. Bull Dogs, on me." He glanced at Freeborn and exited. The Blue Devils ushered in and took positions at the windows and door, while Rose attended to Freeborn.

"Hey, Blue Devils," called out Freeborn. "Who do I have to eat around here to get something to drink?"

One of the guards darted to the fridge, found a drink for Freeborn, and tossed it through the bars. Freeborn growled. Rose tried not to laugh as he slunk back.

Freeborn twisted an iron bar around the door to secure the cage, then sat and drank her soda. It was clear that no one on the outside could open the cage, but there was nothing to stop her if she wanted out.

One thing was sure: Freeborn wasn't a zombie. She was no longer human, either.

Chapter Ten

Dragon found Tandor waiting in front of the station. Cricket opened the door and the team made room as he approached.

The vampire slid in. "Glad you made it through the road block. I had to ditch my bike a mile back."

"Did you eat a cat while you waited?" asked Cricket, pushing him away.

Tandor laughed. "I might have eaten a rat or two." He patted the back of Dragon's seat. "Roll out. We're making a brief stop at the Cliff Dwellings."

Dragon was confused. "Is Rafe there?"

"No. He's at the Citadel. Pallaton confirmed Rafe was taken prisoner last night. The Kaiser forced Rafe to call you this morning and lie to Cadence. The Shadowguard have been watching your camp and the hotel, which is why they're always one step ahead of us."

"Why the Cliff Dwellings? It's out of our way."

"We're meeting with a local werewolf tribe to ask for an escort. You girls ever meet werewolves before?"

"No," said Lotus. "I can't say I want to either."

"We only know werepumas," Monkey added.

Tandor smiled. "Werewolves don't bite. At least, not little girls. The tribe stays in hiding, hunting for toothy types." He chuckled at his own humor. "Don't worry. These people are tolerant of those they consider friendly."

"People? They're animals." Lotus crossed her arms. Her prejudice and negative outlook was uninspiring. She caught disappointment on Tandor's face and mouthed the word, *sorry*.

Dragon utilized a shortcut in Manitou Springs leading through a neighborhood, traveling west under a clear night sky, passing the Garden of the Gods. He wondered if his team thought of the nights they had spent patrolling the Garden. Turning onto a small gravel road, Dragon pulled into a secluded parking lot. He lowered the window an inch and turned off the engine.

"Where are the wolves?" asked Lotus, disappointed.

Dragon didn't need vampire vision to see glowing eyes in the cliff dwellings of the red rocks. "What's the protocol, Tandor? I don't want any trouble. Give us a quick list of do's and don'ts."

"This is the Cheyenne Mountain Wolf Tribe. It's true they are werewolves, but even in wolf form, they retain their human personalities. In other words, they're not wolves and don't think like wolves either," said Tandor. "An infected wolf bit Chayton's grandmother. Believing it a good omen, Chayton had her turn the entire tribe. Fitting, really, as the wolf is the spirit animal of the Navajo. It's an insult to refer to the tribe as a pack, so don't. Chayton likes to pretend he's a wolf, so wait for him to approach you. He'll let you know if you're accepted or not. It's Chayton's way and has nothing to do with the Navajo. He's quite a character."

"They're not like movie werewolves?" asked Monkey. "Won't they eat us?"

Tandor shook his head. "Just like Luna when she's in her cat form, it's still Luna, not a puma. Same thing here. They simply take the shape of an animal, without becoming the animal. I'm far more dangerous."

Cricket tugged on Tandor's hair. "Cut it out, vampire."

Leaving his weapons, Tandor walked to the middle of the parking lot. He held his hands together and bowed low. The cliff dwellings were a small replica of an original Pueblo Indian village, with gift shops, a restaurant, and a museum below.

"I need a smoke." Whisper tried to light a cigarette, but Kirin snatched it out of his mouth and snapped it in half. He grinned and shrugged his shoulders.

"They're coming." Lotus pointed out the front window.

Torches appeared as figures ascended from the lower level, and then from the gift shop. One white and one red wolf trotted out and approached Tandor's extended hands. The red wolf stood with his paws on Tandor's shoulders and licked his face. The vampire chuckled, scratching behind the wolf's ears.

"Wait here," said Dragon. "I'm getting out."

Whisper didn't listen, opening the hatch and climbing out. The girls followed as a group of shirtless young men in tattered shorts fanned out facing the team. Cricket grinned and caught eyes with one.

"This is the one I told you about," Tandor told the wolves, gesturing to Dragon. "He can be trusted or I wouldn't have brought humans here."

The wolves approached Dragon with a soft growl.

"Dragon, this is Chief Chayton and his wife, Chenoa. Remember what I said, let him come close and remain still." He laughed when the giant red wolf growled.

They sniffed Dragon, and Cheyton's head rose to Dragon's shoulders. The white wolf nipped playfully at her mate.

"You've passed the test," said Tandor. "Chayton, this joke is getting old. I already told Dragon that you're not a real wolf. You just look like one."

"They do," said Dragon. He bowed low and formal, a Japanese show of respect. "I am honored to meet you both." He introduced his team. "This is Whisper. The girls are Cricket, Kirin, Monkey, and Lotus."

"I'm Cricket." The petite girl grinned at the young man who caught her eye. "I'm a retriever. I mean, I pick up stuff, you know, for the team. I'm so nervous. We've never met werewolves before."

"I'm Red Hawk," said the boy. "It's nice to meet you."

"Me too, I mean . . . it's nice to meet you, too." Cricket grinned.

The tallest youth snapped his fingers and Red Hawk returned to stand in line. The giant red wolf trotted behind his tribe's formation, becoming hidden from view. When they parted, Chayton stood human form, draped in a red blanket. The chief, no more than thirty, possessed the stoic confidence of a man twice his age.

"It's okay," Chayton addressed his tribe. "These humans are friends of Tandor's. You and I need to talk, buddy. What are you doing here?" He led Tandor to a park bench.

People of all ages gathered around Dragon and Whisper. He counted at least fifty people in the tribe. Chenoa reappeared in jeans and a ski jacket, with a slender, older woman. The woman's red wool cape was draped by her long, silver hair. Her amber eyes illuminated her strong face.

"This is Grandmother," said Chenoa. "These people are from the survivors' camp at Seven Falls."

"Come here, child." Grandmother placed her hands on Dragon's shoulders. "You're so young to be leading others."

Dragon breathed in the scent of wolf, smoke, and vanilla. Her voice was soothing and he liked being in her presence.

"This land was ours before the coming of the Dead Ones and Long Tooths," said Grandmother, "and so it shall it be long after their bones turn to dust. We've meant to stop by your camp and meet Cadence. A great many things have been said about her. When your camp at Pike's Peak fell, we feared you had all been killed. Now that the Long Tooths have taken up residency at the Air Force Academy, we must be careful who is allowed into our camp. Will you accept something to drink?"

"Yes," Dragon said.

Chenoa brought Whisper to stand before Grandmother. The old woman turned from Dragon and embraced Whisper. When she stepped back, the women of the tribe surrounded Dragon and Whisper, pushing them closer together. Grandmother approached them holding a bowl in her hands.

"Do not be afraid," said Chenoa. "You must drink what is offered. It will help you see things clearly."

A cup was placed against Dragon's lips and tilted as he drank. The liquid was cool and tasted like water and iodine. Dragon was surprised when a girl began sprinkling them with vanilla.

"The oil will cover your human scent. Vampires smell like vanilla to each other, and to us," Grandmother explained.

After the girl finished anointing Dragon, he felt warmth spreading through his body. Whisper glanced at him, looking puzzled and feeling the same sensation. Grandmother raised her hands and the werewolves howled, lifting their voices in song.

Dragon saw golden spirits taking shape around them. He thought no one noticed until he caught Chenoa's gaze.

"I see them," said Dragon, overcome with emotion.

"As do all of us. The drink has opened your eyes," said Chenoa. "Our ancestors are always with us, and now they will be with you and your team. Only you and Whisper will see them, and only if they want you to. We can sense the females in your group are closed-minded and wouldn't understand, nor appreciate this gift, but you and Whisper are different. You both realize there are greater powers at work. Grandmother is the one who showed us how to see them."

"Will your husband take us to the Citadel?"

"Yes, I will," said Chayton, joining his wife. "I'm told your girlfriend was bitten by a Dead One. I don't know if Rafe can save her, Dragon, but we'll take you to the Citadel. We've found a tunnel that leads under the academy. The vampires don't use it." He paused. "It's not going to be easy once you get inside. We'll take you to the entrance, but I won't risk my tribe going in with you. If you free Rafe, we'll be waiting for you and will return with you."

"There are many tunnels beneath. Some new, some old," said Chenoa. "We don't know who built the new tunnels. They run from the Academy all the way to the Cheyenne Mountains. We never stay in one camp for long, but the tunnels are a good way for us to get around when we're close to the city."

Revived and filled with energy, Dragon watched Grandmother lead the children downstairs. Chenoa waved farewell and followed the rest of the women. Dragon noticed a necklace with teeth hanging around Chayton's neck.

"Yeah, I know. Pretty disgusting. These fangs were taken from the Kaiser's last wife," said Chayton. "The vampires have been here for several months. A patrol came looking for new recruits and they grabbed my twin brother, so I took the Kaiser's wife. Pallaton is now a Shadowguard and hunts us. Vampires don't like the taste of our blood, but we're certainly not friends. The Kaiser is evil, as are most vampires."

Tandor laughed. "I heard that, Chayton!"

"You were meant to," he said. "It's hard for a vampire to not want to drink human blood. Strong wills, resolve, and compassion are the only reasons why the Dark Angels are able to be with you at your camp. The oath they take helps, but its motivation more than anything else. You're lucky the Dark Angels are around to help."

"I know," said Dragon. "I'm also lucky Tandor is friends with the Cheyenne Mountain Wolf Tribe. I appreciate what you're doing for us, Chief."

"Then let's get going."

A howl sang in the night as the men shifted into wolves, following their chief.

"Get back to the vehicle," said Tandor. "We'll take Interstate 25 and meet them at Monument Creek. Moon Dog and Red Hawk will ride with us."

A large black wolf with a white-tipped tail, and a small red wolf trailed the girls to the Blazer. Kirin and Monkey opened the hatch for the wolves, then jumped in the backseat.

"Grandmother liked you," Tandor said to Dragon and Whisper. "Her blessing is special. She may look frail, but she's Chayton's second-in-command and a capable warrior, as strong and fast as any vampire."

Dragon spotted the werewolves turn toward the Garden of the Gods. He knew they would reach the meeting point long before they arrived and couldn't help envying them for their speed and strength. In that moment, he wished to be one of the tribe.

Chapter Eleven

Every sound and shadow caught Thor's attention as the Vikings hiked the trail. A body lay beside a creek, head in the water. Thor approached, but Logan grabbed his arm, motioning for the team to hold.

Thor watched Logan examine the faceless body. His coat sported a large red *A*. Another corpse floated nearby.

Logan turned to Thor. "Want me to fish him out?"

"I'll do it," said Thor. He laid the crossbow on the ground before wading out.

Thor hauled the corpse to shore and rolled it over. A pair of dull, gray eyes met his own and he shivered. The soldier tried to bite Thor's steel-tipped boot. Reacting, Thor stomped its head until it was slush. Raven marched to him with a disapproving glare.

"I know," said Thor. "I'll be more careful."

"One screw up is all it takes," Raven said. "Let Logan fish out the next one. I don't care what happens to him."

"I heard that." Logan gave Thor and Raven a dour look before examining the remains. "This one is a zombie. The next one might be a vampire. I figure Rafe is behind this. Someone knew the easiest way in and out of camp, along with guard rotations, knowing who would be at Midnight Falls and who would be dumb enough to follow. The Elite and A-Team didn't put up much of a fight. If you had a proper scout, you would have noticed the Shadowguard aren't covering their tracks. We are meant to follow, so I suggest we go back to camp."

Thor frowned. "I have a scout," he said.

"And that's me," said Baldor, pushing his way through the team. "I'll take it from here, scavenger. I've noticed you've been rubbing out footprints with your boot when you think no one is watching. The Shadowguard came through here with Blaze and Star. They are leaving a trail and they're dragging their prisoners. Why are you fouling up the trail, Logan? Don't you want us to find our friends?"

Raven stepped closer to Logan. "Answer Baldor. What are you trying to do, Logan? Why are you covering up tracks?"

"Because this is a bad idea and I think we should turn back," Logan said, stepping around the body. "If you want to continue, send your scout ahead. Your little team of Vikings is no match for the Shadowguard. I've advised you to turn back, so don't say I didn't warn you."

"It's my call," declared Thor. "I say we push on. Move out, Baldor."

Baldor marched on, eyes wide and his weapon ready. Loki and Heimdall followed. Odin crept forward with caution, peering through his rifle's night-vision scope. Raven, Dodger, and Smack brought up the rear with Logan and Thor.

"Have any of you killed a vampire before?" questioned Logan.

"Zombies, you shoot in the head," Raven gruffed. "Vampires, you shoot in the head or the heart. Both, if you can. Thor and I killed one a few weeks ago around here."

Logan snorted. "If we do find Star and Blaze, they'll already be turned. You can count on that."

Thor snarled and connected a haymaker with Logan's jaw. Logan spun and met the ground on his back. The rest of the team kept walking past Logan as he stumbled to his feet. No one stopped the scavenger when he stomped past and disappeared into the gloom.

"Logan's trouble," said Raven. "I don't trust him. It was a mistake to let him come along." She spat on the ground.

"We're not following you, Logan," said Loki, laughing. "You're going the wrong way, idiot."

Thor caught up to Smack and pulled her to a halt.

"Hey, hot stuff," said Thor. "I need a messenger. Cadence needs to know what we've found up here. There are probably more zombies and vampires back on the trail. You want me to send Dodger instead?"

"I got this, sergeant." Smack glanced back in the direction they had come. She checked the magazine in her rifle, clicking it back in place. "Don't worry about me. If anything with glowing eyes jump out, I'll shoot first and ask questions later."

"I'm not kidding about zombies or vamps," said Thor.

Smack took off running, the moonlight guiding her nimble steps. Thor watched until she was out of sight, then caught up with his team. Raven stood beside another body on the trail, recognizing it as one of the A-Team. With its midsection missing, this one would not turn.

Two more of the A-Team were shredded on the trail ahead, but still no sign of the Elites or Logan. Thor wanted to turn back, but he had to find Star. She had trusted him with her life.

Thor changed the order of his team, sending Heimdall to the back, and caught up with Baldor. His scout seemed more bloodhound than human. He had a curious way of walking hunched over, eyes pinned to the ground. When Baldor crouched low, Thor raised his fist and his team paused. Baldor examined the tracks, confirming their direction, then resumed.

The next time Baldor crouched, Thor raised his weapon. Feeling stalked, every sound set him on edge. Baldor gave a nod and pointed off the trail as Logan emerged from the brush holding a knife damp with blood.

"Find a friend?" quipped Thor. "Stick with the team, scavenger. We're not your babysitters."

"I served in a special branch of the F.B.I. recovering and capturing supernatural beings," said Logan, falling into step. "I don't need a babysitter, and pretty boy is following a cold trail. The Shadowguard are long gone. If your ego wasn't in the way, you'd have realized that and turned back by now."

"Baldor has the scent," Raven hissed, brushing by Logan. "Shut up and keep moving. You make too much noise, Mr. F.B.I."

"They're traveling with a Maker. I killed a vampire. Rafe has to be behind this, and you know it," said Logan.

"Where's the body?" Raven challenged.

Thor cocked his head. "A dead vampire won't confirm we've been trailing a Maker. If you're so anxious to go back, then leave. We're going on with or without you."

A scream ahead of them jarred the team into defensive positions.

"I believe that's Baldor," said Logan. "That's my cue to leave." He saluted Thor, backed away, and vanished into the shadows.

Loki and Dodger lit the trail and found Baldor, motionless. The team formed a circle facing outward. Engulfed by glowing eyes circling like fireflies, their gunfire pierced the lonely night air unsuccessful.

"Stay tight," shouted Thor.

He heard Heimdall's war cry and the clank of steel, realizing his friend made his mark. Seconds later, Heimdall was abducted by a vampire. Logan ran past, laughing.

He ran with the vampires, not after them.

The realization that Logan worked for the Kaiser hit Thor hard. He assumed Logan's warnings were based in fear. Vengeful, Thor fired at Logan, striking the vampire carrying Heimdall instead. Logan continued ahead as the vampire fell. Heimdall rose to his feet, dazed and confused.

"Make your shots count," shouted Thor. "Heimdall, get over here."

A helicopter rose from beyond the cliff, hovering at the edge. The sudden roar of the blades buffeted their senses. Thor saw people inside, and he searched for Star and Blaze to no avail. He spotted Logan still running for the chopper. Thor pulled the trigger again and again, enraged, not realizing when the gun responded with empty clicks. Two vampires appeared, seizing Heimdall, and ran for the cliff's edge, easily traversing the gap to the Black Hawk.

"Keep up with me, guys," shouted Thor, charging forward. He fired at the chopper with a fresh clip, killing one vampire. "That's more like it!"

The next moment, a net engulfed Thor and he dropped to the ground. He was helpless as Raven was captured and dragged away in a net.

"Your turn," said a female vampire appearing beside Thor. She picked him up and ran swift toward the chopper.

The thunderous whirl of the chopper filled Thor's ears. They were close. He knew it was impossible to escape, but Thor refused to give up, struggling to free himself. The unmistakable roar of a werepuma brought surprise and relief.

Four large werepumas bolted from the trees, with Luna in the lead. The lithe cat ripped into Thor's captor, finishing the vampire in seconds. Thor watched as Luna drop her kill and bound for Dodger. In a reflex of self-preservation, the Shadowguard dropped Dodger and ran toward the chopper. Luna continued to dodge bullets from the helicopter as a black werepuma assaulted another vampire. Thor became a spectator as the therianthropes ripped through fleeing vampires.

Rising to his elbows, Thor saw Raven was hostage to a tall blonde vampire. A short, formally dressed vampire stood near the chopper, with yellow eyes radiating a supernatural evil. Thor knew—this was the Kaiser.

The helicopter lifted and picked up speed. Helpless, Thor watched as his friends flew north, toward the former Air Force Academy.

"Get this net off me," shouted Thor.

Loki rushed to cut him loose and Thor burst forward in a rage of despair. Luna trotted over, licking her chops.

"Luna, you were freaking awesome," Loki exclaimed, his chin

bleeding. "The pride killed ten of those blood suckers, Thor. I wish they'd caught Logan. Did you see him laughing when he ran by us? He wasn't a prisoner. Why would he do it?"

"I saw it too," said Thor, hoarse. "We can discuss this later with Cadence." He paused, grimacing, feeling his ribs were cracked or broken. "They got Raven and Heimdall. Was anyone else taken?"

"Uther, and a few soldiers." Loki started to reload. "The Kaiser went after our best fighters. There's something about him . . . feels pure evil."

Thor nodded. "I got the same feeling."

Luna and Loki followed as Thor joined Dodger and Odin beside the mangled body of Baldor.

"Why kill Baldor?" Dodger choked back his agony. "I don't understand. They were taking prisoners. Why did they have to kill him?"

The werepumas gathered in close to the group, and the black mountain lion nuzzled Dodger. He threw his arms around her and let out a loud sob. Odin collapsed in shock and two other cats comforted him. Thor covered the grizzly remains with his coat, as tears flooded Odin's face.

Luna growled, standing next to Thor.

Thor kept his hand pressed to his ribs, breathing easier with the pressure. "They wanted us to hear Baldor scream. Dammit! If I had listened to Logan, this might not have happened."

Loki realized the weight of their situation. "The Kaiser has everything we don't, including a helicopter. How can we stop them if they return?"

Thor gave a grim nod at the group, not knowing the answer. "Each of you fought well. If it hadn't been for you, Luna, we'd all be on that chopper. Or . . ." His eyes burned as they fell toward Baldor once more.

Luna stood, transformed into human form. Loki placed his coat around her shoulders. Able to express her grief as a human, she sobbed as Thor held her.

"They took Raven," cried Luna. "I've lost her."

"I'll get her back, Luna. How did you know the Shadowguard were here? I thought you were up in the mountains."

"Vampires have a distinct odor." She lifted her head from his shoulder. "The scent was on the wind, and we came as fast as we could."

"Did you know Freeborn was bitten?" said Thor.

"No! We've been hunting for two days. Are you sure Logan is helping the Kaiser? This is a horrible betrayal."

Thor set Luna back. "It makes sense. Logan let the zombies into the Peak. We lost our camp, and now he's led the Kaiser here and taken some of our best people."

"We'd stay at camp, but people are still afraid of us." Luna wiped a hand across her face. "We are able to sense things we couldn't before. It was more than just the vampire's scent on the breeze. We could feel it coming, like a storm. I don't know what the Kaiser is, but he's far more than a mere vampire, Thor. The Kaiser was the storm, the true evil we all felt."

"Things won't ever be the same," lamented Loki. "Will they? The Shadowguard won't stop at this. They'll keep coming, until there isn't anyone left."

"A coyote told us the Kaiser is collecting fighters for the Death Games," said Luna. "They have been going on in Denver and a few other big cities. Zombies. Humans. Vampires, and therianthropes. The Kaiser has no prejudice concerning who dies in the arena, as long as it's exciting."

Dodger looked at Luna. "Then we're all at risk."

"We've held out this long. Vampires can be killed. They aren't immortal. If you can see them, you can fight them.

"Another reason why your pride should keep close to the camp for a while. We can't see vamps at full speed and we can't kill them quickly," said Thor. "If you don't mind, I'd appreciate an escort back to camp. Besides, we'll need help getting Odin back."

"I understand," Luna replied. "It's not a problem."

Loki's coat fell as Luna turned. Barbarella carried Odin on her back as Sheena and Skye flanked the group. Thor collected the remains of his teammate into his coat. Baldor was loyal and brave, and had always looked after the group. He had saved Thor's life more than once, and this was a crushing loss for everyone. He would be given a proper burial. It was the least they could do for him.

Chapter Twelve

Dragon's team met up with the wolf tribe not far from Pulpit Rock Park. The tribe had pulled vines back, revealing the mouth of a cave. A nauseating odor permeated from within.

"Good thing werewolves can see in the dark," said Cricket, moving toward Dragon. "It would make it easier if they could talk while in their animal form, though. Red Hawk is nervous and I get the feeling that not all of these tunnels are natural."

Dragon shared a bottle of water with her. "We're all on edge, Cricket. Chayton said some of these tunnels are new, but I don't understand how the Shadowguard don't know about them. They have to be man-made."

The sound of a low-flying helicopter approached and they scurried inside the cave. A Black Hawk followed Interstate 25, due north.

"The Shadowguard must be scouting the area," said Tandor.

"Do you know the layout of the Academy?" asked Dragon.

"Not well. Chayton says he can get us inside of the Citadel. The tunnel takes us under the science building, and once inside, we're to find the music hall. I know the general path. Don't worry about the tunnels. If they weren't safe to use, the wolves would not go in."

"Take a wolf by his tail and let him guide you." Cricket grinned at her friends. "Don't worry, they don't bite." She took hold of Red Hawk's tail and wiggled it. The wolf turned and licked at her hand.

"You girls ready for this?" asked Tandor. "What about you, smoker? Think your lungs will hold out to the Citadel and back?"

Whisper shrugged. "Don't worry about me. I'm young."

With a sharp howl from Chayton, Tandor motioned the team to follow the chief. Dragon took hold of Moon Dog's tail, each team member following suit. Dragon led his team, with Tandor bringing up the rear. Dragon depended on Moon Dog. When the wolf's tail went limp, he discovered the tunnel expanded and grew wider. When the tail gave a sudden jerk, he learned to duck and watch his step.

After walking for what seemed like miles, an orange light appeared. Moon Dog yanked his tail out of Dragon's hand, and the wolves gathered sniffing near a large, green door. Chayton glanced at Dragon, who opened the door to a small maintenance room. Three orange lights in sconces illuminated furniture and a rack of workmen coats covered with a fine layer of dust.

Moon Dog and Red Hawk followed the group, while the remainder of the tribe stayed. Once inside Dragon shut the door, leaving the wolves to wait for their return.

"Smell that?" Tandor sniffed the air. "This is the science building, used by the tribe as a hiding place until the Kaiser arrived. There are things in this building we don't want to disturb. Draw your weapons and stay quiet. This is Shadowguard country now."

Whisper tightened a silencer to the end of his rifle, while the others drew their swords. This time Tandor opened the door, standing back as Dragon entered a dim hallway. He led the team along the hall, turned a corner, and came to another door. As he reached to open it, Tandor pushed him back, and placed his ear against the door.

"Yep. I thought I smelled zombies," said Tandor. "Pallaton says the Kaiser uses cyborg zombies in the arena. This must be where they are kept. If I'd known we'd be coming this way, I would have asked Pallaton for directions myself. Stay tight behind me. They're in holding cells, so we should be okay."

The vampire opened the door without making a sound. Dragon entered an enormous room, with a high ceiling and the scent of rotting flesh. It had been cleared of all work tables, and the stained floor led to twelve white doors on either side where former students conducted experiments. Dull orange lights glowed above each door, illuminating numbers *1* through *24* in bright red. The group walked in a straight line toward the next door. Dragon hung back, caught in a moment of curiosity. He picked his favorite number, looking in the dirty window of the door marked *11*.

"You don't want to do that," Tandor said, appearing beside Dragon. "We need to keep going. The slave quarters are in the music hall and Pallaton said Rafe will be there. Do not agitate the captives."

With a quick look through the window, Dragon spotted a face, half of it outfitted with metal and a red, telescopic eye. The cyborg spotted Dragon and thumped on the door. A face appeared at every window.

"Move," Lotus pleaded.

Tandor opened the exit door and the team waited, allowing Dragon to lead them downward through the stairwell. A vampire guard lay on the ground, missing his head. Motioning silence to everyone, Tandor descended and approached another door. They entered and traversed a long maintenance hall to the music department. More guards were piled outside the door, covered with blood.

Tandor motioned the team to keep moving and Dragon could hear the room was filled with zombies. He led the team through the last door, and climbed three flights of stairs. He was sure he saw a Navajo spirit waving him on and, opening a door, he walked onto a stage. The smell of paint and dust was thick, and the theater curtain was closed. Musical instruments lined the wall in a far corner. The team took positions hiding behind an old stage set, while Dragon and Tandor entered a carpeted hallway. Doors with small windows lined the narrow hall, each room dimly lit. Dragon could see men, women, and children sleeping in each room. In Room 16, Dragon found Rafe lying on a cot, eyes closed. His chest showed deep wounds that were slow to heal.

Rafe opened his eyes and was at the door in a flash. As Dragon reached for the doorknob, Rafe pointed toward a surveillance camera.

"We're busted," said Tandor. He used the hilt of his sword to break off the knob, and a siren screeched throughout the building.

"Nice!" Rafe stepped into the hallway, annoyed. "Now the entire academy knows you're here. Get moving, you idiots. I'm not crippled."

Followed by the two vampires, Dragon ran from the hall and back onto the stage. Whisper waited on the far side, holding the door open. China Six, Moon Dog and Red Hawk were far ahead of them. Rafe knocked Dragon aside as he ran out the door. Whisper fired a single shot over Dragon's head before following and, looking behind, Dragon watched a guard drop to his knees as more poured into the room.

Return fire raked the stage. Dragon rushed for the door, tripping over a snare drum and falling hard. Eyes glowing violet, Tandor was quick to pull Dragon to his feet. A stabbing pain in his ankle prevented Dragon from running, and he held on to Tandor. The vampire gasped as a round pierced his shoulder, knocking him back.

"Get out of here," yelled Tandor, lifting his sword. "I'll hold them off."

Not waiting for a response, he turned and charged the enemy. Dragon limped toward the door as he heard steel on steel. The stage lights burned, revealing numerous armed Shadowguard circling the stage. A guard appeared in front of Dragon, blocking his exit.

For a moment, Dragon again saw a shimmering form walking among the vampires. A warm sensation swept over Dragon, and all fear and pain faded. A guard shot at Dragon, missing.

Crying out, Dragon rushed the enemy with his swords flashing a dizzying array of silver. He twirled and connected with a leg and torso, slicing deep, then spun in combinations of skilled maneuvers, diminishing the ranks of the vampires.

The stage curtains parted, and a small audience of vampires filled the audience.

Applause and cheers erupted as Dragon struck down one guard after another, only to be replaced with more glowing eyes. Dragon fought, able to anticipate the vampires' moves and match their speed. Bodies dropped in rapid succession as he began moving faster than his opponents. He lost sight of Tandor, intent on killing until the last vampire fell. At last, Dragon stood alone on stage among the bodies. Drenched in blood, the audience stood to their feet in ovation.

"Bravo, bravo," exclaimed a voice from the front row. Dragon squinted to see a short, bald man in a tuxedo. His black eyes danced, and his fangs were longer than any other vampire Dragon had ever seen.

"You must be the Kaiser," Dragon said.

The man nodded. "Indeed." He gestured at guards standing nearby. "Please disarm, Master Dragon. It's been exciting watching your team slip into the music hall. I've been watching in the security room, but when you started performing, I had to bring a few friends here to watch."

Guards moved to apprehend Dragon, but the teen tensed, raising his blades. The Kaiser coughed, and several more raised their guns, too far away for Dragon to cut down. He had matched the speed of vampires, but he didn't feel like trying his luck against a wall of bullets.

His swords were presented to the Kaiser as a blonde, muscular vampire leaned down and whispered to the Kaiser.

"I agree, Aldarik," said the Kaiser, looking up at Dragon. "He is a magnificent fighter. I am surprised to find Master Dragon is more than a match for the Shadowguard. Yet, I wonder if you could defeat him. Shall we put you to the test?"

The blonde vampire smiled. "Nothing would please me more."

Dragon met Aldarik's gaze. "Give me back my swords."

Lieutenant Aldarik reached for the hilt of a saber, worn on his hip.

Another vampire appeared on stage, standing before Dragon and waved off a fuming Aldarik. The vampire turned around, and Dragon stared at Chief Chayton's twin, though the similarity was only physical. The werewolf was noble and kind, but his fanged twin emanated darkness.

"Captain Pallaton, move out of the way," shouted the Kaiser. "You're spoiling the fun. Why are you here? I ordered you to seek out the wolf pack."

"Tribe," Pallaton corrected.

The Kaiser lowered his voice. "Did I offend you, captain? Truth is, wolves run in a pack. They're not a tribe. Your brother is nothing more than an uneducated dog."

Pallaton stepped aside. "Regardless, we've seen enough fighting tonight. The kid should fight in the arena. There's no profit in letting him kill Aldarik. You'll need a new champion and I'll be out a lieutenant."

Leaping into the air, Aldarik landed on stage. His eyes flared, fangs extending. "If you haven't the guts to kill your own brother, captain, I'll gladly go in your place. A wolf is a wolf as far as I'm concerned, and I have no problem killing them. In fact, I enjoy it."

"I think not, Lieutenant Aldarik. I want to bring prisoners back, alive." Though Pallaton's fangs were exposed, his eyes remained a dark shade of brown. It was clear he was able to maintain control of his anger. "The humans traveling with my brother won't be hard to track. I wanted to see Dragon fight and I'm impressed."

"You're stalling!" shouted Aldarik.

Pallaton and Aldarik faced off.

"Stop this at once," demanded the Kaiser. "Captain Pallaton, you will leave now. Bring back prisoners. I want the wolf tribe for the Death Games."

Saluting, Pallaton left the stage with a several guards. The Kaiser slid a finger across the edge of Dragon's katana, laughing when he sliced his finger. He sucked the wound.

"Be careful, Kaiser," said a sultry, female voice. "This human killed a host of your guards. Of course his sword is sharp. If you don't mind, I want to take a closer look at this young man."

"Be my guest, Salustra," said the Kaiser.

A voluptuous woman in a formal black gown ascended the stairs with grace. Her face hid behind a red veil, with gloves and heels to match. She paused before him and her eyes glowed a dazzling shade of violet.

"I've never seen anyone fight like you, Master Dragon," said Salustra. "Who are your people?"

"My father was Chinese," Dragon said. "My mother was Japanese. Both were Olympic medalists and proficient in the ancient arts. They taught me."

"They certainly did." Salustra slithered up to Dragon, placing her hands on his arms. "You are gold, darling. Pure gold." Her eyes stopped glowing, turning a softer shade of lavender. "It shall be my pleasure to be your guardian. We can't have a champion staying in slave quarters." She glanced at the Kaiser. "I will keep Master Dragon in my quarters, where he will be safe. Do you have any objections, Kaiser? Of course, if you want him . . ."

The Kaiser appeared on stage, standing next to the tall female, though Dragon never saw him move. Dragon tried to comprehend just how dangerous this man was.

"I will allow you to keep Dragon, for now, Salustra," said the Kaiser, using a giddy, high-pitched voice. "But not forever. Dragon is not a pet. He is a warrior and destined for greatness in the Death Games." The Kaiser took Salustra by the hands, kissing each one.

"Master Dragon, my friends come from all over the world. They wish to be a part of something wonderful," continued the Kaiser. "Of course, I don't want to spoil all of the surprises. It's taken some time, but here we are, rulers of the new world." He leaned forward, his voice becoming deep—too deep. "I know you believe help is coming, but trust me, Senator Powers isn't coming. No one is."

"Then why don't you just turn us all into vampires?" said Dragon.

The Kaiser flashed an angry look, raising his pitch again. "What fun would that be? I don't intend to storm your little camp and turn everyone into vampires." He laughed, some of the audience joining in. "Your pitiful little group is much easier to manage while you tuck yourselves into the safety of the Falls. When I want one of you, I'll reach in and take one."

Salustra took Dragon by the arm. "Come with me, Dragon. The Kaiser is quite the conversationalist. He'll be at it all night if we let him. Let me show you to your new quarters."

"Bye now," the Kaiser called out. "We'll be seeing you soon, Master Dragon."

Dragon descended the stage beside Salustra. He held his head high, intent on getting out of the theater alive. Much to his surprise, Salustra led him through the front door of the building, into the chilly night air. Frost covered the grass and Dragon's breath expelled in white clouds, yet he didn't feel the cold. The stars were bright and a waning moon hung in the sky. No guards offered escort and Dragon considered trying to make a run for it, until he saw a string of human prisoners being ushered across the lawn.

The prisoners were cloaked in black hoods, but Dragon watched one particular prisoner. By her gait and boots, Dragon knew it was Star. Blaze followed, cursing and fuming. The Tiger required an escort to keep her in line. He stepped toward his friends, weaponless, but knowing he had to help.

"Don't concern yourself, Dragon," said Salustra, placing a hand on his arm. "You wouldn't make it ten yards before the Shadowguard brought you down with a tranquilizer. Sharpshooters are stationed on every rooftop. We can't have our new main attraction injuring himself trying to be a hero. I take it you know these humans?"

"Yes," Dragon said, bristling with anger. "These are my friends."

"The Kaiser has been busy tonight. I wasn't asked along. Not that I mind," she said, with a laugh. "I don't like being involved in violence. I only like to watch the Death Games. You're fortunate I spoke up when I did. Aldarik wanted to kill you. He occasionally competes in the Death Games, and has never been defeated."

"Can't you help my friends?" pleaded Dragon. "They have Star. She's my best friend. I have to do something. I can't just—"

"You're unarmed. What will you do, break Star's chains? Pick her up and run away with her? What about the others? You'll do far more for them here, by keeping the Kaiser happy. I know it seems cruel, but if you're here, you can keep your eye on them. Leave and they die a worse fate than you could imagine."

Dragon watched the line of hooded prisoners enter the music hall. "I'll kill the Kaiser one day," he said. "That's a promise."

Salustra squeezed his arm. "Maybe. One way or another, for now, we're all slaves of the Kaiser."

He wondered what she meant as they turned and walked in the opposite direction.

Chapter Thirteen

Groggy from the tranquilizer, Blaze was unable to see from beneath the smelly hood. She watched the Vikings try to rescue them, then Logan jumped in and the hood was placed on her head as they flew off. He had betrayed them. On the flight to the Citadel, the vampires talked about Rafe's capture and torture. Blaze found it remarkable that Rafe said nothing about the camp.

"Keep moving," said a guard standing close by.

The grass under her feet turned into cement, and Blaze tripped on purpose. The guard grabbed her arm and pushed her forward. *Nasty blood-sucker*, she thought, as a door squeaked open and the line continued forward. Blaze paused to listen to the soft music playing, and received a shove. She stumbled into Raven, hearing her muffled curse.

"Take them into the theater," said a vampire. "The Kaiser is waiting."

As another door opened, Blaze felt her heart pounding in her chest. Applause filled her ears as cement gave way to carpet. The line came to a halt and a rough tug pulled Blaze up a flight of wooden stairs. She bumped into Raven a second time, hearing no objection.

"Good evening or should I say good morning, as dawn is approaching?" said a man with a deep, booming voice. "Welcome to the Citadel. It's time for the meet-and-greet. Remove their hoods, and let us see the new slaves!"

She blinked as bright lights assaulted her eyes. Blaze stood in a large theater between Raven and Star, and before a ravenous vampire audience. Uther and the Elite stood to the side, along with five Freedom Army soldiers. Blaze heard a sniffle and realized the leader of China Six, so calm and brave in battle, was crying. Her sobs unsettled Blaze and she inched toward Star, nudging her with an elbow.

"Stop crying," said Blaze, in a hushed voice.

The vampires in the theater gasped when she spoke. Star looked at Blaze in terror.

"What's this? You may not speak unless I give you permission!" The Kaiser moved to Blaze, flashing his eyes and bearing his fangs with vehemence. Blaze found her nerve and glared back at him. If she was going to die, she would do it facing her enemy without fear.

A smile crept onto his face. "You're a spirited little thing. What is your name, little girl?"

"Blaze."

"What is your special skill?"

"Attitude," she said.

The Kaiser's forehead creased with his frown. "Let me rephrase the question. What is your preferred weapon of choice? And don't be cute, I don't like it. What weapon do you use in battle?"

Instead of answering, Blaze struggled to get free. She refused to yield before him, knowing she was doomed no matter what she did or said. His eyes glimmered and Blaze imagined the Kaiser sinking his long, pointy fangs into her throat.

"Tell him," said Raven, through gritted teeth. "You'll get us all killed. Tell him that you use a crossbow."

Blaze rolled her eyes. "You just did."

The Kaiser pointed a chubby finger at the two girls. The moment he looked at Raven, his features softened and his eyes glistened. "Oh, my," he said, breathless, his words slow. "I like you."

Blaze seethed as he sauntered over to Raven. The Kaiser and Aldarik studied Raven with lust. Raven, for all her pride and bravery, shuddered with her eyes locked on the floor. The lieutenant reached out his hand, only to be pushed aside by the Kaiser.

"This one is for me, Aldarik," said the Kaiser. "You may pick another."

"Only the best for you, my Kaiser," replied Aldarik, turning his attention toward Star. "I'll take the China Star."

The Kaiser nodded. "So be it, Lieutenant Aldarik. She is yours." He clapped his hands. "What shall be the fate of the others? Guardians speak up now. We have a fine selection of soldiers up for grabs."

Blaze looked at her captured friends. Heimdall and Uther appeared furious as Aldarik led the young men forward. The Freedom Army soldiers were ignored.

"These six are the Elite," said Aldarik. "Battle trained, young, strong, and considered the finest warriors among the humans. Despite their appearance, I found it easy to take them in battle. The soldiers offered no fight at all when Pallaton plucked them from the barricade. Unfortunately, I encountered resistance from another team and they were eliminated." He shook his head. "What I would have given to see them fight against Aries of Athens."

"You wasted precious human blood, Aldarik. I ordered the Shadowguard to return with the finest, and you've brought me puppies." The Kaiser seethed with anger. A few vampires in the audience whispered, but no guardians raised their hands.

Aldarik fiddled with the hilt of his saber, acting remorseful, but Blaze could tell it was feigned. The vampire had the air of a sociopathic murderer. He killed for sport.

"We'll talk later, but for now," said the Kaiser, pointing at Raven, "I want this exotic beauty taken to my quarters. Perhaps I have found a suitable replacement for my wife. Take her away!"

Star cried out as guards appeared and hauled Raven off the stage. Raven resisted and Blaze knew the Viking girl wouldn't tolerate being pawed by this maniac. The moment she had a chance, Raven would move to kill the Kaiser. The opportunity almost made her wish she was the one chosen.

"Now for this one, with the eyes of ice," said the Kaiser, turning to Uther.

Uther, bleeding from the wire around his wrists, glared at his captors with defiance. Aldarik pulled him out of line.

Uther remained steadfast. "You'll be sorry you ever set foot in our camp. If Cadence doesn't kill you, Thor will. All of you will be dead and buried long before the flesh rots from my body. We will be avenged, mark my word."

At Aldarik's signal, the guards moved in and struck Uther with their rifles. He held firm until the butt of a rifle struck the back of his head. He slumped to his knees, his face and head swollen and caked with blood.

"I have heard about the Elite," the Kaiser said to the crowd. "Uther is their leader, but now he is my slave. I promised that I'd give you a wonderful show on Halloween evening. We shall enjoy watching the Elite fight some of the best Class A fighters in the Death Games." He waved his hand in the air, addressing the Shadowguard. "Take the Elite to their quarters. Leave them bound as punishment for their leader's insolence."

While Uther and his team were removed, the soldiers and Heimdall were brought forward. The large Viking fought against his bonds and cursed his captors. His skin glistened with blood, and his hateful eyes defied the vampires' authority. Blaze was proud as he showed the vampires not all humans could be beaten into submission.

"Thor will come for you," shouted Heimdall. "You will all die for what you did to Baldor!" He spat at Aldarik and the crowd booed.

Heimdall growled with fury and charged forward, intent on reaching the Kaiser. Before the guards or Aldarik could react, the Kaiser faced Heimdall, lifted his tiny hand, and smiled. The giant froze in his tracks, wide eyes glued on the Kaiser, unable to move or blink. Blaze and Star exchanged a look of amazement. An audible gasp rose from the crowd, followed by wild applause. The Kaiser circled Heimdall, twisting a large ruby ring on his left index finger.

"Take these so-called soldiers to the pens," the Kaiser shouted. "This one tried to strike me and will fight in the zombie melee. We'll see what he can do against forty of the hungriest zombies."

Aldarik snapped his fingers and guards led the Freedom Army soldiers out of the theater. The Kaiser produced a handkerchief from his pocket and dried Star's tears. Blaze let out a hiss that startled the Kaiser. He gave her a sharp look, before returning his attention to Star.

"You have chosen well, Aldarik," said the Kaiser. "Everyone, this is Star, leader of the infamous China Six. They are the same team that arrived this evening to rescue the traitor, Rafe."

Star gasped, but didn't say a word as the vampires shouted insults.

"Come now, my friends. Rafe didn't want to be part of our club, and he will be brought to heel soon enough." The Kaiser waved the crowd silent. "China Six, I might add, was led here by Master Dragon. Many of you saw how he fought tonight, and you will see him again in the Death Games soon!"

The audience applauded. Blaze wondered what happened during Rafe's escape, and if Dragon was a captive, where was Whisper? Star's look of alarm kept her from causing a commotion.

"You have claimed Star as your slave, therefore you may remove her from the stage," the Kaiser continued. "Do with her what you want, Aldarik. But be careful. She is more dangerous than you think. Pallaton might have taken Star without being wounded, but allow her to sleep beside you unchained, and you may not wake from your rest."

"I can handle her." Aldarik grabbed Star by the arm, hauling his prize across the stage. Star caught sight of Blaze, abject terror on her face, before being led out the stage door.

Alone on the stage, Blaze incensed the audience and stuck out her tongue. They shouted, shook their fists, and cursed her. Feigning boredom, Blaze lifted her eyes to the balcony expecting to see more bloodsuckers. Instead, a lone figure sat in the furthest corner. The Kaiser followed her gaze, but the person ducked out of sight. Her heart skipped a beat. *Whisper?*

"You want to know my special skill?" diverting the Kaiser's attention from the balcony. "I'm an archer. Maybe you've heard of me? I'm Blaze of the Fighting Tigers. Yesterday, I killed a horde of zombies, the same ones you sent to take out my team. Before that, I fought in the Battle of the Peak and slaughtered hundreds. I've even killed a vampire or two, but I'm not keeping score. You all look the same to me. Butt ugly, with fangs and nightlights for eyes."

"Aren't you the least bit afraid of me, little girl?" The Kaiser walked over to Blaze, interested. Too interested. "No? I don't know why Aldarik brought you here. Archers aren't cause for concern. Especially not a tiny, poorly decorated one like you. I wanted Cadence, or Highbrow. Now, who should I give you to?"

A few hands were raised in the audience, but the Kaiser ignored them.

"I'm done playing around with you batfreaks. Take me to my cell and give me some chow," said Blaze. "You want me to fight in the Death Games? As long as I get to kill vamps, I'm your girl."

"Very well," said the Kaiser. "I'll give you to Pallaton. He'll know how to handle a savage." He motioned to his guards. "Take this repulsive brat away and lock her up."

"You're the repulsive one," Blaze shouted. "Drinking blood and eating babies makes you lower than the zombies, you little imp."

The guards made the mistake of grabbing Blaze by the arms. She leveled one with a kick and put a boot in the other's groin. The audience cheered, eager for a fight. Her revolt didn't last as two more guards joined in to help, dragging her off the stage kicking and screaming.

Blaze glowed with rage as the vampires tossed her into a cell. A board covered a window opening in the door, and a light a cot furnished the small space. Framed pictures of dead musicians spotted the walls, and it smelled like a gym locker room. She plopped on the bed and noticed scratching on the wall. It read: *RAFE.*

She was in Rafe's cell. Her thoughts led her to believe that Rafe has been rescued. Hope stirred her emotions and calmed her angst.

Chapter Fourteen

The Dark Angels were tasked with building a wall between the hospital and the lab, requiring a lot of construction and busy vamps zipping about. With all the commotion and increased demands on Rose, she needed some assistance. She placed Ginger—a tall, red-haired vampire with medical training—in charge of tending to minor injuries. The Vikings soon arrived for treatment. Rose treated Odin first, then ordered him escorted to their RV and placed under observation. She sent Loki on an errand, and then examined Thor's ribs.

"Is Thor going to be all right?" asked Luna.

Upon examination, Rose confirmed his ribs were bruised. She noticed a patchwork of old scars crisscrossing his back from the late Captain's disciplinary measures. Thor winced though Rose applied minimal pressure to the bruised area.

She turned to Luna. "He'll be sore for a while, but he'll be fine. I appreciate what you did for the Vikings tonight. Will your pride stay in camp for a while?"

"It's too chaotic around here, Doc. We'll only be in the way. Cadence wants us here, but I'm taking the pride back into the mountains. We won't be far." Luna shifted and bolted through the door, roaring as she vanished into the darkness with her pack.

"I like that girl," Rose said, as she wrapped a brace around Thor's ribs. "With a little rest, you'll be back on the front lines in no time."

"Rest?" Thor said. "I'm going to the Citadel and rescuing our friends."

"Not today," said Rose. "How about something for the pain? Micah and Ginger brought fresh supplies."

Rose held up a syringe. Thor nodded and closed his eyes as Rose sunk a needle into his vein.

"Big guys get big doses," she said. "Better?"

"A little." Thor caught her arm, keeping her from walking away. "Do you think the Kaiser will turn Star into a vampire?"

"It would be the kindest thing he could do . . . to all of them." Thor wanted the truth and Rose wished she could forget. Every Dark Angel knew what the Kaiser did to his prisoners.

"Come on, Doc. I have to know," said Thor.

"Some will feed his troops. The Kaiser knows how to sustain human life for a long time in order to supply his people with fresh blood. There is a place he keeps cold where humans are kept in a state similar to a coma. Every day they provide a pint of fresh blood, until they are expended and replaced. They feel no pain, but I know they dream." Rose had to look away from Thor when his gaze became too intense. "Most fight in the Death Games, and a rare few are kept as personal slaves."

Thor lowered his eyes, unable to respond.

"Ginger?" Rose motioned at the vampire, who was attending to another patient. "When you're done, help Thor to a cot. I want him to rest."

Cadence entered the infirmary sipping a cup of coffee. She had recently showered and changed, and her hair hung straight and full, resting on her shoulders. Rose had given her a shot of iron and Vitamin B earlier, but she still looked anemic.

"How are you holding up, Thor?" asked Cadence. He didn't look up. "Highbrow is making the arrangements for Baldor's funeral. I'll clear your duties so you can attend. In the meantime, Aurora will stop by later with breakfast if you're hungry. You can go back to your RV as soon as Rose releases you."

"Odin is there," said Thor, finding his voice. He stared at the ground. "I can't deal with him right now. I'd rather stay here."

Rose reached into her lab coat and handed Thor a bottle of pills. "Take one every four hours for pain, if needed. Trust me, you're going to need them. It'll take a few weeks to heal, minimum."

"Hey, commander," called out Freeborn.

The Tiger removed the bar she had bent to lock the cage, setting the door aside with a loud *clang*, and strolled out. The Blue Devils came to attention and aimed their rifles at Freeborn.

"Stand down," shouted Cadence. Guns lowered and a few angry words later, Echo led her team outside.

Freeborn hurried to Cadence and they embraced. Rose motioned for the Dark Angels to halt construction and take a break. Ginger cleaned up her work area and joined the vampires, giving Rose, Cadence, and Freeborn privacy.

"Damn, you stink girl!" quipped Cadence. "But it's wonderful to have you back among the living. Did you get a steroid shot? You nearly broke my back."

"Sorry." Freeborn was embarrassed. "I can't help it."

Thor waved her over, and before he could get a word in, Freeborn lifted him from the table and set him on his feet.

"I weigh two-hundred and sixty pounds," said Thor. He grabbed Freeborn by the arm and led her to the cage, the pain medicine was kicking in fast. "Impress me. Bend the bars again."

Freeborn grabbed two bars in her hands and pulled them apart, as if they were made of rubber. She bent the iron bars back into shape and turned around with a big smile on her face. Thor took a seat, shaking his head in disbelief.

"Okay, out with it," said Cadence. "What's the diagnosis on Freeborn?"

"Your blood works opposite from the virus. Where the original virus causes human DNA to break down, your blood supercharges cells and causes growth on a large scale. Her hair and nails are growing faster and her bones are denser. Hearing and vision are heightened and Freeborn is at least as strong as a vampire. Fortunately, she doesn't require blood to replenish her body."

Cadence looked impressed. "She's no longer a zombie? So what you're saying is that my blood cured her?" Cadence considered this news for a moment. "Then I am a Maker? Any idea what my blood would do to an uninfected human to, say, someone like Thor?"

"Highbrow asked the same thing," said Rose. "I'm to report to him directly about the results of my findings. He's worried, Cadence, and with good reason. Looking at slides gives me an inkling of what's going on, but until I've tested it on an uninfected human, I can't give you any answers."

"Tell her about the Shadowguard you killed," said Freeborn.

"A drop of your blood killed a Shadowguard on contact," she said. "You and Freeborn don't have to worry about vampires. Your blood causes immediate regression of a vampire's nervous system, resulting in instantaneous death."

"It's like you have chameleon blood," said Freeborn. "It changes into what we need. I can't wait for Dragon to get back from the Citadel. He's going to be so happy he when finds out I'm okay."

Cadence looked at Rose. "Is she cleared for active duty?"

"In a day, maybe. I'd like to observe her a bit longer," said Rose, "I don't think we need to worry about Freeborn's feeding habits, however, I am concerned about the alteration in her DNA. You asked what would happen if Thor took her blood? I think his bruises would heal and he'd become as strong Freeborn."

"Do you want to be a lab rat?" Cadence asked Thor.

Thor looked excited, still looking at the bent iron bars. "Absolutely!"

"Out of the question," said Rose. "Now I know why Highbrow is so keen to keep you and Freeborn separated from the camp. I can't do this without using proper protocols. We may end up killing Thor instead of turning him into . . . I'm not even sure what Freeborn should be classified as."

"Doc, just admit it," Cadence said, trying to convince her. "You could run tests for weeks and still not have all the answers. We don't have that luxury. There's a lot more vampires than humans. Suppose Thor becomes as strong as a vampire? I can build a new team to fight the Kaiser."

"This type of haphazard scientific dabbling might work for the Kaiser," Rose said, stern, "but I expect more from you, Cadence. You actually care about your people. Please, don't order me to do this. It's a mistake. What if we kill Thor?"

Cadence stood unyielding, and Rose knew she wouldn't convince her. She felt caught in the middle of a private war between Highbrow and Cadence.

"Seven people were killed last night," said Cadence. "More were captured. This is a direct order, doctor. I won't have a staff doctor who doesn't follow orders. Just do it. I'll take full responsibility for whatever happens."

Thor spoke up. "I don't get it. Why don't you have super powers, commander?" He paused. "You know some athletes would set aside their blood in storage before a game or a race. They would get a shot of fresh blood after their game, and would recover faster. Something about oxygen in the blood. Anyway, it revitalized athletes and many of them became champions. If it worked for them, why wouldn't it work for you?"

Cadence removed her coat and laid it on the table. Pushing up the sleeve of her thin blue sweater, she turned toward Rose. "Give Thor fresh blood, Doc, but use some of your stored blood on me."

Rose sped to her work station, gathered supplies and returned to the humans before they noticed she ever left their side. Freeborn, however, saw her every move. Sterilizing a spot on Cadence's arm, Rose drew a vial of blood and covered the extraction point.

"Get on with it, Doc," said Cadence.

Rose cleaned a spot on Thor's shoulder and gave him the blood she had just drawn from Cadence. Pulling a stored vial from the fridge, she injected Cadence. Freeborn pulled up a chair and watched her two friends, waiting for changes.

"In theory, I've injected you both with foreign antigens." Rose sighed with guilt. "Your bodies will either accept it or try to fight back. Both of you need to lie down. I'll have Ginger monitor you for any changes. I'm going for a walk."

Ginger came back in and at Rose's nod, she helped Thor lie on a cot. She sat beside him, monitoring temperature and pulse. Cadence plopped onto a second cot, and they both looked exhausted.

Dawn was on the horizon, splashing pink clouds across the sky. Freeborn joined her, and the look of contentment on her face kept Rose from sending her back inside. Taking a moment to enjoy nature always helped Rose, which was also one of Freeborn's favorite things to do. The Blue Devils watched the doctor and Freeborn, under Highbrow's orders to watch the infirmary and keep eyes on Freeborn. Rose didn't want them following and asking questions she wasn't prepared to answer.

"It's all right," Rose called out, relieved when they remained where they were.

Rose and Freeborn ascended a short set of stairs and found a bench facing the waterfall. The sound of cascading water was peaceful as they sat silent watching the sun rise over the canyon walls. Walking back, they found Picasso and Lachlan unloading a truck with the Blue Devils. She imagined the remainder of the Dark Angels would soon arrive at their new residence.

"Morning," shouted Lachlan. "It's a beautiful day!"

Two golf carts drove by and parked in front of the mess hall. The

Bull Dogs climbed out of one, as Highbrow arrived with Nomad and a small girl in the other. Fearful of Highbrow seeing them, Rose turned toward Freeborn, but she had vanished. Nomad piggy-backed the girl to Rose.

"The kid's got a sticker in her finger, Doc," said Nomad. "She wanted to come see you so you could remove it. Apparently using my teeth isn't good enough. Plus, someone told her a secret." His face grew serious. "You have lollipops."

The girl giggled and pointed at a box that Micah was holding. He placed the box labeled CANDY outside the mess hall and went back for more.

"Talk about perfect timing," said Nomad, setting her down. "Breakfast comes before sweets, Melanie. You know the rules. Betsy will be furious if you get a cavity. I'm the only dentist, and I use pliers."

"Hush, No-mie." The little girl was missing her front teeth. With a shriek of delight, she headed for the box of candy and Micah handed her an oversized red lollipop. "Thanks."

"Only one," shouted Betsy, with a trail of small children following close behind. With short blonde hair and a ready smile, it was hard to imagine Betsy had been a scavenger. "Come in for breakfast, Melanie. I'm making pancakes."

Nomad and Betsy were loved by all, and had assumed the role of guardians for every kid in camp. Melanie held up her arms until Betsy caved, carrying her and leading the rest of the group into the mess hall. Micah followed them in with a box of supplies. Freeborn appeared behind Rose, eyes closed, absorbing the sun. Nomad walked over to Rose, arms out, gesturing for a hug.

"You need a bath," said Rose, grinning. "You smell like motor oil and axle grease, and you have morning breath."

"Comes with the job, Doc," Nomad remarked. "Sturgis and I worked an all-nighter getting a new armored vehicle ready to roll. Seems Rafe was rescued last night and is with the Cheyenne Mountain

Wolf Tribe at the Cliff Dwellings. Sturgis and I are heading over after I've had coffee and breakfast. There's plenty of room for two more."

"If you're asking, I'd be delighted to come along, Nomad," said Rose. "But I need breakfast, too."

"I can help with that," Picasso said, reaching into his coat pocket. "I've got a little surprise for you, Rose." He withdrew a bottle of blood. "We did it! We successfully created synthetic blood. It's nutritional, full of proteins, and slakes the thirst for human blood." He grinned at the scruffy biker. "Not that anyone would want to eat you, Nomad. You don't smell that tasty."

"I'm not," said Nomad, with a grunt.

Rose took the bottle, removing the cap. She sniffed at the contents before consuming it. Not as delicious as what she was used to, but better than living on animals. She decided it wasn't bad, handing the empty bottle back to Picasso, licking her lips.

"Wow, I feel energized," said Rose. "Doesn't taste that bad either."

"I thought you'd be pleased," said Picasso, in triumph. "I'm working on the flavor and the consistency. It's as close to real blood as we can get, but taste is important."

"That's it for my appetite. Thanks!" said Nomad. He grimaced and pointed at Rose. "Doc, you have a drop on your chin. I'd wipe it off, but I'm a bit squeamish right now."

Laughing, Rose wiped it away. Freeborn opened her eyes, turned toward them, smiling wide.

"Well, look who's up bright and early," said Nomad. "Come here and give an old man a proper bear hug." He pulled Freeborn against his chest, yelping when she hugged back full strength.

"Sorry," she said. "You okay?"

Nomad twisted and turned. "The kink I've had in my back is gone. You better freshen up if you're going with us to pick up Dragon. If you're both good, we might stop at a store. Promised Betsy a new dress and some of those fuzzy boots."

"Think I can go, Doc?" asked Freeborn. Rose nodded. "I'll meet you guys back here in a few minutes. Don't leave without me."

The Blue Devils scrambled to follow Freeborn. Picasso and Nomad gave Rose a questioning look, and with her nod, Picasso sped past the Blue Devils. After Freeborn's transformation, the Blue Devils and the Bull Dogs concerned Rose. Accompanied by Nomad, Rose entered the mess hall where Highbrow was standing at the head of the line, watching coffee drip into a large pot. Sterling whispered something in his ear and Highbrow nodded, and then the lieutenant hurried off.

"Morning, Doc," said the captain. "You get anything to eat?"

"Yes," Nomad called out. "She had ketchup. Bring me a cup of coffee, will you captain? I take sugar and powdered creamer. Lots of it."

Rose missed the flavor as she watched everyone eating pancakes. The biggest drawback of being a vampire was the diet in her opinion.

"Nomad thought I might join the team going to pick up Rafe," said Rose. "I wouldn't mind taking a break. I thought we might take Freeborn. She's anxious to see Dragon."

Highbrow tossed his beret onto the table, hair plastered to his head. "I don't like being the one to put a damper on things, Doc," he said, "but you and Freeborn should stay in camp." He lowered his voice. "I can't risk having you captured. Plus, I'm a little nervous letting Freeborn out of her cage, though the camp would probably be safer with her gone."

"I can't tell her that." Rose received a stern look. "It would mean so much for her to go. Staying here would break her heart."

"No can do," he said with his mouth full. "Nomad can handle it without you. I'm not taking any chances, so don't make me pull rank on you."

"Hey, captain." Micah sat next to his friend. "I'm about to head out and pick up the rest of the fence. You need anything from the old camp? We're going to the top for books from the professor's cabin. Looks like you've been nominated to be teacher, Nomad."

"Betsy's idea?" said Nomad, grumbling, taking a sip of coffee. "Why that woman thinks I can teach school is beyond me. I didn't even finish high school. Stories I can tell, but math? Forget it."

"You'll make a fine teacher," said Rose. "So tell us, when are you planning to propose to Betsy? I don't suppose one of the things on your list is an engagement ring?" Nomad blushed. "I thought so. Now I really want to go with you."

"Fine," said Highbrow. "I give in. You can go, Rose."

Rose smiled. "Thank you, captain."

Slipping out of the mess hall, Rose reached the infirmary door as Lachlan was exiting. As Rose entered, Ginger stood in the door to the lab, waving her over.

"We've got a problem," said Ginger. "I've taken an inventory of all of the supplies. If Raven kept accurate records, then you're missing three vials of blood. Micah and I think Logan stole Cadence's blood. I told you not to get involved with a scavenger."

"He wouldn't do that," said Rose.

"Considering everything Logan has done since he's been here," said Ginger, "that's precisely what I think. I knew the day we met Logan Bennet that he couldn't be trusted."

"Bennet? How do you now his last name and I don't?"

"Because he talks in his sleep," Ginger said. "Micah and I are kind of an item these days and he doesn't know I was seeing Logan. I want to keep it that way. Okay?"

Rose wished Ginger hadn't told her either. Ginger knew Rose had an interest, but didn't realize Rose had been seeing Logan. Questions began to ping in Rose's head. Noticing Ginger's strange look, Rose grabbed her coat and left without saying another word.

Chapter Fifteen

Thor was alone in a store, filling up on supplies and food. Zombies ambled about, oblivious. When he finished, he stepped outside into a normal world. The smell of pine filled the air, people were driving to work, walking their dogs, and doing . . . normal people things. He mounted his fresh supply on the back of his motorcycle, climbed on, and turned the key.

Thor heard a sinister click. The bike exploded.

He woke up panicked, still reeling from the nightmare.

Thor noticed sunlight streaming through the windows, and the scent of the nasty pine-scented cleaner the Dark Angels sloshed in their mop buckets. He sat up and threw his blanket off, deciding to remove his brace. He realized the pain and bruising in his ribs and chest were gone.

"Cadence?" Thor turned toward the empty cot. He swung his legs off, donned his boots, and grabbed his sweater. Looking around for Rose, he found Ginger instead.

Ginger held a mop and a disgusted expression. "Rose went with Nomad to pick up Rafe and China Six. You must not be that important," she said in a snide voice. "The Blue Devils went on break and haven't returned. If you would get out of here, I could clean your sheets."

"Why are you mad at me? I didn't do anything."

"Exactly! I took your dirty dishes back to the mess hall. I also cleaned your boots, which, by the way, left mud all over the floor. You look like a hobo with that beard, and you need to trim your nails. You have claws."

Lifting his hand, Thor felt the thick new growth on his jaw, and Ginger was right—his fingernails were long. He reached up with both hands and slid them through his hair, trailing the strands past his shoulders.

"Thanks," said Thor, louder than he meant to be.

Ginger flinched. "Don't shout at me. Get out of here before I start mopping you up. Micah could use some help up on the ridge. You're the biggest guy in camp, so carrying fences shouldn't be a problem."

Full of energy, Thor darted out the door. The sun was bright, but he was able to look directly into the fiery orb. Taking his time, he looked around the camp. He had never noticed how majestic the canyon appeared in daylight, or the crisp lines along the colorful leaves. A bouquet of aromas filled the air and penetrated his senses. He distinguished every scent and sight, including the nearby latrines in desperate need of cleaning.

Thor took off running at blazing speed. A squirrel ran across his path and he let out a shout, not stopping until he reached the Pillars of Hercules, running a mile in less than a minute. Cupping his mouth, he gave a loud yell that bounced off the cliff walls, echoing through the canyon. He turned and ran back toward the camp, veering at the sound of teenagers training with Destry.

"Hey, Thor!" shouted a familiar voice.

Loki waved as he crossed swords with Xena and Phoenix.

"Man up, Loki. You will never win a fight like that. You're always on defense. Attack them. It's not like you're going to hurt an Amazon."

"I know what I'm doing," shouted Loki. "Watch this!"

Thor knew they were toying with him. Xena grinned when a disarmed Loki lunged for his sword. Phoenix blocked his path and knocked his feet out from under him. Loki landed with his face in the grass, pushing himself up on elbows while they laughed.

"Not fair," whined Loki.

"What a baby! Come on, Phoenix. Help the crybaby to his feet."

Xena pulled him to his feet and Phoenix brushed the grass out of his hair. She patted him on the back and planted a kiss on his forehead.

"You'll be all right," said Xena. She pointed to Phoenix's sword. "Just you and me. Let's see if you can give me more competition than the baby."

"Loki's improving," Phoenix said. "Give him time." She retrieved Loki's sword and handed it back to him.

"Thanks. You too, Xena." Loki hurried to meet up with Thor. "Hey, I thought you were laid up?" He dabbed his coat sleeve on the reopened the cut on his chin. "Doc said you bruised your ribs. Why are you out of bed?"

"Okay. Get ready. I've got to show you guys something."

Thor threw his arms over his head and jumped . . . high. Xena stumbled over her own feet and Phoenix's cheeks flushed when he landed, light as a cat. She jotted to him and put her hand on Thor's forehead, checking his temperature. He grabbed her arms and gave her a quick kiss on the cheek. Xena and Loki laughed as Phoenix let out a whimper. She kicked him, but Thor felt nothing. When he let go of her arms, he realized he had bruised her arms.

Loki looked shocked. "Did I just see you . . . ?"

"I'll do it again. Pay attention."

Thor jumped, and this time he flew over Loki's head, landing in a crouched position behind him. They looked as stunned as the patrols who were no longer training, but now watching the show.

"Just warming up before the big game." Thor winked at Loki. "Wanna tag along? I've got to find Cadence."

"We saw her earlier," Phoenix said. "You on steroids?" She squeezed Thor's right forearm and gulped. "You feel like iron."

"If one of your strays gets stuck in a tree," Thor said, laughing, "you know who to contact. It'll be my pleasure." He pointed at Loki's chin. "That's a nasty cut."

Loki glanced at the blood on his coat sleeve. "Oh, crap," he said. "It's gotten worse." He dabbed at it, wincing. "Phoenix, come help me."

The Amazon reached into the pouch on her belt, produced a bandage, and stretched it across his chin. "You need stitches, but this will do for now."

"Thanks. We better get out of here, Thor. Destry looks like he's about to wet himself. You two want to come along?"

The Amazons shook their heads and resumed swordplay. Thor and Loki took the road toward the RVs and Destry whistled everyone back to their drills.

"You're getting pretty close to those two," said Thor. "Amazons don't normally hang out with punks like you."

Loki shrugged. "Hey, they like me," he said, grinning. "Did you hear the Dark Angels were up at the Peak? I heard it's covered with skeletons." He gave Thor a mischievous look. "Odin's still in bed. He wouldn't get up even to hang out with Amazons. I mean, seriously?"

"Odin looked up to Baldor," said Thor. "I know you can just switch off your emotions, but try to show a little compassion, Loki. You're human, too. Keep that in mind."

"Yeah, well, Raven isn't around to mother Odin, and I'm not about to." Loki tramped along, hands in his pockets. "What's the big deal? Lots of people are dead. Raven would've forced him out of bed and made him wash windows. Odin needs motivation. I think he's doing a good job getting out of work detail."

Thor turned to ask Loki to check on Odin and realized he had walked so fast that he left the skinny kid far behind. He waited for Loki to catch up and tried to wrap his thoughts around all the changes he was experiencing.

Thor was overwhelmed with excitement. He envied the vampires and Luna's pack for their exceptional powers, and now he was as strong as any of them. He wanted to plan a rescue mission to the Citadel right away. Together with Freeborn and the Dark Angels, Thor knew they would be able to rescue Star and the others. Being superhuman was what he had wished for, and it felt amazing.

Thor got tired of waiting and took off in a flash, slowing down when he approached Betsy having a picnic with the kids. Betsy smiled and offered Thor some hotdogs and a bottle of water.

"It's such a nice afternoon," said Betsy. "I'll be giving the sermon this evening. Are you coming to the funeral?" She reflected, "It never gets easy, does it? We lose people, but we still miss them long after they're gone."

Thor heard little of what she was saying as he devoured his food. Betsy shook her head and offered him another, which he gobbled down. Four kids sat across from him, eyes wide, watching him inhale his food. Loki caught up and wedged himself between the children. He was drenched with sweat and shaking from running so hard. He grabbed a hotdog and started munching as Thor powered down another bottle of water, then tossed the empty bottle to the ground.

Melanie shook a finger at him. "No, no," she said, in a tiny voice. "No trash! Bad, hairy Thor."

Betsy picked the bottle up as Loki negotiated with the little girl over a bag of chips. "That's enough," said Betsy. "I'm sure you big boys have something better to do than hang out here. I'll see you later."

"Thanks, Betsy," said Thor as the two scurried away. "You need to bulk up, Loki. You're too skinny."

A crooked grin appeared on Loki's face. "Give me whatever you're taking and I won't need to."

Arriving at the Tiger RV, Thor walked in without knocking. Cadence and Highbrow were entwined on the couch and looked up, startled. Highbrow scrambled to his feet, embarrassed by being caught off guard.

"Sorry," said Thor. "I can come back later." He paused. "No. Actually, this can't wait. Cadence, I need to talk to you in private."

"Get out!" Highbrow pointed to the door.

Thor backed out of the RV and shut the door. Loki had overexerted himself to keep up with Thor and was relieving his gut at the steps of the RV. Highbrow descended the steps and stepped in the vomit.

"What the hell? What do you two want? You're supposed to be in the infirmary, Thor." Highbrow glared at Loki. "Is this your mess?"

Loki sat up and saluted. "Sorry, sir. I had a hard time keeping up with Thor. You should have seen him. He jumped clear over my head. The commander is going to freak . . ." He lurched and lost the remainder of his stomach at Highbrow's feet.

"Dammit, Loki! What are you yapping about?" demanded Highbrow. Cadence walked out and slid her arms around Highbrow, but he pushed her away. "Not now."

"Like we're a big secret." Cadence rustled Loki's hair. "You okay, buddy?" She joined Thor at the picnic table. "Guess you're not feeling any pain, and that's a pretty thick beard there. Any other changes?"

"Loki says Thor jumped over his head," grumbled Highbrow, wiping his boots off. "These two are stoned. Having drugs gets you five demerits, and you both get ten for coming here without an invitation. Loki, you're supposed to be on guard duty at the barricade. Last night's events don't give you an excuse to screw around."

"Aurora took my place. I was practicing with Xena and Phoenix, and they aren't on guard duty. Why do I have to be?"

Cadence interrupted them. "Everyone calm down." She put her hand on Thor's shoulder. "You look healthy as an ox. Are your ribs healed?"

"How could they be?" said Highbrow. "Would someone tell me what's going on?"

"Just show him." Loki stood up. "Jump, Thor. Jump!"

Thor picked out a tall oak and jumped, sailing through the air until he slammed into the tree. His arms circled around the trunk, and he peered down from over twenty feet. Grabbing a branch, he swung away from the trunk and landed. Loki applauded and Thor whooped as he skipped back to the group.

"Whoa there, fella," said Cadence. "We talked about this, remember? Don't start doing crazy things. People are going to notice."

"Yeah," Thor said. "Sorry. I guess I lost my head."

Highbrow glared at Cadence. "Stop talking in code. Does this have something to do with Freeborn? She better be back in her cage or I'm throwing her in the brig."

"Freeborn?" Loki stood. "I heard how she broke off the door to her cage. What did Rose give her? How about it, commander, can you hook me up with some super juice? Is it vampire blood?"

"It's not vampire blood," said Thor. "It's better."

Highbrow turned on Cadence. "We're not talking about this outside," he fumed. "Get inside, you idiots, before someone hears you!"

He grabbed hold of Loki's shirt and hauled him into the RV. Thor followed behind Cadence and sat on the couch beside Loki. Highbrow stood back to the counter, arms crossed. Cadence closed the door and leaned against it, crossing her arms and leveling a warning look to Highbrow.

"Sit down," said Highbrow. "I want to talk about this."

For a moment the couple stared at one another, neither giving in, until Highbrow finally looked away. Loki snickered.

"This isn't a laughing matter," said Highbrow. "I want it clear that what's said here, stays here. Loki, give me your word. Whatever you hear remains a secret. This is classified information. If you tell anyone else, I swear, I'll have you whipped."

"Man, calm down," said Loki. "I'm not going to tell anyone."

"Cadence please, sit down," said Highbrow, climbing onto a stool. "Let's talk about this. For starters, tell me how you're feeling, Thor? Are you on pain killers?"

"I feel great," said Thor. "I'm not on any drugs. I don't need them."

Cadence walked to the couch and sat between Thor and Loki. She placed her arms on the couch behind Thor and Loki, crossing her legs and regarding Highbrow matter-of-fact.

"Do you really care how Thor feels?" asked Cadence.

"Look, I just want to know what's going on," said Highbrow. "I asked Rose to let me know what your blood does to an uninfected person. Did she use Thor as a test subject? She did, didn't she? On your orders!" He glanced out the window, seeming nervous.

"I'm the commander," said Cadence, ice in her tone. "If I want to order a full-scale assault on the Citadel, then that's what we'll do. If I want to test my blood on willing soldiers and create superhuman fighters, we will. Who do you think you are? You're my second-in-command. I call the shots. You follow orders."

Highbrow took it hard. "How could you say that? I thought we made decisions together?"

Cadence appeared relaxed, but her voice was rising. "You asked Rose to report to you, and you only. I'd call that going behind my back, captain. Your behavior is insubordinate. Yes, I gave Rose a direct order. My blood works. Freeborn and Thor are both living proof that I'm some kind of Maker, only I'm not making vampires, but superhumans."

"A Maker? I knew it. I knew you were going to pull something like this the moment my back was turned."

Cadence stood, detached and collected. "When I'm dead and gone, you can run this camp however you want, but right now, I'm in charge. Maybe you don't like hearing that, Highbrow, but it's a fact. My camp. My rules. My blood. I intend to win this war."

Highbrow slid off of the stool brimming with aggression. Thor got to his feet, prepared to step between them and stop Highbrow.

"Why, Cadence?" demanded Highbrow. He clenched his fists, still looking to the window. "You know how hard I've tried to keep our camp free of the infection. Please tell me it stops here. Swear to me you're not planning to give your blood to anyone else. You can't infect humans with another form of the virus . . . one we know nothing about."

"Freeborn is cured. She and Thor are both healed. Maybe you don't like the idea of my blood actually being able to help people, but it works, Highbrow."

"You're a carrier, dammit," said Highbrow, disgusted. "You aren't healthy or normal anymore. One drop of your blood kills vampires and cures zombies. Give it to a human and you create a superhuman. You could infect the entire camp if I don't contain it now, and then everything will be turned upside down. Logan has betrayed us and is probably informing the Kaiser. Your blood and these changes put us in danger." His eyes grew cold, his nervous tremble disappearing. "You being here puts us all in danger."

Thor noticed Loki peering out the window. Something held his attention.

"Look around, Highbrow," Cadence said. "We're in a world where nothing makes sense anymore. It's time for the human race to evolve. Maybe this is what God intended all along."

"Rules and regulations are the only thing that separates us from the monsters. Why can't you see that?"

"I'm ordering Rose to give my blood to the Fighting Tigers. They're the best team in camp. Dragon too, if he wants it. The next time the Shadowguard attack, we'll be ready."

Loki let out a shout and jumped off the couch. "We gotta go. The Blue Devils and Bull Dogs are outside with Lieutenant Sterling and Destry. They've got Dodger and Smack on the ground."

"It's a setup." Thor leveled his gaze at Highbrow. "You bastard! This has nothing to do with us, does it? While you've been making nice with Cadence, your team assembled. You're not taking us into custody. Come on, Cadence. We'll get you out of this."

"Stay put," shouted Highbrow. "All of you."

Cadence threw her arms around Highbrow, holding him back. "Go, Thor!" she shouted. "Take Loki and get out of camp!"

Opening the door, Thor grabbed Loki before he could run. With his arm around Loki's waist, he plowed through the soldiers, scattering them across the ground. Sterling shouted and someone shot.

Thor didn't look back.

Chapter Sixteen

Nomad drove his new battle tank down Memorial Highway. Rose sat beside him in the semi-truck outfitted with a flatbed trailer, spiked rims, and a snowplow. Sturgis sat in the back with three other soldiers. Nomad was having fun knocking cars and zombies off the road with the massive rig.

"Must you?" questioned Rose, wincing. "You could try to miss a few. They're not bugs, Nomad."

He patted Rose on the shoulder, laughing.

"Nomad rides his bike the same way," said Sturgis. "Better move when he's on the road. Nomad was one of the toughest sons-of-bitches in our bike gang. Now don't you fret, Doc. Nothing he does can wreck this truck. I built the engine myself. We can go faster if you like."

"I would like to arrive in one piece, thank you."

"Relax and enjoy the ride," Nomad said, chuckling.

Rose closed her eyes and leaned her head back, finding it somewhat comforting that she felt sick for the first time since becoming a vampire. All she needed was to go for a ride with Nomad.

The big truck pulled off an exit ramp, knocking aside a school bus. There were fewer zombies the closer they drove to Manitou Springs, but more vehicles littered the roads. Nomad cut a path and made his way to the gravel road leading to Cliff Dwelling. He came to a jarring halt and laid on the horn. Several werewolves ran toward them, and Rose watched amazed as they morphed into men.

Opening the gate, they stepped out of the way as the diesel engine growled forward. As the truck pulled into the parking lot, wolves dashed up the steps from the lower level. Rafe came up after them, followed by the girls of China Six.

"Something went wrong," said Rose, reaching for the door handle. "Tandor isn't here. Nor is Dragon or Whisper."

"I'm sure they're around here, Doc." Nomad threw open the driver's door, jumping down. He walked toward the girls. "Ladies, I've come to take you home!"

The anxious girls ran to Nomad, giving him a hug before climbing into the rig. As Rafe walked through the wolves, they growled and snapped. Rose greeted Rafe with a hug and kiss.

"I'm so glad you're alive. I was worried about you." Rose stepped back and handed Rafe a backpack. "Looks like the Kaiser didn't go easy on you. You're weak. I brought supplies so you can eat."

"What's in here? A rabbit?" Rafe opened the backpack and took out a bottle. "Synthetic? How does it taste?" He removed a cap and took a sip, grimacing. "Like crap."

"Just drink it," Rose said, aware the red wolf was watching. "It works. It will help you heal faster, so drink all of it." She watched as Rafe drained the contents. "Where are Tandor and the others? What's happened?"

"Ask the chief," said Rafe. "My rescue was poorly prepared and poorly executed. I'm lucky to be out of there, no thanks to these mongrels."

"Hush! Go get in the truck." The wolves growled louder, and Rose wanted to avoid an incident. "I need to speak with Chayton. His tribe is upset and we don't want to leave on bad terms. Maybe I can smooth things over."

"Good luck with that. The truth is, they just don't like me," groused Rafe. He walked over to the truck and regarded Nomad with disdain.

"Why did they send you, scavenger? Is your nose that far up Highbrow's backside?"

"Nice to see you too, Rafe." Nomad pointed at the flatbed. "No room for you inside. Sorry. Guess you'll have to ride in back with the soldiers."

Rose approached the large red wolf. His amber eyes were level with her shoulders. She lifted her hand and waited for Chayton to greet her. The growling stopped and he wagged his tail. Out of instinct, Rose scratched Chayton under the chin, feeling a recent wound.

"Things didn't go well, did they?" asked Rose. "I'm sorry, chief. I should have known Tandor would come to you for help. Please accept my apology for Rafe's behavior. Will you speak to me?"

The wolf stood, becoming a man.

"Your apology is accepted, Dr. Rose. You and Tandor are friends of our tribe." Chayton motioned at the line of werewolves. "We lost five men getting your people back here, and Pallaton took our cousin, Huritt, prisoner. Tandor, Dragon, and Whisper never made it out of the Citadel."

"I'm sorry for your loss," Rose said. "I appreciate what you have done, and so does Commander Cadence. It doesn't excuse Rafe's behavior, but he was tortured. You know as well as I do what the Kaiser does to his prisoners. Pallaton—"

"My brother did what he was commanded," said Chayton. "Huritt will be missed. Tell the commander I've kept my word. We helped save her friend, but Pallaton will come here looking for us, so I'm taking my people into the mountains." He put his hand on Rose's arm. "My brother is not your friend. Be warned. Pallaton cares only about himself. He has always been this way."

Rose knew Pallaton played it safe, but could not think the worst of him. "Thank you, Chief. Can we do anything for your tribe before we leave?"

"No. Leave and do not return. It's not safe here," said Chayton. "I'm sending two of my tribe back with you. Moon Dog and Red Hawk have asked to remain with the girls as their protectors. They, too, are brothers."

Gazing at the truck, the chief smiled when Cricket stuck her head out the window and gave a whistle. She blew a kiss to the chief. "Thank you, Chief Chayton!" she called out. "I'll take good care of them both! We love you!"

He let out a soft chuckle. "That one is precious, but tell me about Dragon's girlfriend. Were you able to save Freeborn, or is she now a Dead One?"

"I found another cure," said Rose. "Cadence's blood. The camp was attacked last night by the Shadowguard. They killed a number of people and abducted the best fighters. Having Rafe back will help with security. There's a lot going on at the camp right now, and I wish we had more time to talk."

"I do as well, doctor," said Chayton. "I'm interested in knowing more about Cadence. Perhaps another time." He paused. "If Cadence finds a way to rescue her people, be sure to tell Tandor that he's always welcome with our tribe, as are you and China Six."

"I will, and thank you," said Rose.

Chayton transformed into a wolf again, and Rose knelt and bowed her head. The wolves sniffed her face and hair, and one licked her face before running downstairs again.

"The wolves like you," said Nomad, helping Rose to her feet and walking toward the truck.

"Some of their members were killed last night getting the girls out of the Citadel. Tandor, Dragon, and Whisper didn't make it out. The chief doesn't know if they're alive or dead."

Rose climbed in back with the girls. The wolves crammed into the front seat while Cricket rode on the floor beneath them.

"I hope you don't mind that we brought friends," said Cricket. "Red Hawk saved my life."

"Let's go, Nomad," Rose said. "If we can have vampires and werepumas in camp, we can certainly have werewolves. Red Hawk and his brother will be welcome in our camp."

A mile later, Nomad cursed as an engine light flashed and the truck chugged to a halt. Rafe pounded his fist on the cab and glared in the back window, fangs out and eyes glowing.

"Sturgis, we have a problem," said Nomad.

"Alternator." Sturgis sounded unhappy. "I'll fix it."

Nomad opened the door. "Best get the toolkit out of the back and switch out the battery with the spare. Come on, I'll help."

"Wake up, people." Rafe pounded on the roof a few more times. "We have company."

Nomad let out another curse, grabbing his gun. The soldiers fired on the incoming creatures, while the girls filed out, ready to fight.

"Rose, stay inside. This could be a Shadowguard ambush." Nomad looked at Moon Dog and Red Hawk. "I'd appreciate you two staying close to Rose. If the Shadowguard are nearby, they'll do their best to get to her."

Moon Dog and Red Hawk nodded, growling. Cricket jumped out and prepared to join the fray. Rose admired China Six, poised and cool, though they had to be exhausted. A soft growl and a gesture from Moon Dog revealed more zombies were approaching from the rear.

"Rafe," shouted Rose. The vampire looked her way. "The soldiers need help. Can you handle that many zombies?"

"Please," said Rafe. "This won't take long."

He waited until the zombies were close before dealing with them vampire-style. Rose watched the battle from inside with the werewolves.

"I'm sorry your tribe got involved," said Rose. "Tandor is like my brother. I know how it feels to lose someone you love."

Without warning, Moon Dog jumped out of the window, followed closely by his brother. Rose witnessed Cricket engaging a zombie with a crowbar, as another slid by Rafe to attack her from behind. Moving with speed and fury, the wolves ripped into the zombies.

Kirin slammed against the cab of the truck and saw Rose through the window. "Get out and help. There are too many of them." She returned to the fight, limping.

Not waiting for a second invitation, Rose scrambled out and landed on her feet. She ran toward Rafe and tore into zombies with her bare hands. The black werewolf was beside her as she sped through the horde, decapitating all zombies within her reach.

Nomad and Sturgis closed the rig's hood and motioned for everyone to climb in. The team had laid waste to the monsters, but more were sure to come.

"We've got Shadowguard following," Rafe shouted. "Don't try to find them. Trust me, they're out there. I'm sure the zombie ambush was their idea of a good time."

Lotus snorted. "If you saw them watching, why didn't you fight them?"

"Uh, I was busy killing zombies, flower girl," said Rafe. "As hard as you humans fought to keep the zombies off Nomad and that old man, Rose and I killed more than all of you together. You're lucky it was zombies and not Shadowguard. Once again, the Dark Angels saved the day."

"Protecting us is supposed to be your job," said Kirin. "If you don't like it, you can go back to the hotel. Camp was nicer without you around."

Rose grew tired of the fighting. She turned to face everyone. Rose knew it was time for them to face the truth.

"Last night Star was abducted by the Shadowguard," said Rose. Everyone fell silent, and the tension turned to sadness. "So were Blaze, Raven, Heimdall, a few soldiers, and the Elite. The A-Team was slain near Midnight Falls. I was going to let Commander Cadence tell you what happened, but with all the love I'm feeling in this truck, I decided it couldn't wait."

"Star and Dragon are both in the hands of the Kaiser," cried Cricket. "What are we going to do without them? What's going to happen to us?"

They all stared at Rose. She caught Nomad's gaze, but it was his smile that gave her confidence to keep talking.

"We're going to stop fighting and pull it together. We've got to get through this alive," said Rose. "That means we have to put aside our petty differences, prejudices, and dislike for one another and start acting like a team. And that goes for you too, Rafe. Defeating the Kaiser may seem impossible right now, but if we are to stand a chance, we will have to work together. It doesn't matter anymore if we're vampire, human, mountain lion, or wolf. We're in this mess together, and that's just how it is, so deal with it."

Nomad smiled at Rose and rolled on toward camp.

Chapter Seventeen

During the night, Blaze heard cries and screams coming from the other cells. There were more humans imprisoned at the Citadel than she realized.

Following her unsuccessful attempt to break out, a guard was posted outside her door, accentuating the cell's claustrophobia. She hated being watched, and sleep eluded her because of it.

Blaze had no way of telling time, little food or water, and no toilet. She was exhausted and too hungry to show her enthusiasm when the Shadowguard placed her in a long line of prisoners, and draping her with a light blue scarf.

She followed the group until they came to an abrupt halt, at which point she turned to yell at the guard, only to realize they were alone. There were more prisoners than she imagined, and found relief that she didn't know anyone. A large man with a red scarf tied around his arm stood in front of her. He looked like he hadn't shaved for months and was every bit as smelly.

"I'm Bob," he said.

"I'm Blaze. You know where they're taking us?"

The big guy shook his head. Blaze looked along the hallway, finding at least five surveillance cameras. Imagining the vampires watching filled her with a yearning to escape. Feeling trapped was too much, and she decided to make a run for it.

Bob started crying, which surprised Blaze and kept her from running.

"Hey, knock it off," said Blaze. "Why are you crying?"

"Me and my buddies came in on a bus from Arkansas," he said, shuddering a breath. "The driver said he was taking us to a safe place with no zombies or vamps. I should have known better and stayed in Little Rock."

"Was your driver a vampire?" Blazed rolled her eyes when Bob nodded. "I didn't come in on a bus. I came in a helicopter."

"You a champion?" Bob wiped his eyes with the back of his hand.

"In my own way," said Blaze. "The point is, if they brought you here all the way from Arkansas, the vamps place some value on your life. You're big and hairy. Use that to your advantage. Growl and snarl a lot. If they want a show, give it to them. Did all these people come from Arkansas?"

"No," he said. "From all over the place. Some people come from Los Angeles, Atlanta, Philadelphia, Kansas City. I learn a lot about people by listening to them talk in their cells. Where are you from?"

"Right here," said Blaze. "Our camp used to be on the Peak, but we moved it."

"Really? I thought you were on the game circuit?" said a man in glasses and a dirty business suit behind her. "They're turning the football stadium into an arena. Who is your guardian?"

"What's a guardian?" asked Blaze.

"Slave owners are referred to as guardians. We all have a guardian. The color of the scarf signifies your owner."

"That's news to me, but then I didn't know there were other human survivors until now," Blaze said, digging for more information. "Were all of you bussed in here? How did the vampires get things set up so fast?"

"Call me Mr. Smith," said the guy with glasses. "I can't believe I took you for a national fighter. Not everyone was bussed in. Many were captured in nearby towns. We're being led in for breakfast, and you'll get another meal this evening. Tomorrow they'll watch us compete and decide what event you'll be fighting in. Everything will be broadcast live on TV."

"No way," said Blaze. "I don't believe it. When did they start broadcasting on TV? For that matter, are they controlling the country, because I thought they were only in Colorado?"

"This week vampires have officially made their presence known in every major city in the U.S. I don't know everything, just what they tell me, but vampires have been around for a while. It's just another form of the virus. I only know because I used to work for the Kaiser. Mr. Rafferty and Big Mike are two vampire lords controlling most of the U.S., and there is another named Salvatore D'Aquilla who arrived this morning from Italy."

Everyone was trying to listen as the line began to move. Doors opened at the end of the hall and the prisoners were led into a gym.

"Where are the armed forces?" asked Blaze. "How come no one has fought back and killed these guys? Please tell me someone is fighting back somewhere in the world."

"I don't know. I was the Kaiser's attorney," said Mr. Smith. "All I did was handle money transactions since the vampires still use cash. In a way, they have restored civilization. Unfortunately, an agreement with the Turk went sour and I was blamed for a financial oversight. I was given the choice to fight in the arena or be executed. At least in the arena, I have a chance to survive."

"Who's the Turk?"

"Another lord."

"Do they all have stupid names?" Blaze groaned when Mr. Smith nodded. "I don't want to fight in the arena. This is crazy. We're not chained and there are no guards, so I'm sure I could make a run for it. Why don't you and Bob come with me?"

"Where would we go, Blaze? Back to your camp?" said Mr. Smith. "I think I'll stay here. It's time for breakfast and I'm starving."

"Well, I'm not sticking around long enough to fight in the arena," said Blaze. She spotted a door in the hallway and ran toward it.

A small group of people followed Blaze into a storage room with a small window, racing to cram through. Blaze left them to their struggle and tried to get back to the hallway. Bob grabbed her, pushing through the crowd, and escorted her back in the direction they had come. A riot erupted behind them.

A siren blared and Blaze and Bob ran until they found an exit leading outside. They slipped behind the gymnasium and continued past the music hall toward the central section, hoping to find transportation. Rounding a corner, Blaze pulled Bob behind some bushes, avoiding a marching platoon of vampires. Blaze spotted an empty truck parked near the curb and dashed toward it with Bob on her heels. Jumping in, she found keys and fired it up as a group of prisoners burst through the gym door to the welcome of gunfire.

The rear window was shot out by a rooftop sniper and Blaze took a sharp turn, maneuvering through a courtyard filled with boxes and new furniture. She felt like she was in a demolition derby. Driving faster, excitement built as she neared the main road, freedom within reach.

A hand reached in, ripping Bob from the truck. He cried out and Blaze grabbed a gun from the front seat, blasting the vampire at the passenger window, then scattered a squad standing in the main drive to the academy. Ahead of her she saw two trucks blocking her path. She ramped onto the lawn and sped toward the burned-out apartments. As she reached the apartments, the number of vehicles in pursuit increased along with a chopper.

A vampire reached Blaze, pulling her from the careening truck a moment before it slammed into the side of a building. The explosion showered flaming debris around them as the vampire held her in his arms and ran back toward the academy. She fought and managed to strike him in the face, causing him to drop her. She rolled hard, coming to a stop at the feet of her enemy.

"Don't move," said an angry voice.

Blaze looked up to see Lieutenant Aldarik aiming at her head. Yanked to her feet from behind, Shadowguard bound her hands and shoved her forward.

"That was an exciting, yet futile attempt," said Lieutenant Aldarik. "I'm taking you back to your cell. If you didn't belong to Pallaton, I'd kill you. I don't like troublesome humans."

"I don't like vampires, so that makes us even," Blaze said, falling in step beside Aldarik.

Aldarik glared at her. "Be silent, human."

"Who are you guys?" said Blaze, ignoring his instructions. "Where the hell did you come from and why did you come here? And why do you all wear those stupid uniforms? It's just doesn't work for you."

"I said be quiet!"

"So. Haven't you noticed yet that I don't take orders well?" Blaze stopped walking and Aldarik leveled his aim at her again. "Hey, I'm not resisting. I only want to know what's going on. Why are you in Colorado Springs? Why did you take me prisoner?"

Seething, Aldarik grabbed Blaze and she sank to her knees as his fangs grazed her neck.

"I wouldn't do that," warned a commanding voice.

Aldarik let Blaze go and she crumpled into a heap. She was lifted to her feet and held close by Pallaton. Aldarik laughed as his fangs rescinded, flashing his eyes. Blaze pressed in to Pallaton. She didn't know his intentions, but for the moment, he wasn't Aldarik.

"She's your fighter," said Aldarik. "I wasn't going to bite her, captain."

"I don't like my property being mishandled. Do what you want to the others who tried to escape and get this mess cleaned up, lieutenant."

"That girl killed one of my men!" Aldarik pointed an accusing finger at Blaze. "I want her punished. Whip her, now!" He snapped his fingers and a guard handed a whip to Pallaton. "It's the only way to handle unruly humans."

Pallaton tossed the whip aside. "Aldarik, take your men and return to your duties. I'd no more whip one of my fighters than bite them. Watch your tone and remember who give orders here."

The captain led Blaze to his vehicle and removed the ropes from her wrists. Shadowguard passed them, glaring. Aldarik laughed with derision as he walked by, his gaze piercing Blaze.

"Never try that again," said Pallaton driving toward the gym. "I may not be around the next time. Lieutenant Aldarik knows you belong to me, but that wouldn't stop him from sucking you dry when my back is turned. He isn't a Maker, so one bite from him would have turned you into a zombie, unless he snapped your neck. You've fought too hard and too long to end up as a zombie. Don't you agree?"

"You're my owner and I'm your slave. I'm not in a position to disagree with you."

"I'm your guardian. You're my fighter. Class B, too." Pallaton sounded impressed. "Most fighters start out at Class F, if they're decent. You remember Tandor, don't you? He's one of mine, and a Class A. He'll be fighting in the Death Games on Halloween night, as will you, Blaze."

"Can't you just let me go?" Blaze gave him a pleading look. "I want to go home. Please."

Pallaton drove around the large courtyard and turned toward the gym.

"I'd like to," said Pallaton. "But the Kaiser wouldn't approve. Normally, I don't associate with my fighters, but I made an exception for you. You're the only fighter who tried to escape, and you almost made it. You did something truly amazing, Blaze. I've done what I can by giving you a Class B rating. If you win your match, you'll live to fight another day. That much I can promise."

"What about my friends who were brought here? Star? Raven?

Dragon? I know I'm asking a lot of questions. I just want to know what's going on."

"Dragon will fight Halloween night. Salustra is his guardian and he's ranked as a champion," said Pallaton, pulling up to the curb as two guards approached. "Anyone you see dressed trench coats are Shadowguard. My men tried to reach you before Aldarik's men, but were too late. He wants my job and will use any opportunity to advance. If you had escaped, he would have used it to gain favor with the Kaiser and attempted to replace me. Star belongs to Aldarik, I'm sorry to say, and Raven is the Kaiser's new mistress. I doubt you'll ever see them again, Blaze. Not unless you win your match and win me a great deal of money. I can only protect you if you win. Now go with the guards and return to the gym. Eat your breakfast and try not to get yourself killed."

Blaze reached out and placed her hand on his arm. His fangs extended at her touch and he removed her hand, giving her a nod. "Sorry," she said. "I just—"

"I understand," said Pallaton, "and you're welcome, but don't ever touch me. It's hard enough to smell a human. I don't want to hurt you."

Blaze lowered her head and went with the guards, though she had no intention of fighting in the Death Games. The moment she had another chance, she would run. She had to get back to camp and tell Cadence everything.

Chapter Eighteen

"What you're proposing is a rebellion," said Luna.

Thor stood on the cliff, cloaked in shadow as he watched the camp below. Patrols monitored the road and were stationed throughout the grounds, while the Dark Angels set the fence in place. The werepumas had found Loki and Thor when they fled camp and brought them to one of their supply dens. While the small pride kept watch outside the tunnel, Luna spoke with Thor.

Luna continued, "The entire camp is already on lockdown and the Tigers are restricted to their RV. There will be no turning back and Highbrow will either kill you, or at least exile you from camp for good. Are you sure?"

"Yes," he said. "Cadence's blood is our only chance at fighting back and Highbrow doesn't have the right to deny us this opportunity. I'm going to the infirmary to get what we need."

Luna nodded. "Okay then. How can we help?"

"No one suspects you're involved," said Thor. "Your pride can enter camp and find anyone else who wants to join us." He patted Loki on the shoulder. "I know you're itching to talk to your friends, pal. When you guys explain what we're doing, I know at least China Six and the Amazons will join us."

Luna motioned to the main road as a patrol truck modified with high-watt lights illuminated the canyon walls.

"There's a path at the Pillars of Hercules they haven't closed off, so after you have recruited people, bring them through there," said Luna. "Meet my pride back here, and we'll take you to our new winter camp on the south side of the Peak. There's fresh water, and plenty of room for everyone."

"I didn't think it would come to this." Thor leaned back against the rocks. "People I love are prisoners at the Citadel or being detained in camp, or dead. "I just want the blood vials, and to get out with anyone who wants to join us. I'm not interested in taking control of the camp. Cadence will join us if we can free her, and she is all we need to start over."

"We can do this," declared Loki. "Black Beard and Caesar are my buddies, so I'm sure some of the Buccaneers and War Gods will join us. I'd ask the Bull Dogs, but they're loyal to Highbrow."

Thor nodded. "Then let's do this."

Minutes later, Thor scaled down the cliff with Loki on his back. The two knelt behind a dumpster as a battle truck drove past, scanning the canyon walls with search lights. Razorbacks were above the overlook point, armed. The Bandits had been positioned outside of the tunnel where Betsy watched the children, and teams stood beside the waterfall and outside the infirmary.

"Are they looking for us or the Shadowguard?" said Loki.

"The Dark Angels are all at the ridge. I'd say their main concern is the Shadowguard, not us. We were seen leaving camp, not returning." Thor put his hand on Loki's arm. "Bring everyone you can and meet me behind the infirmary when you're done. I'll figure out how to get to all the Tigers and bring them with me."

"I'll do my best." Loki sprinted away.

Thor made a dash for the infirmary, moving fast. The Blue Devils were standing guard, but Echo and her team didn't notice him. Thor found an open window, and slid into the lab. There were no Dark Angels in the lab, and the only lights on were from equipment and computers. He made his way to the fridge, broke the lock, and opened it to find all manner of labeled vials and bags of blood. He rummaged through the shelves until he saw a tray labeled *Cadence*. Pocketing six vials, he slunk back to the window when he heard the door open and froze.

"How did you get in here?" asked Picasso. He glanced at the open window, shut the door and approached Thor. "So the rumors are true. Did you find what you wanted?"

Thor lifted an eyebrow. "Yeah, I did. What's the deal? Why aren't you turning me in?"

"Because I believe in Cadence. Highbrow arrested her, Freeborn, Smack, and Dodger. Freeborn is in the brig, but the others are in the Tiger RV," said Picasso. "While I agree with what you're doing, I suggest you avoid being seen by any of the Dark Angels. We can't get involved, Thor. Rose wants to stay here, so she's staying neutral on everything. We can't afford to be kicked out of camp."

"You never saw me, and I was never here," said Thor, as he slipped out the window.

Thor hid in the trees behind in the infirmary, a short distance from HQ and the waterfall. The Dark Angels had three RVs set up nearby, but no one appeared to be inside. From where he was hiding, he could hear voices on the stairs beside the waterfall. Thor pressed flat to the ground and peered up to see Highbrow and the Bull Dogs returning from Midnight Falls. The vampires were working hard on the ridge above, clearing trees and installing additional high-voltage lighting on either side of the cliff.

"We're here," said Loki, creeping up behind Thor.

Xena, Phoenix, Dodger, Smack, and Freeborn crouched behind a wall of bushes. Loki had done the impossible, freeing the two youngest Tigers. Dodger grinned from ear to ear, a glint of darkness in his eye.

"We couldn't get to Cadence," said Loki. "I managed to get Dodger and Smack out of the RV, but it was Dodger who freed Freeborn from the brig. He knew the guard."

"Where is Cadence?" asked Thor. "Is she okay?"

"Highbrow has the commander at the barracks," said Freeborn. "Luna and the pride are going to try and rescue her."

Thor was frustrated with the entire situation. "Isn't anyone else joining us? Where are Black Beard, Saber, and Caesar?"

"They're interested, but they won't join us unless we come back with Cadence's blood. They want to be transformed before they join our revolt," said Loki. "I tried to get Odin to come with us, but he just put a pillow over his head and refused to talk. Did you get Cadence's blood? I'm to meet back up with the Buccaneers and War Gods. They're waiting at their RVs."

Thor reached into his coat pockets and produced the vials of blood. Everyone grew quiet and nervous as he distributed a vial to each team member. Freeborn stood guard, while each pulled the rubber stopper from their bottle.

"You don't need a lot," whispered Thor. "Take a drop and save the rest. If in doubt, take another drop, but don't overdo it. We need the rest to give to anyone else who will join."

Xena went first, tapping three drops in her mouth. The rest of the group did the same, acting as if they would sprout wings or horns.

"Nomad should be getting back soon," said Thor. "China Six will join us when they learn Star was taken. Xena, go with Phoenix and meet them at the front gate. Make sure you get to China Six before Highbrow does. I know Dragon will join, and if he joins, the others will too. Picasso said he's on our side, but the Dark Angels are staying in camp and don't want to be involved, so steer clear of them. Rafe will join us, guaranteed, but he's it."

One after another, each person placed their hands over the next, building a tower of unity. Thor put his hand on top. He could smell the excitement.

"This is a rebellion. Our rebellion," said Thor. "If we're going to survive, this is the only way."

Their hands launched upward and separated at the same time.

Xena grabbed Loki by the arm. "You best come with us, Loki. I know your friends said they'd join us, but you shouldn't be going on your own. We all need to pair up. It's safer that way. Freeborn can go with Thor, and Dodger with Smack. Once we turn the others, we can join back up with Luna's pride."

"Just be careful," said Thor. "I don't trust the War Gods, so forget them. Black Beard and Saber are cool. If we can get them to join us, the rest of the Buccaneers will do the same."

The two Amazons and Loki moved out, keeping to the trees. Smack and Dodger each hugged Freeborn. Both kids were quiet and taking the mission serious. Freeborn turned away and knelt beside Thor.

"What's the plan?" asked Freeborn. "Who do you want to approach? Echo has been good to me. She's a Blue Devil and all, but I think she'd be someone to ask."

"Not a chance. The Blue Devils support Highbrow and Echo doesn't like me. I pissed her off too many times in the past. The rest of the team can ask around. I thought we'd go into HQ. Cadence has weapons and supplies in her cabin that we'll need. Wait outside the window and I'll hand everything to you."

They moved through the shadows, sneaking up behind headquarters. Thor opened the window and slid inside, landing on Cadence's cot. No one was inside, but he heard chatter on the short wave radio Destry had repaired. Thor grabbed everything he could lay his hands on. He passed boxes of food, water, ammo, and weapons to Freeborn, bagging the radios, along with some clothes and a few maps. Freeborn ducked a search light as it swept the side of the cabin. Thor tossed several duffle bags out and went back for the short wave radio.

"We got it all," said Thor. "You ready to haul this up the stairs?" He paused noticing a strange look from Freeborn. "What's wrong?"

"Highbrow called me a monster. Suppose that's what we are? We really don't know what Chameleon Blood will do to us."

Thor lifted an eyebrow. "Is that what you're calling it? Chameleon Blood?"

Freeborn nodded. "I'm worried, Thor. This strain of the virus mutates fast. It might have serious side effects. We could all end up zombies."

"Change is scary, but we're doing the right thing. Now come on. I need you."

They loaded up and snuck around the cabin, where they spotted the Razorbacks guarding the stairs. Thor could hear Highbrow and the Bull Dogs talking near the golf carts. With a nod at Freeborn, he ran past the Razorbacks unnoticed, reaching the top of the stairs in a single breath. He didn't hear Freeborn behind him on the path and went back to see what happened. She was kneeling at gunpoint, encircled by the Razorbacks. Highbrow and the Bull Dogs joined them, and moved against Thor.

Three shots struck Thor in the stomach and shoulder as the Bull Dogs opened fire. Despite the pain, he sped to the newly built Moon Tower, ten yards from the fence line. The Dark Angels saw Thor as they helped Lieutenant Sterling raise the fence, but remained silent. Thor passed through the opening, evading Sterling's sight and giving the vampires a grateful nod. Grimacing at the pain, he jumped the creek at Midnight Falls, and followed the path to Luna's cave.

The scent of burning flesh on the breeze caught his attention and Thor came to a deep pit in a grove of trees, still smoldering with charred human and vampire remains. He sank to his knees and let the bags and radio drop to the ground. Tears covered his cheeks as he gazed into the pit. On Highbrow's orders, the funeral involved stacking the vampires and humans, including Baldor, and burning them together. It was unforgivable.

Gunfire echoed through the canyon and Thor wondered who they were shooting at, but saw he was not being followed. Opening his coat, he probed the wounds in his stomach and shoulder, slick with blood.

He kept waiting for the pain to grow intense, expecting his last breath. When he didn't die, he checked the holes again. His muscles were constricting, pushing the bullets out of his body. Thor sat for several moments, soaking in the knowledge that his body healed within minutes of being shot.

At the sound of growling, Thor turned to see four werepumas trotting from the east. Barbarella had been shot in the shoulder and was limping. Skye sniffed and snarled as she walked around the smoldering pit, her bright eyes glowing.

"Was anyone else hurt?" Thor wiped the blood on his pants as he rose to his feet. Luna sniffed at his clothes. "Don't get close to me. I'm covered in blood. It kills vampires. It might kill you."

A flock of birds scattered from the trees as Smack and Dodger rounded the path carrying backpacks over each shoulder, neither tired or out of breath. Dodger groaned and held Smack as they stared at the remains of former friends in the pit mixed with their enemies.

"We've got to move past this right now. What happened?" asked Thor. "Was anyone else shot or captured?"

Smack shrugged. "Destry opened fire on the pride, keeping them from the barracks. The War Gods and Buccaneers were with us, but they ran the moment Destry started shooting. I think most realize Sterling is running the camp, not Highbrow, and are too afraid to join us."

"Where are Loki, Xena and Phoenix?" asked Thor. "Are the rest of the Amazons coming or not?"

"No," said Dodger. "Like Smack said, they're afraid of Lieutenant Sterling. Loki went with Xena and Phoenix to the garage to wait for China Six and Whisper. We told Loki to meet us here once he gets everyone to join us. Where's Freeborn?"

"Captured," said Thor, hanging his head. "I'm not leaving without Cadence, though. We're going to have to go back and rescue her. We need to rescue Freeborn, too." He offered Smack a reassuring smile. "I won't leave without the Tigers, kiddo."

"Hey, you're covered in blood. You were shot!" Smack pulled back from Dodger and pointed at Thor's bloody clothes. "Why aren't you dead?"

Transforming to human form, Luna said, "I'm wondering the same thing. You heal as fast as we do." She leaned toward Smack. "You also give off a scent that's similar to vampires."

The entire pride transformed as Barbarella's wound began to heal.

"No one volunteered to be a werepuma," Barbarella said. "We were bitten, so we didn't have a choice, but we're happier this way. Highbrow can't see that, and he doesn't realize we're the same people. Destry didn't even ask why we were there, he just opened fire on us. We won't go back. Now that they're expecting us, it's too dangerous."

"We're not afraid, but you three move faster than we do," said Skye. "When you lead a team to the Citadel, we'll go with you. You can count on us, Thor."

Luna gazed up at the night sky. "Dodger and Smack can help us take the supplies to a nearby cave," she said. "Are you sure China Six will join us? Lotus doesn't like werepumas and avoids us. Something about her bothers me. Always has."

"Dragon will convince his team to join us," Thor responded. "I'm not worried about China Six, nor should you be. When the girls take the Chameleon Blood, they'll be different, too. They won't think twice about you being werepumas. Why don't I go back to the garage and wait with Loki and the girls? Just don't go far."

"We'll be close by," said Luna. "Promise."

The pride leapt into animal form and hit the ground running toward higher country. The Tigers followed close behind with the supplies.

Thor took the path toward the Pillars of Hercules, hoping he could save Cadence and Freeborn.

Chapter Nineteen

Dragon escorted Salustra to dinner, and the two complimented each other in dress. He was shocked to see the sizeable gathering, adorned in formalwear and jewels. Tables draped in white were set with silver plates, gold stemware, and crystal vases filled with white roses. The guests glided toward the tables, finding their seats.

"We're at the head table," said Salustra.

A stringed quartet entertained, as champagne was served. The Kaiser sat on a golden throne in the center of the room, with Raven on his right, stunning in black velvet. On his left, Star accompanied Aldarik in a silver dress and diamond collar. Pallaton sat between the lieutenant and Salustra's seat. Dragon caught a glimpse of Star as he offered Salustra her seat. Star sat stoic, yet Raven smiled and flirted with the Kaiser. Dragon wondered if she was still human.

"You look beautiful this evening," Pallaton said. He waved for service and provided Salustra with a glass of champagne. "I see you've brought your pet."

Salustra patted Dragon's arm. "Don't pay any attention to Pallaton. He switched the place cards. We should be seated next to the Kaiser."

Dragon was busy studying the room and didn't care where he sat. The banquet hall was filled with guests, and armed guards were stationed at every door and in every corner. His friends were so close that Dragon considered trying to make a break for it, knowing full well the Kaiser expected such foolish impulse. Without weapons, he doubted he would get far. He noticed guests watching him and, wanting to blend in, accepted a glass of champagne.

At the other end of the head table, he spotted two children. Queen Cinder and Lord Cerberus. Logan sat near Cerberus, caught Dragon's stare, and offered a smirk. He felt his temper boil. The clanging of silverware against crystal brought his attention to the pretentious little monster occupying the throne.

"Ladies and gentlemen," squeaked the Kaiser. "Thank you for accepting my invitation to this, our first Halloween gala. Most of you are local, however those who traveled from afar have provided me a great honor." He paused as the guests clapped, then held his hand toward the two vampire children. "Allow me to introduce our local royalty. I present to you, Queen Cinder and Lord Cerberus. If I am correct, quite a few of you here were made by them."

Guests raised their hands, acknowledging they were the children's offspring.

"While I have ordered the elimination of all Makers, with the exception of current company," the Kaiser continued, "be assured that each of you have my affection and trust. I want you to think of Cinder and Cerberus as my family."

More applause filled the room. There was no mention of Rafe, and Dragon wondered if the Kaiser was embarrassed that one Maker had slipped through his pudgy fingers. He finished his glass of champagne and reached for another, finding the company of this many bloodthirsty vampires unsettling. He expected any minute to be dragged from the table and forced to fight.

"I'd now like to introduce you this beauty," said the Kaiser, pointing to Raven. "This is Raven, the newest member of my family. Raven, please say hello to my friends."

"Hello, everyone," Raven said, rising to her feet. The crowd went wild when she blew them a kiss. She looked at the Kaiser with adoration, and glowing yellow eyes.

"A special thank you is in order to Agent Logan, formerly of the F.B.I. We've known each other a long time. He has proven to be most resourceful through the years. I don't want to give him all of the credit for making tonight possible." The Kaiser laughed. "However, with Logan's help, my Shadowguard successfully raided the survivors' camp at Seven Falls, acquiring new fighters for the games. I'm sure you can smell the two humans at my table. Star is Lieutenant Aldarik's new mistress and Master Dragon is Salustra's new fighter."

The audience applauded. Star stared at the crowd, not saying a word. Dragon resisted the urge to grab a spoon from the table and shove it through the Kaiser's eye socket. He forced himself to relax at Salustra's gentle tap on his arm.

"Tell us, Master Dragon, how you managed to kill so many Shadowguard." said the Kaiser. "You look like an ordinary human, only you're not. What makes you so different from all the little mice at Seven Falls?"

Salustra laughed loudly. "Dear Kaiser, let's not spoil the mystery about Dragon's magic. He fights Aries of Athens tomorrow night, and I'm planning on winning a large sum of money. Some things are best kept secret."

"You're right," the Kaiser said, grinning wide. "On Halloween night, you will see Master Dragon in action. Determine for yourselves what makes him so special. If you gamble wisely, you may leave the Citadel a lot richer than when you arrived."

Dragon was unsure, but he thought he caught a menacing look in the Kaiser's eyes as he blew Salustra a kiss. She might not be a favorite in this court after all. The vampires made a big deal of their Makers, and most of the Dark Angels had Salustra's violet eyes. Only Micah and Ginger had green eyes, so he knew they'd been turned by someone else. Dragon wondered if she didn't join the Dark Angels at Seven Falls because she was part of the Kaiser's family, or if she, too, was a prisoner.

"I will give you ten humans as payment for a front row seat, my Kaiser," shouted a rotund vampire from one of the tables.

"Make that fifteen humans," said another. "I want to taste Master Dragon's blood when Aries rips him apart."

"That's the spirit," the Kaiser said. "Mr. Rafferty and the Turk will both have a front row seat. What about you, D'Aquilla? You came all the way from Italy. Do you want to sit next to my beautiful Raven in a box seat? What do you say?"

A tall man with gray hair stood from a table filled with beautiful women. "I will give you twenty humans if I am allowed to sit next to Raven," he said, gazing at Raven. "Surely European blood is more valued. Americans all taste the same. Like hamburgers."

The room rippled with laughter.

"Why pay in humans?" Dragon whispered to Salustra.

"Zombies are worthless because there are so many of them" she explained. "No one gambles with therianthropes since they are considered animals. Pets. Only humans have any real value because they are who we feed on and are in great demand."

As the wagering continued, the room was buzzing with theatrics. Dragon was stunned. Zombies inhabited every known city, and now he realized vampires did as well. He didn't like to think of himself as a food group, or their currency.

Hearing a rustle at the head table, Dragon spotted Star rising. He jumped to help her as she stumbled toward the door. As a guard lowered his weapon to block their path, Star slumped against Dragon. He noticed her pupils were as large as plates. She had been drugged. Escaping with Star in her current condition would be difficult.

"Where do you two think you're going?" said Aldarik.

Sensing Aldarik's movement, Dragon shoved Star into the arms of a guard and ducked as Aldarik swung. Dragon dropped and spun, extending his kick and knocking Aldarik's legs from under him. Aldarik hit the floor hard, but was on his feet in an instant, dagger in hand.

"Stand back," shouted the Kaiser. "Let them fight."

Aldarik lifted his knife and charged. Dragon shifted his feet, blocked Aldarik's movement and knocked the blade from his hand. Aldarik crashed to the floor and into Dragon's submission. A small crowd gathered around the two combatants, shouting bids. Dragon released Aldarik and stood, adjusting his tie. He scanned the room until he found Star back in her seat.

"You'll pay for that, slave," said Aldarik, shamed.

Charging again, he avoided Dragon's strikes and seized his throat. Dragon landed two knifehands into Aldarik's diaphragm, knocking the wind from his lungs. Aldarik released his grasp and staggered backward. Moving forward at blurring speed, Dragon landed a knee to his opponent's neck, sending Aldarik tumbling further backwards. The crowd cheered and Aldarik rose to his feet. Dragon attacked again, battering the taller man with hard blows to his chest and ribs. Aldarik defended with an attempted sweep and Dragon jumped, landing another kick to the vampire's chest. The two moved and countered, unwilling to surrender, until a commanding figure stepped between them, ending the fight.

"Enough," demanded Pallaton. "This is a dinner party. Not the arena. We're not savages."

With a snarl, Aldarik slunk back to his chair while Dragon bowed in respect to his opponent, and to Pallaton. The captain gestured for Dragon to take his seat, and the room quieted. The music resumed as guests returned to their seats, and dinner was served.

"Master Dragon, are you not curious about the fate of your friends?" asked the Kaiser.

"I assume they will fight in the arena. But if I may ask a question . . . What are you doing in Colorado Springs? You could go anywhere in the world, but you came here. We can't have the only survivor camp in the country."

"Why not Colorado Springs?" said the Kaiser. "It's a lovely place."

"Then you plan to stay here for a while?" Dragon wiped his mouth and tossed his napkin onto his plate. "I'm sure the camp at Seven Falls seems like an easy mark. You came away with a few good fighters. It won't be so easy the next time."

"I have no intention of attacking your camp." The Kaiser smiled. "Of course, I would like to meet Commander Cadence and Captain Highbrow. Your camp is the only one that has offered resistance, though not very successful. If your commander would surrender, I might spare your people."

"Yeah, right," said Dragon. Having nothing further to say, he leaned back in his chair.

Pallaton stood and approached Dragon. "I have instructions to escort you to the slave quarters. The Kaiser wants you to see the living conditions of the non-classified slaves compared to how a champion lives." He caught Salustra's eyes and shrugged. "Don't worry, Salustra. I have no intention of letting anything happen to him. The Kaiser does insist though. It's that or you both return to your room. Now."

"Very well." she said, annoyed.

Dragon followed Pallaton into a hallway filled with Shadowguard, and was immediately placed in handcuffs and leg chains. The Kaiser anticipated an attempt to escape. Pallaton selected several Shadowguard to accompany them to the slave pens, leaving the remainder posted on the upper level.

Dragon expected to see humans, not zombies, corralled by an electric fence. Many of the zombies were former Freedom Army soldiers he had known at Pike's Peak, and good men and women who never made it to Seven Falls. The Captain was among them, his uniform almost unrecognizable under the dried blood and gore. He still had both arms and legs, and, smelling fresh meat, swept through the weaker zombies to stand at the fence. Black discharge dribbled from his mouth, and rotting flesh hung from his face. His eyes were covered with a gray film, yet he seemed to recognize Dragon.

"This was your former captain?" asked Pallaton. At Dragon's nod, he continued. "We brought these zombies back from the town of Cascade. They'll open the games."

"Why doesn't the Kaiser just kill the zombies?" asked Dragon. "If he intends to restore civilization, then clearing them out would be a good way to start. I don't want to kill people in the arena that I used to know. The Captain and the Freedom Army soldiers don't deserve this. They gave their lives protecting us. You can't tell by looking at him now, but at one time, the Captain was a good man and in charge of caring for a lot of people."

"Then what happened to your camp? There are so few that remain alive."

"War," said Dragon. "War against the zombies, scavengers, and now your kind. He did his best. Cadence merely picked up the pieces."

Dragon walked around the corral, observing the captain as he pushed through the dead. Zombies didn't hold memories, nor did they have the capacity for conscious thought, yet his former leader was behaving opposite from what Dragon knew about the living dead. If Dragon had the means to tear down the fence and not get electrocuted, he would release the zombies and escape in the chaos.

"Your Captain failed to protect his people," said Pallaton. "The Kaiser won't make that mistake. Denver, Los Angeles, New York City, and Atlanta are now major vampire strongholds. We came here because Colorado Springs is centralized, and from here, the Kaiser can rule North America."

"What about the U.S. government?" Dragon pressed. "The Kaiser made it sound like Seven Falls is the last of the survivors, but there has to be more. With all the vampires I've seen around here, you've found plenty."

Pallaton snorted. "Many more, but as for the government, I don't think it exists. We've looked for them. If the President is alive, I assume he's at sea with the Navy, and that's where they'll stay. The Kaiser is expanding his borders unopposed and unchallenged. He's killed most of the Makers in North America, except for a select few. D'Aquilla rules Italy, but he'll branch out in time. Your friend Rafe is an exceptional vampire. It's a shame he'll only be recaptured and sent to the arena. My point is, you're hopeless and outnumbered."

"The Dark Angels fight for us," said Dragon.

"There aren't many Dark Angels and the Shadowguard continues to grow."

"This can't last," said Dragon. "The Kaiser will deplete all of his resources at the rate he's going. When the government resurfaces, and they will, vampires will be the first to go. You're far more a threat than zombies." He paused. "Say what you will about the Captain, but he kept the camp at Pike's Peak running for a year. When the National Guard fell back, he offered safety, and he stayed when he didn't have to."

"Well, he didn't offer much resistance when we captured him," said Pallaton. "It's not that difficult to catch zombies. They're stupid creatures, though I must admit, it's curious that he seems to remember you. Put him in the arena and he'll act like all the others. I'm not a fan of the Death Games, but they provide entertainment for the troops, if nothing else."

Turning away from the zombies, Dragon looked toward the exit. Pallaton followed his gaze and laughed.

"Fearless and brave to the end. You are an unusual human," said Pallaton. "Why not try to escape? I thought if you saw the Freedom Army soldiers kept here that you might try. Tomorrow night you will fight Aries of Athens. Aries is one of the first to fight in the Death Games. He's different than the others. For all your speed and skill, not even you will be able to defeat the European champion."

Dragon looked Pallaton up and down. "I feel sorrier for you than I do for the Captain or myself. Zombies can't think. They don't know they're prisoners, but they'll fight for food. Me? I can leave any time I wish, Pallaton, and you know that. Bringing me here doesn't frighten me, nor does it leave me without hope. I have friends waiting for me and when I'm ready, I'll leave by the front door. But you," he said, shaking his head, "you're stuck."

Pallaton's eyes and fangs betrayed his emotion. "We're through here," he declared.

Chapter Twenty

A thin crescent moon hung its cautious gaze in the sky as Nomad pulled up to the barricade. Rose stared out, amazed by what had happened during their absence. More dead zombies than she had ever seen were burning. The Panthers and War Gods continued to add more to the pile as the Bull Dogs fed the fire's hunger with kerosene and even more bodies. Micah was the only Dark Angel present, standing as a lookout on top of a vehicle. Highbrow and Sterling stood at the open gate with a group of soldiers, as patrols occupied the guard towers.

Rose had informed China Six about Freeborn's condition and the earlier attack on the camp. They were visibly shaken about the loss of both Star and Dragon, and she knew Highbrow would be troubled to hear that Whisper, Dragon, and Tandor weren't coming back. The captain lifted his hand, waving the vehicle through the gate. Nomad pulled up outside the newly built garage and parked behind a modified armored bank truck. The doors to the garage were open and Nomad could see several people welding a metal cage over the windshield of a truck.

Nomad opened his door. "Everyone out!"

Sliding out of the truck, Rose stepped aside as the soldiers and girls climbed out. The soldiers walked toward Highbrow, while China Six and the wolves tracked in the opposite direction. Rafe shut the door and leveled a disapproving glare at Highbrow.

"I better go sort this out," said Nomad.

"You do that," said Rafe, smoothing back his blonde hair. "I have no intention of talking to Captain High Horse. I'm going to find Cadence."

Rafe sped into the distance and Rose transferred her attention to the girls of China Six. Her vision allowed her to see the girls standing in the shadows of tall pine trees, talking with Loki and two Amazon team members. Rose knew something was amiss as they followed Loki through the trees. She accompanied Nomad and was relieved when he wasted no time filling Highbrow in about Chief Chayton, the battle on the highway, and Rafe sighting Shadowguard following them. Something other than their tardy arrival seemed to have both Highbrow and Sterling agitated, and she didn't think it was zombies.

"Go after Rafe," said Highbrow, glancing at his lieutenant. With a crisp salute, Sterling recruited a few men and gave pursuit. "You're confined to the garage, Nomad. Coming back this late is unacceptable. I'll make an allowance, this time, since it's you. Pull another stunt like that and I'll toss you out of camp."

"Captain, you can't be serious!" said Rose, intervening. "Nomad hasn't done anything wrong. The enemy is at the Citadel, not here. We're all on your side."

Highbrow crossed his arms. "I'm in control of the situation, doctor. You'll be escorted back to your RV. I won't need you in the lab tonight. For the time being, it's closed."

"Do I get guards, too?" asked a sarcastic Nomad.

Highbrow stepped forward. "Things are going to change around here," he said, irritated. "Personally, I don't care whether Rafe stays or goes. If he causes trouble, he'll be asked to leave. The same goes for anyone else who disobeys a direct order."

Nomad shook his head and turned toward the garage. The scavengers were on thin ice since Logan's betrayal, yet Rose felt sympathy for

Highbrow. He was doing his best. Wanting to comfort him, she patted him on the arm, and he returned a thankful smile.

She started walking, wanting some time to mull over the events of the day before she returned to work at the lab. Within moments, a golf cart wheeled up next to her and the captain waved her over.

"Get in," said Highbrow. Odin sat quiet in the back seat. "You know how I feel about you and the Dark Angels, Doc. You're the only person I know who has tried to help this camp. Of course, I realize I'm asking a lot, but I need you on my side. I'm depending on it."

Several trucks rolled past, transporting armed patrols to the main gate, and others marched along the road or manned guard shacks. Security lights illuminated the road and every RV. Frightened, people peered through the windows of their trailers, hiding when they spotted Highbrow. There were no campfires, no groups roasting marshmallows, and no music playing. As they drove past the Tiger's RV, Rose saw the Bull Dogs standing guard and assumed Cadence and Freeborn were being held inside.

"What's going on, Highbrow?" questioned Rose as they pulled up to the infirmary. "You have the camp in lockdown. Is this about the Shadowguard, because I could understand that? Or, is this about Freeborn? Have you arrested her?"

Highbrow turned off the engine. "While you were gone, Thor and Loki stole Cadence's blood and gave it to several others. Both Cadence and Freeborn were part of the rebellion. I've had to lock Freeborn in the brig, and Cadence is in the infirmary being guarded by the Dark Angels. I don't know where Thor and Loki are."

"How many were infected?" said Rose. "Do you have any idea?"

"I know the names of the rebels," said Highbrow. "I also know that Cadence gave you a direct order to infect Thor with her blood. Instead of leaving camp, you should have stayed to monitor your patients. I made it clear I wanted to know what would happened if a healthy person was infected with her blood, but this isn't how I wanted to find out. Thor changed, like Freeborn. I don't know what they are, but they're not human. To avoid the virus spreading further, I've ordered the rebels shot on sight if they return to camp."

Rose felt her pulse quicken. "Please don't tell me someone has been shot," she said. "There's a better way to handle this, Highbrow. You don't have to shoot your own people."

"The werepumas are involved," said Highbrow. "Both Thor and Barbarella were shot."

Rose gasped.

"Their bodies haven't been found, so I assume they've healed from their injuries. So far I've learned that Cadence's blood can cure a zombie bite, but it also changes the host into some type of superhuman, with the same strength, speed, and healing ability as a vampire or a therianthrope. In short, Doctor, you've created a new type of species."

"That wasn't my intention." She shook her head, feeling guilty for the turn of events. "After seeing the way Freeborn reacted, Cadence decided to give it to Thor for his injuries. Her intention wasn't to create a new species, nor was it mine. We thought we'd found a way to heal people."

"By infecting people with the virus?" asked Highbrow. "I want to preserve the human race, Rose, not alter it. I'm disappointed. You both let me down."

Rose wasn't sure what to say, knowing she had betrayed his trust, but as camp doctor she was under Cadence's authority. "I'm sorry," she said, knowing it wasn't enough. "I warned Cadence about the risk. If I had thought Thor would lead a rebellion, I wouldn't have left. I'll understand if you think the Dark Angels should leave camp."

"Now that I've taken command, things are changing fast," said Highbrow. "I intend to use every means possible to ensure my camp remains safe. Asking the Dark Angels to leave is the last thing I want to do. I need your help, Rose. You are the camp doctor and it's your job to help every man, woman, and child. There's no way to undo what you've done, but you can make certain it doesn't go further than this."

"What do you intend to do with Cadence and Freeborn? You can't ask them to leave. If you do, you'll only make things worse. Most of the teams worship Cadence and would follow her to the grave. Sending her away will divide the camp and destroy your friendship. You need Cadence more than you need me."

"I thought I did," said Highbrow. "That's changed now."

Highbrow stepped out the cart. The Blue Devils appeared and surrounded the door to the infirmary, armed and in defensive position. Picasso stepped outside, took one look at Echo and her team, and went back inside. Rose walked toward the building, but Highbrow blocked her path.

"We're done playing games, Doctor," said Highbrow. "The only way to make sure my people remain safe is to destroy the lab, along with every blood sample you have in your possession. I no longer care about finding a cure. Go inside and talk some sense into Cadence. What you two have done is a crime against humanity and against God. I expect her to address the camp and tell them her blood is dangerous, that she is dangerous. Anyone infected is to turn themselves in. I'll decide what to do with the rebels once they're secured."

"Shouldn't you go inside and talk to her, Highbrow?" suggested Rose. "You're putting me in the middle of an argument. I'm afraid you'll send the wrong message if you exile the rebels and destroy the lab. It's also the infirmary. People still catch colds and scrape their knees. I can get rid of the blood but you need to resolve this with Cadence, and unify the camp."

"What I need is your cooperation." Highbrow's tone turned hostile. "If you want to remain here as camp doctor, do what I ask. Cadence will either abide by my rules or she will be asked to leave. Right now, I think she needs to apologize to the camp. If someone can't follow my orders, they can leave."

The Blue Devils were joined by Lieutenant Sterling and the Bull Dogs. Rose hurried to the building and stepped inside. The majority of the Dark Angels were inside and armed. Picasso closed and locked the door behind Rose, and the vampires surveyed the gathering crowd beyond the windows. Lachlan stood beside Cadence with his galloglass in hand. Cadence was armed and furious. Rose noticed Rafe was present, but Micah and several others were missing.

"I thought we agreed not to take sides," said Rose. "We're here to protect the humans and offer medical assistance. Highbrow wants Cadence to address the camp. If she'll apologize and help round up the rebels, Highbrow will allow us all to stay."

"I'll do nothing of the sort," Cadence asserted. "This is my camp. Highbrow isn't capable of running things without me. I'm not about to help him arrest Thor or the others."

"Rose, it's not as simple as you think," said Picasso. "We took a vote when Rafe arrived and have decided to stand with Cadence. You asked Rafe to lead the Dark Angels and he didn't have to take a vote, but he did. We believe this is the right thing to do."

"Don't make it sound like I give a damn about Highbrow or his camp," said Rafe. "The only reason I called for a vote is because I didn't want to force anyone to pick sides. We've been waiting for Micah to return, but he must still be on the ridge. I'm sure he'll side with Highbrow, but the rest of us want Cadence to remain in command. If anyone is leaving, it's High and Mighty."

Ginger peeked through the curtains. "The crowd is growing," she said, concerned. "It looks like everyone is camp is coming here. What are we going to do?"

"Not back down," said Rafe. "Are you with us or not, Rose?"

Rose locked eyes with Rafe. She asked him to lead the Dark Angels in order to unify with the humans. It was a mistake. They had to remain neutral—the camp wouldn't last a day without the Dark Angels. News of division would prompt an attack.

The situation played right into the Kaiser's hand.

"We agreed long ago that one person would lead the Dark Angels," said Rose. "I'm prepared to reassume my position as leader. I say we disarm and follow Highbrow's orders. Step away from the door, Ginger. We're not getting involved and that's final."

Rafe laughed. "You're asking me to resign? Do we need to take another vote or do you want me to pretend I care what you think? You're not thinking clear about this. Cadence needs our help. If we do nothing, we are siding with Highbrow."

The Dark Angels watched as Rose and Rafe debated, not sure what to do. Ginger turned from the door and joined Rose, and most of the vampires followed her decision. Lachlan, Picasso, and six others sided with Cadence.

"Please take the lead, Rose," said Rafe, sneering. "I didn't enjoy being in charge anyway. It's obvious what we need to do. If you decide to support Highbrow, I won't stop you. But I'm not staying either."

"Rose is right, Rafe," said Cadence. "The Dark Angels need to stay neutral. This is a problem between Highbrow and me. I'll talk to Highbrow, but it won't resolve anything. I'm not letting him arrest Thor, or anyone else for that matter. I'd rather leave camp than see anyone else harmed. And I will not apologize."

"Highbrow is afraid, Cadence," Rose said. "He's afraid the virus has created a new species. By your own admission, you believe this to be the case as well. Unless amends are made, the infected will have to leave camp. Where will you go? Please reconsider what you're doing here, Cadence. Highbrow needs you."

"Cadence, you better not surrender," said Lachlan. "If you do, I'll shoot you myself." He winked playfully.

Cadence cocked an eyebrow at him. "You could try."

"I second that, Irishman." Rafe faced the commander. "It's your call, Cadence. Do you want to make up with that wet biscuit or do you want to march out of here with your head held high?"

"Oh, I'm marching out all right," said Cadence. She walked over to Rose and held out her hand. "No hard feelings, Doc. I understand why you're staying, and I approve of your decision. Keep the camp safe. Highbrow will need you more than ever once I'm gone."

Rose shook hands with Cadence. "I'm sorry," said Rose. "I didn't want this to happen. Highbrow intends to burn the infirmary down, along with the blood samples, equipment, all of my research. I'd rather not do that, and if you agree, I think Lachlan should take what he can carry back to the hotel. There's too much valuable information in my files. I still think I can find a way to use your blood and create a cure that won't change people into . . . whatever your blood is doing to them. If you still want my help, I'm offering it."

"Of course I do," said Cadence. "Lachlan, take everything you can and leave out the back window. Anyone else who wants to help can do the same. I won't expect you to stay at the hotel. You can come back here. I'll give you a few minutes and then I'm going out to talk to Highbrow. Picasso? Rafe? I'd like you both to come with me."

Setting his sword aside, Lachlan started bagging up Rose's research. The rest of the vampires scurried to box up equipment and supplies. Everything that held value to Rose's work was packed up and hauled out the back.

"Some of these vials contain dangerous materials," said Rafe, studying them. Rose had brought more than just one form of the virus. "We'll take what is needed and leave what we don't need."

When they finished loading everything, half the vampires followed Lachlan out. Cadence, Rafe, and Picasso stepped toward the door. Rose sped to intercept them.

"Let me go first," said Rose. "I'll let Highbrow know you're coming out. Try not to be angry with him, Cadence. Highbrow is only doing what he thinks is best, and so am I. I'm not picking Highbrow over you. The camp is my priority. This isn't personal."

"I understand, Rose," said Cadence, smiling. "I'll try to keep the shouting to a minimum."

The moment Rose stepped outside, a flurry of activity stirred. The Bull Dogs, Valkyries, Blue Devils, and Lieutenant Sterling stood behind Highbrow. More armed patrols were arriving, led by Destry. The War Gods, Bandits, Razorbacks, and Panthers ran toward the gathering as well. Rose tensed as Cadence, Rafe, and Picasso walked out and stood behind her. The ensuing confrontation wasn't what had Rose worried, but that the Shadowguard were watching from the ridge. No alarm was raised, so Rose assumed Lachlan and the Dark Angels had made it past the Shadowguard without incident. Part of her wished the enemy would strike while Cadence was still present.

"Captain Highbrow, I believe Commander Cadence would like to speak to you," said Rose. "I think it would be best in private. I also think you should allow the Dark Angels to bring out the medical supplies for the camp and store it in the mess hall for now."

Highbrow smirked and drew his weapon. "I'm not stupid, doctor," he said. "Have all of the Dark Angels stop what they're doing and come out so I can get a headcount. We're burning this lab now. We can build another hospital and get other supplies."

Picasso ducked inside, and came back out with the remaining Dark Angels. Micah arrived with the others that had been working on the ridge, and Ginger joined him.

"What now?" said Cadence. "If you want to talk, then talk, Highbrow."

"Commander Cadence," said Highbrow, in a formal voice, "I have assumed command over this camp. As of this moment, you are no longer in command of the Freedom Army. Will you stand down?"

Rose moved to speak with Highbrow. "This needs to be in private." She hadn't counted on him grabbing her arm. "What are you doing? I thought you wanted to talk?"

"Making it clear that you're on my side, Doctor," said Highbrow. "Have you thought about my offer, Cadence? If you have something to say, then say it in front of the camp. I think everyone deserves to hear your side of this. Well?"

"When Pike's Peak fell," said Cadence, "I'm the one who brought us here. I've done everything possible to ensure our safety. It's because of me that Rafe brought the Dark Angels here to protect us. You won't be able to protect this camp without us."

Highbrow and Sterling had orchestrated the perfect military coup. Their forces advanced and encircled Cadence, Rafe, and Picasso.

"Let's keep this simple," said Highbrow. "Since I know Cadence won't surrender or take orders from me, you have one choice. Leave camp. Now."

Cadence stepped forward. Lieutenant Sterling snapped his fingers and every armed individual pointed their weapon at their former commander. With a snarl, Rafe stepped in front of Cadence to shield any attack. Rose jerked her arm out of Highbrow's grasp.

"The Shadowguard are watching us," said Rose. "I know you can't see them, Highbrow, but there are scouts on the ridge. Everything will be reported to the Kaiser. Are you sure you want him to know what's going on?"

"It is what it is," said Highbrow. "I'm waiting, Cadence. What is your decision?"

"So, this is how it's going to be?" asked Cadence, moving from behind Rafe. "You are so desperate to take command. Take it, Highbrow. I'm not going to stand in your way. I'll pack my things and leave, but I'm not leaving without Freeborn. I'd have preferred to talk to you about this in private, but since everyone is here, then let's keep this simple. Tell Sterling and your soldiers to lower their guns and I'll get my things at HQ, while you send for Freeborn."

"Someone already cleared out your possessions," Highbrow said. "That's how I knew you intended to leave." He lowered his gun. "I didn't want it to be this way, Cadence. I'm doing this for the good of the camp."

Rafe pointed at Highbrow. "You're an idiot," he said, angry. "You're not fit for command. The moment Cadence leaves, the Shadowguard will pick this camp apart. The Kaiser wants fighters for the Death Games, and he needs fresh blood. When you end up in Room 16 at the Citadel, be sure to write your name on the wall, like I did."

"Be quiet, Rafe," said Cadence. "You're not helping."

"Cadence!" shouted Freeborn. The tall girl came from behind the mess hall, accompanied by the Buccaneers who joined the ranks of soldiers and patrols. She glared at Highbrow and joined Cadence. "No cage can hold me. You want us to leave, we'll leave. But I'm disappointed in you, Highbrow. The Fighting Tigers were your family."

Highbrow was moved, but didn't break. "You want me to be the bad guy," he said, "but I'm not. All I want is to make sure humans stay human. I want this camp to survive. The one to blame is Cadence. She had a choice, Freeborn. So did you."

"Yep. Just like your father," said Cadence. "Abandoning people runs in your blood, I see."

Highbrow raised his aim at Cadence. Confusion and anger filled his eyes. "When the zombie outbreak occurred," he said, "no one knew what to expect, so we banded together. People from all walks of life came together, trying to survive. We rebuilt. I might not be able to control the spread of the virus, but I can control what happens here."

"We're with you, commander!" Thor called out. A group of misfits led by the large Viking stepped out of the shadows. Thor's leather coat was zipped up, but the bullet holes and dried blood were visible. Rose was desperate to discover everything that had happened to Thor, but it was not the time or place. Cadence's blood changed Thor, and she wasn't the only one that noticed. Highbrow and Odin both stared in disbelief. For a moment, Rose thought Odin would join Thor, but he remained with the captain. Thor's group joined Cadence, followed by the werepumas.

"Take care of yourself, Rose," said Rafe. "Come on, Picasso. Let's get outta here."

Rose never believed Picasso would leave her side, but if Cadence had promised to rescue Tandor, then she understood why.

A commotion behind Highbrow revealed two soldiers dragging a stocky figure through the crowd. Sarge was thrown on the ground in front of Cadence. Released from solitary confinement, he was dirty, unkempt, and less burly than a month ago. Sarge looked around, rolled his eyes, and cackled like a mad man.

"Take Sarge with you," said Sterling, glancing at Destry. Sarge and Destry had been best friends. Destry hung his head in shame. "We don't want him. He's all yours."

Cadence pulled Sarge up by the arm and allowed her eyes to communicate disappointment to Highbrow. "You're throwing away a human?" she demanded. "Just like that? So much for your lofty idea of protecting your own."

"He's useless," said Highbrow. "We can't waste food on him any longer. It's all about give and take here, and Sarge only takes. Keep him or dump him into the nearest gutter. I don't care, he's your problem now."

"You're breaking my heart, Highbrow," said Cadence, handing Sarge to Thor. "I'll take Sarge with us and anyone else who wants to join me. I won't turn anyone away! If you want your freedom, if you want a voice, if you want to know you still have rights, then come with us. I'll do my best to keep you safe. I give you my word, and everyone here knows my word means something."

Highbrow walked to face Cadence as everyone watched, breathless. The hope in her eyes wrenched Rose's heart. "From this day forth, you are dead to us. Goodbye, Cadence."

Whatever hope Cadence allowed to surface hardened into cold

resolution. She removed her blue beret, the icon she had strived so hard to attain, and let it fall. The others with her tossed their berets to the ground in anger. No one joined them, choosing the comfort of the camp over the unknown beyond the gate.

"See these people get the supplies they need and escort them out of my camp, lieutenant," said Highbrow, firm. "Let them take any vehicle they want. No one is to interfere or get in their way. Just let them go."

Sterling saluted. "Yes, sir." As Highbrow turned away, the lieutenant smirked.

Soldiers and patrols formed lines on either side of the road. Rose watched Cadence lead her group through the crowd. She had never felt more proud of Cadence. Walking with her head high into the unknown with her small team, Cadence left without a single shot being fired.

Chapter Twenty-One

Pallaton and five guards accompanied Blaze to a large auditorium for breakfast. Twice as many prisoners than the day before sat under heavy surveillance. Blaze wondered if her guardian was a good guy or just another fanged sociopath. He let her sleep late today, a privilege not afforded anyone else.

"You will sit with my fighters," said Pallaton, indicating a group of people crowded together. Most had the look and confidence of experienced fighters, Tandor among them.

Pallaton pulled Blaze's chair for her to sit, prompting stares from several nearby.

"I will select your meal. Eat only what I put before you. Is that clear, Blaze?" Pallaton pressed. "You'll be training today. I'm teaming you up with Tandor. Learn all you can from him. What Tandor teaches you may save your life in the arena."

"Yeah, well, if you would just drive me home," said Blaze, "that would work too."

Pallaton laughed and gently pushed her into the chair. He placed a plate in front of her, filling it with rare-cooked steak, three poached eggs, and strips of chicken. An overweight fighter enjoyed blueberry pancakes across the table from her. Annoyed, she sat back, envious of a basket of chocolate muffins before her. She reached for one, and Pallaton smacked her hand. He monitored the table, making sure his favorite fighters ate according to his choosing, removing anything he didn't approve.

"How are you doing?" asked Tandor, pushing her fork closer to her plate. He was the only vampire seated with Pallaton's fighters.

"Okay." Blaze picked up the fork and took a bite.

Tandor offered a tolerant smile. "Vampires have come from around the world for tomorrow's fight. Big name fighters have been brought in. We'll need to train hard today if you're to be prepared."

Pallaton returned and placed a protein shake in front of Blaze. She hoped it tasted like fruit, and not chalk. Sipping, she tasted almonds. Many were eating with their hands, so she felt privileged to have a fork and a knife. She spotted Bob and Mr. Smith, though only Bob acknowledged her.

"Is that a new friend?" asked Tandor.

"Kinda." She washed her eggs and chicken down with the thick almond-flavored shake, ending with a loud belch.

"Tandor, train Blaze today," said Pallaton, returning. "I raised her to Class B after she tried to escape and killed a Shadowguard. It's my intention to have her to fight as your partner."

Tandor gave a nod. "I saw D'Aquilla yesterday, hanging around the practice arena. He's brought a tough group in from Rome."

"D'Aquilla has a strong foothold in Italy," said Pallaton. "His consigliore will remain in charge during his absence. He was jealous when he heard the Kaiser has claimed Colorado, Kansas, Nebraska, and Missouri as new territories and he wants to make a strong showing here."

"What about the other vampire lords?" questioned Tandor.

Blaze filled her coffee cup without objection from Pallaton. She noticed he enjoyed speaking to Tandor, and realized they had been friends.

"The Turk has the northern United States," said Pallaton. "Rafferty has L.A. in his pocket, and Big Mike took Manhattan and the east coast. No one seems interested in Canada or Mexico, and Central and

South America are filled with rogue gangs and cutthroats. I don't think any of the vampire lords are attempting to curb the zombie population. They'll need to eventually if they intend to expand their borders."

"Why doesn't anyone want Canada or Mexico?" asked Blaze, wiping her mouth with her hand. As soon as she spoke, she knew she had broken another rule. Tandor quieted and stared at his plate. Pallaton's hand fell to her shoulder and squeezed firm enough to indicate silence.

"It's a shame you got caught up in politics, Tandor," Pallaton said, lowering his voice. "As a crew chief, you could have done more good here than venturing out as an independent." He paused. "Salustra is alive. She's here." Tandor looked up with interest.

Blaze watched blood seep as she cut into her steak. If she had been at a restaurant, she would have sent it back, but a prime cut of beef was unheard of at camp. *Waste not, want not*, she thought. Blaze chewed, and chewed some more. Unable to grind the raw steak with her teeth, she swallowed it whole and choked. Tandor thwacked her on the back and the steak shot out of her mouth and into her coffee.

"You're not a snake," said Tandor.

One of the fighters laughed, and then everyone started laughing, except Blaze. People began to clear the table and ready to begin the day's training. Blaze was not happy about her coffee, and even more so that she would begin training on a full stomach. Tandor waited for her.

"You're supposed to wait a while before exercise," said Blaze. "I don't want to vomit everything I just ate. Can't they let us digest our breakfast before we start?"

"Pallaton did you a favor. He only gave you protein. Those who ate starch and sugar will not be fit for the games. You can always tell a Class F fighter by what they eat the night before a game. Your friend, Bob, isn't expected to live. He was allowed a high-sugar meal."

"You and Pallaton used to be friends." said Blaze. "Is that why he was so nice to you? Is that why he is looking out for me?"

"We're investments," said Tandor, a tinge of anger in his voice. "He was a friend until the moment he chose me as a fighter. Pallaton is only interested in making money. But once, yes, we used to be close. Things have changed."

Tandor remained quiet the rest of the way to the training gym. Blaze imagined they would be taken onto the football field at some point so they could get a feel for the fighting arena. Guards followed close, leaving Blaze no recourse but to follow the other fighters. Pallaton's fighters separated from the larger group to train on their own. She scanned the gym and recognized a few people. Heimdall and three of the Elite had been claimed as Aldarik's prisoners. Uther was owned by the Kaiser and fought against a familiar figure with a handle bar moustache. It was Lieutenant Habit. Blaze thought Habit died at the Peak, but he'd been taken captive, along with several other Freedom Army soldiers.

A coach walked by the line of prisoners and handed each person a weapon. Blaze was given a crossbow and a pouch filled with arrows. A katana was offered to Tandor. Looking around the stadium, she saw armed guards everywhere. It made no sense why the prisoners didn't revolt.

"There are more of us than guards," said Blaze. "Why don't we fight our way out?"

"There are surveillance cameras everywhere. We wouldn't get far and too many humans would be harmed in the chaos," said Tandor. "After your escape attempt yesterday, the guards have orders to kill anyone who runs. I need some space to train with my sword for a while. Go stand in line with the archers and focus on training, I'll join you soon."

When Tandor started to walk off, she followed after him. "What happened to Whisper? Is he dead?"

Tandor turned back and kept his voice low. "Whisper isn't with the prisoners and Pallaton hasn't mentioned him. Why? You think he's still in the Citadel?"

Keeping her silence about what she had seen in the theater the first night, Blaze watched Tandor join Uther and Lieutenant Habit. The men exchanged greetings and engaged in swordplay. Blaze joined the line and watched as two archers let loose a quiver full of arrows against a group of zombies inside a corral. The line moved up each time an archer emptied their quiver. A young vampire was sent in to fetch arrows for the archers. He moved fast and returned with a load of black, gooey arrows.

"You're good," said a girl after Blaze finished her turn. She wore a green scarf and was malnourished. "I came in on a bus with Bob and a bunch of others. You must be Blaze. He talked about you and your camp last night. We didn't have anything like that in Nashville."

Blaze shrugged. "We've held out for about a year now, Nashville."

"Some say the vampires spread the virus," said the girl. "There's always a conspiracy floating around."

"Turning people into zombies doesn't seem to be an effective way of maintaining a healthy food source. Vampires can't feed on zombies, but zombies sure feed on them."

"Oh, the vamps have human breeding farms in Canada. My guardian, the Turk, comes from Chicago. He's been running things ever since the virus broke out. It's a vampire conspiracy, all right. Too many of them."

It was Blaze's turn to shoot again. She stepped up to the line with Nashville. While Blaze hit her moving targets with ease, Nashville was unsure of herself and took too long to shoot. Blaze noticed the vampire coaches were watching, worried for the girl, and decided to offer a few tips.

"You need to shoot faster, Nashville," Blazed advised her. "When you get nervous, your muscles freeze up. Relax, breathe, and pick your shot. If you miss and they get too close, shove an arrow through their eyes, hard. Kill the brain and move on to the next one."

Nashville shrugged. "Yeah, well, I didn't survive on the streets this long without killing a few on my own." She missed her next shot.

Blaze didn't believe the girl. She leaned over the fence and whistled at the zombies. One paid attention and turned toward Blaze. His thin body was pierced with so many arrows he resembled a pin cushion. She wiggled her hand at the zombie. It caught her scent and stumbled toward her.

"What are you doing?" Nashville gasped.

"Teaching you how to stay alive," Blaze said. "When he gets up to the fence, stab him in the head." She kept her arm over the fence until the zombie was close, then pulled away. The zombie gnashed the air where her arm had been and let out a loud, desperate moan. "What are you waiting for? Stab the dumb thing in the head, will you?"

Nashville was shaking hard and fumbled with her arrow. The creature slammed into the railing, attracting two more zombies to the fence. Zombies weren't smart, but they were hungry and could smell human flesh. In a moment the entire horde started toward the fence.

"Look what you've done," Nashville said.

A zombie managed to crawl over the railing and landed at Blaze's feet. She knew Nashville wasn't going to be able to kill the zombie, so she put her foot on the zombie's head, and stomped down hard. Its skull cracked open and she forced her foot through. With a shriek, Nashville dropped her weapon and ran to the back of the line.

"What's the matter? I killed it," Blaze called out.

Lifting her crossbow, Blaze shot another one in the eye and smiled as it fell with a thud. Yet another worked into a frenzy and started to climb over the railing. Blaze noticed that none of the vampire coaches were going to help. Some idiot behind her let an arrow loose, and Blaze ducked and ran for cover. She circled the corral and continued dropping zombies. As she made her way back to the archers, the whole lot was crawling over the railing. Using her crossbow like a bat, Blaze swung hard and clobbered a zombie in the head.

Blazed turned around and yelled at the dumbfounded archers. "Seriously, people. Are any of you knuckleheads going to help me? Zombies don't take time-outs."

A man stepped up to Blaze, lifted his bow and let it zing. He missed. Another woman wearing a red scarf stepped forward and fired at a zombie leaning over the fence. She hit the target and several more archers joined Blaze as the railing came crashing down. The zombies lumbered forward, hungry and in pursuit of their next meal. Everyone ran, except for Blaze, the woman with the red scarf, and the man who was determined not to miss again. Together they unleashed on the approaching zombies, backing up in step with each other and continuing to launch arrows. When they dispatched the final zombie, the two patted Blaze on the back.

"Where did you learn to fight like that?" asked the man.

"I'm a Fighting Tiger," said Blaze. "Ever hear of us?"

The man shook his head. "Sorry. I'm not from around here."

One of the coaches approached Blaze and her two new friends. "You two must have seen action in the past. You're both moving up to Class B with Blaze," he said. "Maybe you won't get eaten tomorrow night."

"That was a close call back there," said the woman as the vampire walked off. She followed Blaze to the water table. "This stuff doesn't seem to get to you. Been on the circuit long?"

"I'm new," said Blaze. She scrutinized the woman, guessing her to be in her thirties, in good shape, and no coward. "You're handy in a fight, lady. Why don't you come with me? I'm headed back to my camp. Both of you can tag along."

The man gave her an odd look. "They're watching us."

Blaze noticed the other archers being rounded up by the coaches. The dead zombies were carried out and the corral was quickly repaired. Replacement zombies were brought in and the archers lined up again. Nashville was back in line and holding a new bow. Blaze hung back to watch.

"You have a plan to get out of here?" said the woman.

"Something like that," said Blaze. She finished her water and wiped a hand across her mouth. "I'm walking out. Right under their noses."

The woman stared down at her water bottle. "They have security cameras set up all over the place. It's hopeless, Blaze. I can only hope to kill my opponent. That's how things work around here."

"Not in my world," said Blaze.

Glancing at the exit again, Blaze started walking, not caring if she was watched or not. No one stopped her. She walked through the tunnel and into the main corridor. It was like any other basketball complex, so she took off toward the main doors. She grabbed the metal bar on the door and pushed when she heard someone say her name. A head popped up from behind a snack counter and Blaze shrieked. It was Whisper. She glanced in both directions, making sure no vampires were coming, and ran to the counter. She toppled Whisper, diving over the top.

"Blaze?" Pallaton sounded angry. It hadn't taken him long to notice she was missing. Vampires were scouring the entryway, and someone opened the front doors and ran outside.

Whisper put his hand over Blaze's mouth. His face was made up to look pale, with dark circles painted under his eyes. He had found makeup in the theater, along with a black trench coat and looked every bit like a Shadowguard. Whisper removed his hand. They remained on the floor, pressed close together, listening to the sounds of footsteps. Whoever it was passed the counter and in the opposite direction.

His lips pressed against her ear. "I'm getting you out of here. Follow me."

Chapter Twenty-Two

It was past midnight, and Thor and Cadence sat in the sport's bar of the Broadmoor Hotel. Thor sipped a cold drink and Cadence enjoyed a cup of coffee. The hotel was in good shape and the bar was impeccable. If Thor hadn't known better, he would have thought management was simply in the middle of remodeling. He didn't mind being tossed out of camp or accused of being a mutant if it meant life in a luxury hotel.

However, with only a handful of Dark Angels to guard the hotel, Thor felt exposed. He caught a brief look at Cadence. She hadn't said anything about Highbrow, and she didn't have to. She wore her emotions for everyone to see. Cadence was hurting, and it was written all over her face.

The Death Games were being broadcast on TV. Tonight's reruns were the last event held in NYC and they were being hosted by the Kaiser himself. Each fight was bloodier than the last, and the first season was being recapped on every station.

"Dinner is served," called Lachlan.

The Irishman entered with a tray of grilled cheese and tuna fish sandwiches. Betsy packed a sack full of groceries before the team left camp, making sure they left with fresh vegetables and baked bread. Lachlan set the tray down and began preparing drinks for everyone.

"Picasso used to fight in the games," said Lachlan. "He won more than sixty fights before he called it quits. In the vampire world, Picasso is a pretty big deal."

Big letters scrolled across the screen: *Watch Tomorrow Night's Halloween Death Fights at 8:00 P.M. EST, brought to you by the Kaiser.*

"Will Federov be there tomorrow night?" asked Cadence. "I guess he's the reigning, and undefeated, international champion."

Lachlan looked up at the flat screen. "Keep watching. Federov is the broad-shouldered vamp in red. His last match is against the Greek champion, Aries. It's coming up next."

"What good does it do to sit here, pretending we're not orphans?" said Rafe. "We should load up the trucks and go to the Citadel. If we're going to free Dragon and the others, that's where we need to be." The former leader of the Dark Angels sat at a card table, playing poker with Luna, Barbarella, and Skye.

Thor turned back to the TV in time to see Federov rip Aries' arms off and throw them into the crowd. The fans went wild, and while Federov waved to the crowd, Aries rushed his armless body and slammed the Russian into the corner of the cage, biting into his neck. It took seconds for Aries to drain Federov dry. The champion dropped to the ground like a deflated balloon.

"Holy crap!" shouted Thor, food falling from his mouth. He turned around to look at the card players. "Did you see that? He sucked him dry!"

"It's barbaric," said Phoenix. "I think I'll take a look around. Come on, Moon Dog." As she made for the exit, the wolf rose to his feet, stretched, and trotted out.

Rafe tossed his cards in. "I hate poker. You're cheating, Barbarella. You keep looking at Skye before you ask for cards, and she's dealing from the bottom for you."

Skye laughed. "I'm not either." Her voice was calm, but she was annoyed. "You just can't play poker, Rafe. It's your deal anyway."

"I love this place! I never want to check out," called Loki. He swept into the room, fresh from a hot shower, wearing a hockey jersey and fuzzy slippers. "The last guy to have my room left behind his travel bags. Guess he was a sports fan, and a bit eccentric."

"It's snowing if anyone is interested," said Lotus, entering the room. Kirin and Monkey were with her. They dove into the sandwiches without reservation.

"I wish I could watch world news," Kirin said. "I'd love to know what's going on in London. Why can't the Shadowguard set up webcams or start posting online?" She turned a sarcastic face. "Oh, that's right . . . we don't have internet and vamps don't care about current events."

Lachlan laughed. "Hey, that's not entirely true. Here's some news . . . in Europe, the animals aren't affected by the virus. It's only here that we have shape-shifters like Luna and Red Hawk. A true werewolf only turns at the full moon, with no memory of their human side, operating purely on instincts and blood lust. They're called the Old Ones. No one knows how long they've been around, but they are so feared by the European vampires, the Kaiser has banned them from North America."

"Why no shape-shifters in Europe?" asked Cadence. "The vampire virus spread to the rest of the world. Doesn't make much sense."

Lachlan grinned. "Makers in Europe don't feed on animals. In fact, D'Aquilla is the only Maker overseas since he's killed all of his competition. The Kaiser is doing the same thing here. He's executed most of the Makers, keeping only those that breed superior offspring. Rafe was supposed to be executed."

"Rafe is the only reason I'm alive," said Cadence. "Don't tease him."

"Thank you," said Rafe. "At least one person here likes me."

"And this is what you call a Royal Flush," Barbarella said, laying out her cards. "I win, again!"

The Irishman walked over and knelt between Thor and Cadence. "The only reason the fights are being aired is for the Kaiser to reach out to other vampires, and to strike fear in the hearts of any human survivors. I happen to believe the U.S. government and a few other world leaders have survived. All Makers have sworn allegiance to the Kaiser. Instead of fighting amongst each other for control of cities, they've agreed to hold Death Games to sort out their differences. In a way, it's civilized. It's better than war."

Thor rubbed his fresh-trimmed chin, thinking about what Lachlan had said. He couldn't help wondering how they'd stand up in the games against opponents like Aries of Athens or one of the Old Ones.

Freeborn came in reading a magazine, and sat down at the bar, grabbing a sandwich and a bottle of water. Thor turned back to the TV to watch a tawny werewolf fight a slender female vampire with a whip in a suspended cage. It wasn't as exciting as football for him, but Thor was riveted. He let out a cheer when the werewolf won.

Picasso returned from a perimeter check covered with fresh snow. "I checked the perimeter as you asked, commander. The rest of the Dark Angels are standing guard and one is monitoring the security cameras."

"Great. Do you have the map I asked for?" asked Cadence. "Hey everyone, let's turn off the TV and sort out the details of this mission."

Picasso spread a map across a large dining table. He had marked places where their team members were being held. Trying to get to all of them was going to be difficult. Freeborn, Phoenix, and Lachlan joined them at the table as everyone else quieted down and turned their attention to Cadence.

"Tomorrow night is when the Kaiser will expect us," said Picasso. "The football stadium is the new arena, and the Kaiser will have tight security. There are tunnels all over the campus the humans can use, while the Dark Angels won't have any problem blending in with the audience. The Dark Angels will have the best chance of getting into the slave pens. They'll have the Freedom Army soldiers and the Elite beneath the stadium prior to game time. Tandor is scheduled to fight during the second half and Dragon fights last. He'll be fighting Aries."

"I assume Pallaton provided this information." Cadence looked up. "Did he mention where Star, Blaze, and Whisper are behind held?"

"No word on Whisper. Blaze has escaped. Pallaton is looking for her, but she's vanished," Picasso said. "Star is Aldarik's slave, so she'll be with him. It'll be even harder to reach Raven, and worse, the Kaiser has turned her. As his new mistress, she'll be in the box with the rest of the vampire lords. If we can get word to Dragon, he might be able to help. Pallaton says Dragon killed a host of Shadowguard before he was captured. Didn't you say he cut his finger in the lab?"

Cadence nodded. "If he's infected with my blood, then he must be changing like the rest of you. Any word on Logan or if he gave my blood to the Kaiser? Do they know about me?"

"Pallaton didn't say anything about it, and I didn't bring it up," said Picasso. "The less Pallaton knows about you and your team, the better chance we have of surprising the Kaiser. I don't think Pallaton would betray us. Then again, he's the Captain of the Shadowguard and expected to follow orders. There's a good chance he knows we're at the hotel, so I think we should find a new location."

"I've been thinking about this too." said Thor. "I played on that field. If Dragon is like us, he won't have any problem getting Star and Raven out of the stadium. Blaze and Whisper may be hiding at the Citadel, waiting for us. Rose said your Maker is still alive. Will Salustra help us? She'd be the one to contact and tell Dragon what we're planning. . . unless you trust Pallaton. And I don't."

Lachlan and Picasso walked to the bar to talk in private, Cadence and Thor joining them.

"I'll take half the Dark Angels and rescue the Elite," said Lachlan. "Picasso, you take the other half and get to the Freedom Army soldiers." He gave Thor a thin smile. "If you're going after Star and Raven, it'll be easier if you sneak into their sleeping quarters. That leaves Dragon. Salustra is his guardian. With her help, we can coordinate with Dragon and have him provide a diversion for Thor."

"That means we need to do this tonight," said Thor. Everyone looked at him. "We go in tomorrow and they'll be waiting for us. Hit them tonight, when they're not expecting it, and we can pull this off. What does the Kaiser have planned for tonight?"

"Another banquet," said Lachlan and Picasso at the same time.

"What about Raven?" Luna joined them at the bar. She wiggled in between Cadence and Thor. "We can't leave Raven there just because she's a vampire."

Thor shifted his conversation to Loki. "Give me the vial of blood back. In fact, everyone who has a vial, place it on the bar." He waited until all six vials were on the bar. "According to Rose, a drop of this will stop a vampire dead in their tracks. We're going to put this on our swords, knives, and ammo. Lachlan, grab me a bowl and set it on the table. Whatever is left can be given to the Elite and Freedom Army soldiers."

"Brilliant," said Cadence. "Let's get it done."

The vampires backed away from the bar, and the werepumas put distance between them and Thor as well, unsure of the effect Chameleon Blood would have on them. Thor poured the contents of two vials into a bowl, and used a bar rag to wipe the liquid across everyone's swords, knives, and arrow tips. He passed it to Xena, who dabbed a trace of blood on the end of each of their gun barrels. Anyone with a revolver covered the tips of their bullets. Leaving the team to their work, Thor walked over to the vampires.

"All it takes is one drop to turn a human or kill a vamp," said Thor. "Be careful handling this, guys." He held out three vials of blood and pocketed the last as a reserve. Picasso, Rafe, and Lachlan wrapped the vials in cloth and slipped them into their coat pockets.

"We need an exit plan," said Rafe. "The Shadowguard have a Black Hawk. Can anyone fly it?"

"I'm a pilot." Picasso offered. "Why don't I secure the chopper and have Freeborn lead my half of the Angels?" He put his hand on Rafe's shoulder. "Find Tandor. He'll be in the music hall. Give the blood to as many humans as you can reach and then meet me at the chopper."

"I suggest we start at the Cliff Dwellings," said Red Hawk. "The Shadowguard know about that place, and they won't expect us to return. The tunnels will be watched, and so will the interstate, but Moon Dog and I know a mountain trail that leads behind the Citadel. They won't anticipate us coming in from the north."

A lone gunshot echoed through the hotel sending everyone into a scramble. Thor grabbed his gun holster, sliding it over his shoulder, and tossed a rifle to Cadence. Freeborn took for the door with the Amazons, and Luna and her pride morphed and circled around Cadence. Assuming it was the Shadowguard, everyone grabbed what they could of their personal belongings and prepared to leave through a window.

"It's Sarge," said Freeborn, reappearing in the doorway. "I found him on the second floor. The crazy bastard broke the lock on his door. He must have found a spare gun in one of the rooms. He's dead. The Dark Angels are in the lobby and ready to go."

"Let's move out," said Cadence.

Thor turned off the lights after everyone exited the bar. He hadn't liked Sarge, but he felt sorry for him. If Sarge had been given Chameleon Blood, Thor wondered if he would have regained his sanity or turned back into the mean-spirited tyrant he was before. It didn't matter now, except the world had lost one more human life.

Chapter Twenty-Three

Rose sat at Cadence's desk, which was covered with maps and a disassembled rifle. On the corner of the desk was a framed Polaroid of the Fighting Tigers taken at the Peak. Rose had left the crowd watching the infirmary burn to the ground and came to the cabin for a break. The camp was in an uproar with the departure of Cadence and her new team. A few people wanted to join Cadence, after the fact, and had gathered at the mess hall to make demands of Highbrow.

When the phone rang, Rose leaned back and picked it up. "Hello?"

"Rose? It's Pallaton. We're headed to the Broadmoor. Get your people out." The line went dead.

Rose hit the receiver button and dialed the Broadmoor. The lines had been cut. All she heard was a busy tone. She hung up, tore off her lab coat, and ran out the door. She found Micah and the Dark Angels at their RVs, watching the smoke rising into the night sky.

"We're leaving," said Rose, her heart fluttering with panic. "Pallaton's sending troops to the Broadmoor. Cadence is there and she doesn't know the Shadowguard are on their way. The phones are out, so we'll have to leave now to get there in time. I'll fill Highbrow in and meet you back here."

The fire from the infirmary cast an orange glow over everyone gathered in the camp. Rose found Highbrow with the Bull Dogs. He seemed out of sorts, which was understandable, and Lieutenant Sterling was nowhere to be seen. As she approached the table, Highbrow sat up straight.

"Pallaton called," said Rose. "The Shadowguard are advancing on the Broadmoor. I'm taking the Angels. I won't let the Kaiser get his hands on Cadence. You need to get up and put your camp on alert. They'll be coming for you next."

Highbrow stared at her, as if his head was in a fog. "It was her choice to leave. I made the rules clear. If you can't follow my orders, then you must leave as well. Is that what you're doing, Rose? Leaving me too?"

"Pull yourself together, Highbrow! The Shadowguard are coming!"

Her shouting set every person within earshot into motion. Odin pulled Highbrow to his feet and got him moving. Everyone scrambled to take positions behind makeshift barricades, in trenches, and in patrol vehicles. Searchlights shined across the cliffs. At least Highbrow's teams knew what they were doing, though he seemed to be in shock. Rose didn't have time for a pep talk. She had let Cadence down once, and didn't plan on doing it again.

Returning to the RV, Rose accepted a rifle from Micah, slid the strap over her shoulder, and led the team on a path to the side of the cliff. The Dark Angels knew what had to be done. In an instant, the vampires scrambled up the cliffs, leapt the fence, and ran across the rocky terrain. Flare guns exploded high above the canyon, creating a red glow that lit up the sky. Rose and her team kept to the cliffs, following an upper trail to the road.

Micah led the way through a neighborhood that hosted zombies on every lawn and porch. The vampires had no choice but to travel by rooftop. Rose pushed her team, reaching the highway and racing through a gathering of the living dead. Zombies spun in every direction, unaware that a group of Dark Angels had slipped through their superior numbers. The vampires sped across a grassy field, filled with crude grave markers and dark mounds, and approached the rear of the Broadmoor Hotel.

Shadowguard marched around the hotel, formations tight. One after another, the Dark Angels jumped onto small cement landings under the windows on the second floor. Slipping in through the windows, the team dropped inside. Micah opened a door and peered into the dark hallway.

"Find Cadence and get her team out," said Rose, readying her rifle. "Regroup at the gas station at Colorado Avenue and Highway 24."

Rose and Ginger made their way to the sports bar, relying on vampire vision to move through the hotel. She saw boards had been removed from a broken window and ducked as a Shadowguard stepped into the bar. His eyes gleamed yellow as he scanned the bar before rejoining the troops. Rose crawled across the floor to a large table. A map was pinned to the wood, and she noted the circles around key locations at the Citadel. She rolled it up and tucked it away. Cadence and her team had been at the bar as she suspected, but all signs pointed to a sudden departure.

Rose and Ginger maneuvered to a piano bar that overlooked the lobby and peered over the marble railing at the entryway. Through the glass doors, they saw military vehicles and troops waiting beside a tank. The tank turned its turret, the heavy gun aiming at the hotel.

"The Kaiser doesn't mess around," said Ginger. "Let's go."

Rose grabbed Ginger's arm and they fled to the stairwell, racing to the third floor as a loud explosion brought down the entryway. Micah and a handful of Dark Angels were searching empty rooms. They found Sarge laying in the hallway, still gripping the revolver he'd used to end his madness.

"They've checked out," said Micah. "So should we. Now."

Fleeing upward, Rose found the rest of the Dark Angels waiting on the roof for her arrival. An explosion on the ground floor shook the entire hotel. Another blast took leveled the front of the hotel, sending bricks, steel, and glass crashing to the ground. The roof buckled as the building took another direct hit. Smoke and fire burst from several holes in the roof.

Rose ran to the edge of the roof and looked down. Shadowguard had taken up position in the field and, upon seeing the Dark Angels, starting firing. Micah motioned for the team to follow as he ran to the north side of the building and jumped, landing on the far side of a swimming pool. The team followed, springing over the fence, and running toward the highway as the hotel exploded into flames.

The team sprinted along Colorado Avenue toward Manitou Springs. Micah ran to the front of the group and brought them to a halt under the bypass.

"Picasso must have gotten Cadence's team out earlier." Micah's face was covered with soot. "I doubt Pallaton gave him a courtesy call. The Shadowguard weren't there to take prisoners. They opened fire, expecting Cadence and her team to be inside."

"That would be Aldarik," Ginger said. "They'll head to Seven Falls next. Which way, Rose? To the Citadel, or back to Highbrow's camp?"

"We find Cadence," said Rose. "I'm determined to help her. I never should have allowed Highbrow to throw her out." She turned to Micah. "Two werewolves were with Cadence's team. Good chance they returned to the Cliff Dwellings."

Micah looked in the direction they needed to travel. "Then what are we waiting for? Move out!"

Following the highway, the Dark Angels reached the Cliff Dwellings. Explosions sent rocks tumbling down the side of the cliffs, shattering across the drive as they ran through the main gate. Gunfire was heavy. The Shadowguard had Cadence's team pinned down.

"This is our fight as much as the humans," said Rose. "Spread out and kill every Shadowguard you see. Our job is to protect Cadence. Find her and get her out."

With her eyes glowing and fangs extended, Rose led her team into a raging battle.

Cadence's team was positioned at the windows of the tourist building, firing back at Shadowguard on the ridge. Ginger and Rose dropped in behind the vehicles parked in the lot and pushed toward the shop. A figure in a trench coat spotted them, charging until Micah stopped him, ripping the enemy's head from his shoulders. The other Dark Angels joined them as Shadowguard converged, spreading violence across the parking lot. Making a run for the small building, Rose jumped onto the roof and screamed as it collapsed under her. She fell through shelves and displays as she crashed to the floor.

Rose picked herself up as a Black Hawk lifted from behind a ridge. Machinegun fire raked across the front of the store, setting fire to flammable goods and cutting a path through the building. Rose saw familiar faces as Cadence was with Loki, returning fire at the chopper. Freeborn was at the back of the store helping the team escape through a hole in the roof. Thor sat dazed in the center of the room amongst a pile of rubble. Rose grabbed his hand, pulling him to his feet as a section of roof fell, cutting her off from Cadence and Loki.

Rose saw the chopper release a missile aimed at the building and she felt a muscular arm encircle her body. Thor jumped with her in tow, landing on the roof and sailing over the side of the cliff as the building exploded. On the opposite side of the cliff, another explosion shook the ground and loosed an avalanche of rocks. Rose and Thor escaped the falling rocks and ran to the highway.

"We've got to get out of here," said Thor. "Picasso and Lachlan took off for the Citadel. I'm not sure who else went with them. The Shadowguard caught us by surprise. The only place to go was into the store."

A barrage of explosions ignited the night sky like fireworks. Freeborn, Smack and Lotus joined them as another figure slid down the side of the cliff, trailed by two furry bodies. Phoenix picked herself up from a pile of rocks, cut and dazed, and hobbled over to the team. Two werewolves remained by her side. Artillery fire from the far side of the cliff continued, and Rose knew none of the Dark Angels, nor any more of Cadence's team, were coming.

Rose felt sick and lost. Her confidence was shot and she turned to Thor. "What do you want to do? The Shadowguard attacked the hotel and I'm sure they hit Seven Falls. Pallaton didn't give us much warning."

"We get the hell out of here," he said, "lick our wounds, and regroup."

"But we left Cadence behind." Freeborn took a step toward the cliffs. "She took a bullet in the chest. Loki went to help her, but they shot him too. I don't know what happened to anyone else."

Thor addressed one of the wolves. "This is your turf, Moon Dog. Is there a safe place for us to go? Somewhere Pallaton wouldn't think to look."

The wolf morphed into human form and, bleeding from several wounds, he pointed north. "We could go to the tribe's new camp at the Cave of the Winds. Chayton will give us shelter."

"Not without my girls," said Lotus, her voice cracking.

Phoenix stepped forward and drew her revolver. "I'll go back with you," she said. "They've got Xena."

"No!" Moon Dog stepped in front of the tall Amazon. "You will not go back. I will not let you sacrifice yourself, Phoenix. We go the caves. Please. There's nothing we can do to help your friends right now."

"You're right," said Phoenix. "It would be suicide to go back."

"We may draw attention to your tribe," said Rose. "Isn't there somewhere else we can go? Somewhere in the mountains? A lodge or a house?"

Moon Dog gave Rose a sharp look. "Pallaton won't attack his brother. Pallaton is many things, but he won't attack the tribe. He would never harm Grandmother. She's the only person Pallaton truly loves. While she is alive, Pallaton will not bring the Shadowguard to Chayton's camp. We'll be safe there."

Thor motioned the group forward. "Let's move out, people."

Moon Dog morphed once more and ran north. A rumble and the chopping of air revealed a helicopter looming over the cliff. Its search lights hit the road as it flew south, toward Seven Falls. Rose and the group crossed the highway and took refuge inside a bus as three more choppers flew overhead.

"We'll wait here to make sure no more choppers are coming," said Thor. "Is everyone all right?"

When everyone took a seat, Thor closed the doors and crouched as a small herd of zombies walked by the bus, attracted by the noise and lights at the Cliff Dwellings. Thor was quiet as he moved through the bus aisle, checking on each teammate. Satisfied everyone was safe, Thor returned to Smack and slid in next to her. Everyone watched the zombies stumble toward the Cliff Dwellings.

"I'm worried about Seven Falls," said Rose.

"They're equipped for an assault. I'm not worried about Highbrow, and he sure the hell wasn't worried about us," said Thor. Smack pressed against him. He held her in his arms, letting her cry against his chest. "Highbrow is the one who sent us away. He weakened our forces and it's his fault Cadence is dead."

"We don't know Cadence is dead," Rose said, refusing to lose hope. "Thor, I was told you were shot several times and yet you survived. I have every reason to believe Cadence will too. I have to believe that we'll see her again."

Thor stood and pulled Smack up with him. "We survived," he said. "You can be sure we killed quite a few Shadowguard. The Kaiser is going to learn we're hard to kill." He gave Rose a broad smile. "Thanks for coming back for us, Doc. I didn't expect to see you again, but it's nice to know you care."

As the team filed out of the bus, Rose glanced over her shoulder.

No one had said anything, but they had all smelled death. The skeletons of numerous children lay over one another in the back seat of the school bus. With a heavy heart, she exited the bus and caught up with the group.

Chapter Twenty-Four

The Kaiser was hosting a private dinner party. Only the vampire lords, their mistresses, and a few celebrity fighters attended. Dragon sat quiet at a candlelit table, while a stringed quartet played. Attendants served each course on silver dishes. Dragon was served roasted chicken, mashed potatoes with gravy, corn on the cob, and white wine. Dragon was the only human champion present. Though he hadn't been tested in the arena, the vampires acted like he had earned his title in blood.

"You're not eating," said the Kaiser. "Is the food not to your liking?"

Dragon looked up. "I apologize. I don't feel very well." Though, it was his dinner companions that were not to his liking.

"Take your wine and retire to the bar," said the Kaiser, using his deep, baritone voice. He glanced at Salvatore D'Aquilla. "Seeing your fighters has probably caused Dragon to lose his appetite. Tell me more about the Spaniard."

Excusing himself from the dining room, Dragon found guards waiting for him in the lobby. *So much for making a grand escape*, Dragon thought as he handed his wine glass to a guard. The guards led him to an alumni room where football fans once gathered to enjoy highlights and socialize. More guards were seated inside. Dragon considered disarming one and killing the rest, but until he was able to rescue Star, he didn't want to leave the Citadel. She hadn't come to dinner with Aldarik, and Pallaton wasn't at the party either, leaving Dragon to suspect both officers were on a mission.

Taking a seat, Dragon noticed all of the guards were watching the Death Games. He looked around the room, noticing a pool table and a few arcade games in the back. Dragon rose and walked to a pinball machine, and as he launched a silver ball into the game, he noticed a shadow in the hallway. Whisper stood there, dressed as a Shadowguard.

"I need to go to the bathroom," said Dragon, loosening his bowtie.

A tap on Dragon's shoulder turned him around, and a Shadowguard reared back and punched Dragon in the nose. He slammed into the pinball machine, holding his bleeding nose.

"What's that for?" said Dragon. "I don't know you."

"You killed my brother." The guard wiped his hand on his jacket. "I owed you one. Glad to see you can bleed." The other guards started laughing.

Walking to the bathroom, Dragon pinched his nostrils together. As the door closed behind him he noticed a window was open, letting in snow and cold wind.

"You in here, Whisper?"

Blaze stepped out of a stall, followed by Whisper. Seeing Dragon's nose, she grabbed a paper towel and tried to help stop the flow. The bleeding wouldn't stop, so Whisper grabbed towels and shoved one into each of Dragon's nostrils. Whisper and Blaze were covered in Dragon's blood.

Dragon tilted his head back, trying to stop the bleeding, and detected the faint odor of vanilla.

"What are you two doing here?" asked Dragon. "Is this a rescue?"

"That's the idea," Whisper said. "They've got the Elite and the other soldiers in the music hall. We can free Uther and his buddies and get out of here. Sound good?"

Dragon measured the risks as he stared at the door. He wanted to see Freeborn more than anything. "I can't leave without Star," he said.

"Raven is a vampire, and she's enjoying her new life, but it's hard on Star. Aldarik has her locked in his room, which changes every night, so I'm not sure where she's kept from one day to the next."

"Then let's go find her." Whisper stole a look out the window. "We've waited all day for a chance to talk to you. Most of the Shadowguard left about two hours ago, so we think they went on another raid. If you're going to escape, it's now or never."

Blaze joined Whisper. "Come with us."

"I have a better idea," said Dragon. "The games start tomorrow at 8:00 p.m. Pallaton gave me a tour of the place, and they keep zombies in pens beneath the stadium. The human and vampire fighters will be taken to locker rooms, and they will put the humans in the visitor's locker room. My idea is that you let the zombies out of their pens and open every door marked with a red X. That's where they keep the cyborg zombies."

Whisper looked at Blaze. "You game to try?" She nodded.

"If you go down to the sewer, there's a manhole that opens up under the stadium," said Dragon. "Just before the show starts, let the zombies out. They'll be hungry, so be careful. Don't try to save anyone, just create the diversion. I'll get Star and meet you back at Seven Falls."

Blaze climbed out the window and onto the ledge. Whisper followed behind her. Dragon watched them lower into a drainpipe and vanish. He shut the window as footsteps approached, running through the hall. Dragon sped into a stall and flushed as the door opened.

"Salustra is asking for you," said a guard, impatient.

Dragon emerged from the stall, pulling the wadded towels out of his nostrils. He watched the guards in the mirror as he washed his face and hands. His nose had stopped bleeding, and as he wiped his hands, he spotted the bloody towels he used earlier in the sink next to him. So did the guards. One of them walked to the sink, grinning, and shoved them in his mouth.

"Yum, yum, love me some prisoner blood . . ." said the guard as he attempted to drain the towel of blood. His eyes went wide, and a moment later, he dropped dead.

"What the hell?" Dragon stepped back as the remaining vampire took aim. "Hey, this isn't my fault. The freak wanted to eat my blood and he choked on a paper towel. Paper is not on your diet, is it?"

The guard looked at his dead cohort, a gleam of fear mixed with anger in his eyes. "It has to be poison. You poisoned him! What was on that towel? Did Dr. Leopold slip you something to test on us?"

Dragon knelt over the corpse, feeling for a pulse. He felt nothing. "He's dead," said Dragon. "Maybe there's poison in the coffee. Might even be on your cups."

Dragon knew he had started to change after being exposed to Cadence's blood, but he hadn't realized his blood was toxic to vampires. He thought of Freeborn. She had been given a full dose of Cadence's blood. She could be cured and waiting for his return.

Dragon headed back to the alumni room, as the guard began shouting for help. Guards ran past him and rushed into the bathroom.

"What's going on?" said Salustra, standing in the door to the dining room.

"Some guard choked on paper towels." Dragon took Salustra by the hand, trying not to act nervous, and placed it on his arm. "Do we have time to catch a movie or would you rather go to the casino? I feel a lot better."

Guards were racing through every hall and Dragon escorted Salustra into the dining room, remaining calm. The Kaiser and Raven were rising from the table, and Dragon saw that Star had been brought in. Raven was delirious, playing with her excessive jewelry, as Star slumped over the table, weak and heavily medicated.

"Where is Aldarik?" asked Dragon. He was relieved to see Star alive, but furious they were keeping her drugged.

"He's in the hallway. He and Pallaton were on a mission together."

Salustra gestured toward the exit, anxious to leave. "Shall we go, my dear?"

"If I may, give me a moment to check on Star."

Salustra moved to admire Raven's diamonds and Dragon hurried to Star. Lifting her head, he checked for bite marks and didn't find any. If he was right, Cadence's blood carried a new strain of the virus, which had been passed to him. Maybe his blood would give Star the abilities he now possessed. If Aldarik attempted to turn her, it would kill him. Being sure no one was watching, Dragon sliced his finger with a steak knife. He pulled back Star's lip and wiped his finger across her gums. She licked her lips and let out a sleepy sigh.

Aldarik stormed into the room, enraged to see Dragon standing over his property. Aldarik raced to her side and as he tried sitting her up, Star's eyes opened wide and her pupil's dilated extreme. She pushed Aldarik with a weak shove and slumped to the table again.

"A guard is dead!" Aldarik pointed at Dragon. "How did you kill him, slave? Did Heston or Leopold put you up to this?"

"I don't know what you're talking about," Dragon retorted. Aldarik flashed his fangs and Dragon feigned disinterest, turning to Raven. "Nice necklace, Raven. Really matches your heart." The Kaiser and Raven smiled and gestured appreciation for his comment.

Aldarik sped toward Dragon, furious, so Dragon took a swift, yet subtle, step away from the incoming threat. Aldarik stumbled and ran into a chair. Snarling, he threw the chair over the table and wielded a knife toward Dragon.

Dragon took a terrified Salustra on his arm and turned to leave. He sensed Aldarik advancing toward them, and spun Salustra in his arms, moving in a dance of grace and speed through the exit. Guards met them as they entered the hallway, forcing them back into the dining hall.

"You killed my guard," threatened Aldarik. He raised his weapon and aimed at Dragon. "Now, I'm going to kill you."

The evening's guests had filtered back into the dining room, amused, watching the spectacle. Salvatore D'Aquilla took one look at the situation and laughed. A cruel smile appeared on Aldarik's face as he pulled the trigger. Dragon pushed Salustra aside, and dropped to the ground as the bullet struck a guard standing behind him. Dragon jumped and kicked the pistol out of Aldarik's grasp, catching it in mid-air. Guards were slow in reacting and Dragon held aim at Aldarik's head before they could apprehend him.

"Tell your men to lower their weapons or you're dead," said Dragon.

Aldarik looked nervous. "You're bluffing. You don't have the guts."

Dragon pulled the trigger and severed Aldarik's ear from his head. Aldarik cried out, grasping the side of his head, blood gushing between his fingers. Dragon maintained his aim, considering whether he should shoot off the other ear or retreat with his guardian. The Kaiser began clapping, and Raven let out a boisterous laugh. Everyone in the dining hall joined the Kaiser's applause.

"Bravo," said D'Aquilla. "Give them swords and let's have a duel. What do you say, Kaiser?"

"A moment, please," said the Kaiser. "Lieutenant Aldarik, are you fighting over a human? If I didn't know better, I would think Star has arranged for your death. I warned you she was dangerous."

"My lord, it's a misunderstanding," said Salustra. "Lord D'Aquilla, I'm sure a duel would be in bad taste. We were going to the casino. Care to join us?"

"Perhaps later, my dear," said D'Aquilla. "While you are lovely as always and it is difficult to deny your company, I want to see the Kaiser's champion fight Master Dragon."

Raven leaned in to the Kaiser, caressing his hand. "What shall we do with these two warriors, my darling? I want to see more blood. I want them to fight."

"If you want a show, then a show you shall have," said the Kaiser.

"Let's move into the banquet hall. The fighters may choose their own swords."

The guests filed out of the dining room, through the hallway and into the larger banquet hall. The guards cleared the center of the room as guests took seats lining the outer walls of the hall. A guard dragged Star in and dropped her on the floor at Raven's feet. Aldarik and Dragon both followed Star's movements, inciting laughter from the Kaiser.

"Place your bets, gentlemen," called Raven. "The winner fights Aries."

"A fine suggestion," said Mr. Rafferty. The robust vampire lord of Los Angeles sat beside D'Aquilla. "I'll take Aldarik. And you, Salvatore? Will you fancy a gamble on Dragon? The odds are not in his favor. What human could beat a vampire?"

"I'll take the human," D'Aquilla called out. He seated his mistresses and moved to sit, and flirt, with Salustra on the front row.

Aldarik threw his coat to the ground. With a bow to the Kaiser, he walked to a rack of swords on the far wall. His eyes set upon a Prussian saber with a Damascus blade and a ruby-studded lion's head pommel. Swords covered the wall from all nations and time periods. Aldarik swung the blade over his head, flashing a sadistic grin and gaining the approval of the female vampires.

Under intense scrutiny, Dragon moved to choose his weapon. He noticed many of the swords were museum pieces, and others still, replicas. One sword held his gaze: a Japanese *nodachi*, boasting an elaborate ivory-carved hilt. He negotiated the long blade through a partial kata to test his grip. It was cumbersome, but he was confident. He felt the spirit of the blade speaking to his own, and knew he held a warrior's history in his hands. Looking up, he saw several golden spirits shimmering behind the audience. Dragon took his place at the center of the makeshift arena and bowed to the Kaiser, then to Raven.

"In my spare time, I have collected some of the world's most famous blades. This is an interesting choice, Master Dragon," said the

Kaiser. "You certainly know your history, or, at least, a well-fashioned blade." He turned to Raven. "Go ahead, my dear."

"To the death," Raven shouted. "Fight!"

Every nerve in his body roared to life like a fire, and Dragon set himself in fighting position. Aldarik circled like a tiger, tossing the heavy Prussian sword between hands.

Vampires chanted, "*Blood. Blood. Blood . . .*"

Raising the saber overhead, Aldarik gave a shout and attacked. Dragon deflected blow after blow as they thrust against him. Finding an opportunity, he swung his blade in a wide arc. Aldarik ducked as the long sword swept over his head. The crowd erupted as Aldarik lunged. Dragon stepped, parried, and sliced Aldarik's back, shoulder to shoulder.

"You'll pay for that," shouted Aldarik.

Dragon prepared to take another swipe as Aldarik charged. Dragon brought his sword upward to block. The blow created an opening and left Aldarik unprotected. The tip of Dragon's blade pierced Aldarik's right shoulder and dissected his flesh. Stumbling backward, Aldarik switched and attacked with his left, chopping and hacking like a butcher. Dragon stepped, avoiding or blocking each attack. Aldarik brought a heavy overhand swing. Dragon side-stepped into a traditional low stance, turned and angled his strike upward. Aldarik's face halved and slid from his neck, spraying his life from exposed arteries. He fell to his knees as his saber clattered to the ground.

The crowd hushed in disbelief. Dragon stood over his opponent and Aldarik gaped at him, shocked and paralyzed with pain. Dragon pulled his sword back and thrust it through Aldarik's heart. Releasing the hilt, Dragon turned to face the Kaiser as Aldarik fell to his side. A crescendo of applause rose from the crowd. Raven stood and approached Dragon.

"Master Dragon will fight Aries of Athens tomorrow night!" sending the guests into ravenous cheers. Raven gave Dragon a hard look.

"I'm sorry it has to be this way. Good luck tomorrow, Dragon. You're going to need it." She returned to her seat and placed her hand on Star's head. "With Aldarik dead, I claim Star as my property."

Dragon stared at the crowd as they dispersed. The golden spirits among the departing guests nodded at Dragon and faded from his vision. As their glimmer faded, he spotted a large, winged shadow shift on the wall. No one else seemed to notice it. The Kaiser, D'Aquilla, and Mr. Rafferty approached him.

"Something is different about you, Master Dragon," said the Kaiser. "I don't know how you defeated Aldarik, but I'm going to find out."

"Fine entertainment, Kaiser. I look forward to tomorrow night," said Mr. Rafferty. He gave Dragon a nervous nod and hurried out.

Salvatore D'Aquilla lowered a thoughtful gaze toward Dragon. "It would take a superhuman to defeat Aries, and perhaps that is what you are. No ordinary human could defeat a vampire, after all."

The Kaiser ushered Raven out of the room, followed by her newly acquired slave. The majority of the guards and Salustra remained in the banquet hall. Dragon stood over the body of Aldarik and pulled the Japanese blade from his body. Wiping the blood clean, he carried the ancient sword to the rack and replaced it, bowing in respect. Salustra met Dragon at the door.

"Thank you for killing that monster," said Salustra. "A few months ago, I tried to escape Denver with my offspring, the Dark Angels. Aldarik killed most of them before he caught me. Rose, Tandor, Picasso and many others escaped, thanks to Pallaton. Rose united them and gave them purpose. I never understood her overwhelming desire to help humans, until I met you," she admitted. "I suppose the Kaiser thought I was more useful alive than dead. I know it's hard for you to trust our kind, but know I am a prisoner, like you."

Dragon suspected Salustra had made most of the Dark Angels. There was no guile or pretense about her, and he believed she was telling the truth. As they walked out of the banquet hall, the hairs on the back of his neck stood. Something dark and evil followed them. He spotted the dark shadow again, moving across the wall.

"You see it, don't you?" said Salustra, holding onto Dragon's arm.

He nodded. "I see it. But what is it?"

Guards opened the doors to her bedroom as they approached. Salustra flipped on the lights and scanned the room, expecting to see the winged creature. Dragon closed the door and she threw herself at him, a look of terror seized her face.

"I can't put words to it," said Salustra, "but I often see it moving through the halls, even when its master is not around." She pressed a hand over her heart. "The Kaiser isn't like the rest of us, nor is he a Maker as he claims to be. He can shift his appearance, much like the voices he uses. I don't know his real name, but I have seen his true form. Believe me when I say, Dragon, that the Kaiser is no mere vampire. He is a demon."

Chapter Twenty-Five

Pushing the manhole cover aside, Blaze surfaced in the ladies' restroom. A flurry of vampires, dressed to seduce, stood at the mirrors freshening their makeup and perfumes, and consuming potent mixtures of infused blood shots. A clock on the wall read 7:50 p.m. Blaze's coat was wrinkled and covered with refuse after spending an entire night and day in the sewer.

"Drug bust! Show the goods, ladies," yelled Blaze, as she emerged from the hatch. "Pallaton reported substance abuse here, and I don't think that's allowed, is it?"

The mention of illegal substances caused the women to scramble. Whisper came up behind Blaze, sliding the manhole cover back into place. Femme fatales fled the bathroom, as two more bolted from a stall, rearranging their clothes. One of the escaping vampires tossed Whisper a pack of cigarettes as an attempted payment for his silence. Whisper and Blaze shared a chuckle.

Blaze felt different since she had seen Dragon, as did Whisper. Both teens were experiencing new sensations and increases in speed and strength.

Dragon was displaying the same changes. Whisper had filled Blaze in on Dragon's feats since being captured, and they had both handled his blood when helping him earlier. Their only guess was they had ingested his blood by accident, or it had seeped into a cut or wound on their hands, and become . . . whatever he was.

Unable to contain her impulses, Blaze pulled Whisper to her and kissed him. The scents of perfume, vanilla, and fresh blood hung thick in the air. Whisper pulled away, smiling, and peered out.

"This is perfect," said Whisper. "It's like a carnival out there. It shouldn't be hard to mix in." A group of young vampires walked by in Halloween costumes, drinking and laughing. "Come on, Blaze. Let's mingle!"

Whisper shed his coat, slipping his rifle to his back, and stepped into the crowd. He snatched a feathered boa from a young girl's shoulders and wrapped it around his neck, as another partygoer plopped an oversized leprechaun hat on his head. Blaze stayed close behind Whisper as they moved with the crowd. Blaze felt a firm hand rest on the back of her neck. She didn't turn around, but knew it was Pallaton.

Every alarm inside of her rang fierce. Blaze reached for Whisper's hand, but he was too far into the crowd. The stranger's hand remained firm as she sensed him drawing close to her. As they walked into the stadium, balloons and confetti fell from the air, and a live band sent the raucous crowd into a frenzy from the center of the arena. Search lights streaked and strobe lights pulsed to the beat of the music. People were intoxicated with the electric atmosphere that swayed and throbbed around them. The Kaiser's festival was in full swing.

"You're in the wrong place," said Pallaton, whispering in her ear. "Come with me, both of you. We're getting out of here." His hand lowered, sliding to her shoulder and sending a shiver down her spine. "I have looked everywhere for you since you disappeared. I never expected to find you here."

"We've been hiding," said Blaze. "Are you turning us in?"

Pallaton took Blaze by the arm and managed to catch up with Whisper, guiding them both through the crowd and into a long hallway, ending in a separate area partitioned by a steel fence. Tour groups were being led along a red carpet, pausing to admire the zombies held within a second fence.

"Last night the Kaiser ordered three attacks," said Pallaton. "One at Seven Falls against Highbrow, another against the Dark Angels at their hotel, and one at the Cliff Dwellings where Cadence took her new team of mutants. I personally led the attack on the Cliff Dwellings and managed to capture most your friends, including Cadence."

"She's here? Cadence is here?" asked Blaze, excited to hear the news.

Pallaton nodded and offered a sad smile. "She is here. I've released Tandor and he'll arrange to free your friends and get your commander out of here. However, they need a diversion. That's where you and Whisper come in. Open the doors to the zombie pens and go straight to the main campus courtyard. Tandor will be waiting at the chopper. It's all arranged."

The urge to hug Pallaton brought Blaze to her tiptoes. The vampire caught her by the shoulders, forcing her to stare at the zombies. Their former Captain and a group of Freedom Army soldiers were in the pen. The Captain watched Blaze with unsettling, gray eyes as though he recognized her.

"One more thing," said Pallaton. "I confiscated several vials of Cadence's blood from the Dark Angels, which I used to lace the fighters' protein shakes this morning. Many human fighters are as strong as you or Dragon now, and hopefully will give the Shadowguard a bit of trouble."

"Why are you doing this?" asked Blaze, turning to face her former guardian. "I thought you were a bad guy."

"Not this evening," said Pallaton. "Besides, I owe my brother a favor, so let's leave it at that. Good luck you two. I must rejoin the Kaiser in his private box, lest he come looking for me."

Blaze blinked and Pallaton was gone. She spotted Whisper in his leprechaun hat working his way through the tour group. While the tour guide explained which city the zombies had been captured in, Whisper lifted the latch and opened the gate to the first pen. Blaze sped around, aware the Captain was watching her, and reached the second pen. She opened the gate and disappeared among the vampires, working her way to Whisper who was busy fending off a flirtatious vampire. Slipping past Whisper, Blaze unlocked the third door before returning to rescue him. The vampire pouted when Blaze pulled Whisper away. Blaze pulled him past the first pen and let out a loud whistle. They both saw the Captain lift his head and notice the open gate.

"We've got to go," said Blaze, tugging on Whisper.

With a loud snarl, the Captain pushed through the gate and led the zombies out of the first pen. The door to the second pen opened and more zombies streamed out, plodding for the vampires. Blaze heard a vampire being pulled down by a pack of zombies as confusion and terror ripped through the crowd. Blaze and Whisper arrived in a dim hallway with doors, all painted with a red *X*. They opened each door as they raced toward the exit. Growls and moans could be heard rumbling behind them as vampires fled screaming. They kept running until they reached the exit, blasting through, exposing the night sky and a light layer of snow on the ground.

They reached the main campus and ducked behind some bushes at the sound of vehicles rumbling near. A company of Shadowguard followed the vehicles, fanning out as the vehicles stopped. The back of the truck opened and a mass of human and vampire prisoners jumped out and started walking toward the arena.

"Let's get a better view," said Whisper. He pulled at Blaze's arm and pointed at a water tower that stood close to the stadium.

With a running jump, Whisper leapt and landed on the tower's platform. Blaze took a step back, jumped, and propelled herself upward. She suppressed her laughter as she flew through the air, landing beside Whisper.

"Did you see what I just did? I bet I could jump even higher!"

"Sh!" Whisper knelt down and peered through the scope of his rifle. "Pallaton was right. Those are our people down there, but they're being taken to fight, not released. I don't see Tandor."

Blaze saw the Black Hawk in a large field beside three smaller choppers. Shadowguard stood guard at each one, but she didn't see Tandor. A line of prisoners were marched past the helicopters, and even with burned clothes and bloody faces, Blaze was able to identify Cadence, Xena, Loki, Dodger, Monkey, and Cricket. A red werewolf and three werepumas trotted behind them wearing collars secured by vampire guards. A group of Dark Angels followed behind them. More Shadowguard came from every direction and fell in formation beside the prisoners, escorting them toward the stadium.

"I see Cadence," said Whisper. "She doesn't look good."

"Where is Tandor? He's supposed to be waiting for us."

Screams from the football stadium caught their attention. Their diversion had worked. Costumed vampires rushed toward the fence, screaming and pursued by a horde of zombies. Vampires leapt the fence and crossed the parking lot, but even more were trapped inside the fence that circled the stadium. As the vampires tried to climb the fence, it collapsed under their weight and the hungry zombies pressed forward. Gunfire erupted as the Shadowguard attempted to stave the tide of zombies.

Blaze saw Tandor, Lachlan, and Picasso emerge from a nearby building. They fired on the Shadowguard and the prisoners ran toward them, all racing toward the Black Hawk.

Blaze and Whisper jumped, running as they landed. They joined the assault on the Shadowguard as they darted to meet the rescue party. A werepuma dashed in front of them, taking a Shadowguard.

"Cadence!" shouted Blaze.

The commander saw Blaze and pointed to the Black Hawk. The propellers tossed up a cloud of dust as they began to whirl. Blaze and Whisper rushed to the commander, running with her to the chopper, and pursued by Shadowguard. A vampire guard reached out for Cadence as he moved to within striking distance. Rafe appeared from nowhere and tackled the Shadowguard, intercepting his attempt. Guards moved in and surrounded Rafe, while Blaze, Whisper, Cadence and the Dark Angels reached the helicopter.

Blaze scrambled on board and helped Cadence inside. Whisper jumped in and made space as the Dark Angels followed him. As the chopper began to lift, Blaze caught sight of a red werewolf and four werepumas circling beneath the rising aircraft. At the approach of Shadowguard and cyborg zombies, they sped across the courtyard, passing Loki and Xena who were trapped in a net. Blaze lost sight of her friends as Lachlan slammed the door. The chopper made a quick exit and flew south.

"That's all that's coming," said Lachlan. He sat next to Whisper and met Blaze's horrified stare. "I'm sorry more didn't make it out, Blaze. We did our best."

Blaze spotted Picasso at the controls with Tandor. Micah and Ginger were seated opposite of Whisper, with Cadence and four more Dark Angels on her side. The commander's coat and clothing were ripped and covered with holes. Blood covered Cadence's chest and hands, and patches of burned skin could be seen on her face and neck. Blaze knew the commander would not have lasted in the arena in her current condition. She looked out the window as the chopper flew over the campus, toward the mountains. Guilt set in deep.

"Dragon didn't get Star out," said Blaze. She glanced at Cadence. "We left quite a few people behind. We'll have to go back for them as soon as we can."

"I know," said Cadence. "It's a miracle any of us made it out. You timed things perfectly, Lachlan. I don't know how you guys orchestrated this, but you did a good job."

Blaze spoke up. "It was Pallaton," she said. "He's the one who arranged for the diversion at the stadium. Whisper and I let out the zombies, but we wouldn't have escaped the Citadel if Tandor didn't make it to the chopper."

"There are other Chameleons," said Lachlan. "I saw them. Pallaton must have given Cadence's blood to the human prisoners."

Blaze cocked a pierced eyebrow. "Chameleons?"

"I'll explain later," said Cadence.

"The ones I saw fighting against the Shadowguard were strong, but they're outnumbered and untrained. I doubt any of them will get far, but we threw a dent in the Kaiser's plans."

"Rafe sacrificed his freedom to save me," said Cadence, sounding bitter. "Kirin is dead. I saw her go down during the assault at the Cliff Dwellings." She touched Blaze's arm. "I know you are grateful Pallaton helped you get out, but he's the one who led the attack. I blame him for Kirin's death."

"Pallaton was my guardian," said Blaze. "He's the only reason I'm still alive. It's not his fault Kirin died. He had to lead the attack and maintain his cover. He's on our side." Not up for arguing, she leaned against Cadence. "It'll be good to get back to camp."

"We're not going back," said Cadence. "Highbrow threw me out. He threw out anyone who took my blood, including Freeborn and Thor—again, I'll explain later. We're headed to Chief Chayton's new camp but we'll only stay for the night, and then move out in the morning. I'll find someplace safe for us, where we can regroup and recover."

A hundred questions tore at Blaze's mind. Cadence looked too tired to question, and Blaze was certain her friend was hurting over being exiled. It was hard to imagine Highbrow could ever separate himself from Cadence. She wondered what exactly had happened while they were at the Citadel.

"I'm glad we have a place to go," said Blaze, leaving it at that. She looked at Whisper to get his reaction about Highbrow, but he was out. It was the first time he'd slept in days.

Whatever happened now, Blaze had faith that Cadence would sort things out. She'd reorganize their team and find a new place for them to call home. She felt everything was going to work out as long as they stayed together and didn't lose hope.

Thor watched a chopper fly overhead and drop down to land in the parking lot. Rose stood beside him as he walked out of the Cave of the Winds. Several werewolves trotted out of the cave, along with Chief Chayton, who was dressed for winter. A side door opened and Lachlan peered out.

"I guess that's your cue to leave, Doc," said Thor. "I don't know why you and the Dark Angels want to return to Seven Falls, but I'm glad you showed up when you did. We wouldn't have made it if you guys hadn't shown up, and for that, you have my gratitude. Highbrow isn't going to change, so don't expect him to welcome you back with open arms. You're infected like the rest of us. There will always be a side of him that doesn't trust you, no matter what you do."

"I have to go back, Thor," said Rose. "The Dark Angels are sworn to protect all humans. It's up to you to take care of your team. Cadence is going to need you now more than ever." She patted him on the shoulder. "We'll be in touch. You can count on it."

Keeping her head down, Rose ran to the chopper as Cadence, Blaze, Whisper, and Lachlan climbed out. The doctor shook hands with Cadence before climbing inside to join the Dark Angels. The chopper whirled away and the small group ran to their friends.

"Thank God you're all alive," said Thor. He had hoped to see Star among the survivors. His heart plummeted. "Is this all that made out?"

Cadence nodded. "A few more might have escaped on foot," she said. "Picasso and Tandor will join us here later. I know you expected us to return with Star, but it just wasn't possible. We'll go back to the Citadel for another rescue, but first, we need time to rest and plan."

Snow began to fall, pushed along by a frigid northeastern breeze, and Freeborn threw a blanket around Cadence's shoulders.

"The storm is going to get worse," said Freeborn. "Come in out of the cold."

Cadence shuffled forward. Her injuries were healing, but her spirit had been shaken. She put a hand on Thor's shoulder. "We will save them."

Even after being exiled by her second-in-command, being captured, and losing several of her friends, Cadence's eyes burned with the will to fight. Thor nodded, knowing she wouldn't crumble after this defeat.

He remained outside as Freeborn escorted Lachlan and Cadence into the cave. Left alone, Thor turned his thoughts toward the Citadel, and toward Star. He gazed up into the vastness of the night sky, searching for answers. Somehow they would find a way to defeat the Kaiser and his Shadowguard and bring their friends home . . . wherever home was.

The fight for survival had just begun.

About The Author

Susanne L. Lambdin is the author of the *Dead Hearts* series of novels. A "trekkie" at heart, she received a "based in part" screen credit for writing a portion of *Star Trek: The Next Generation*: Season 4, Episode 76, titled *Family*. She is passionate about all things science fiction, horror, and high fantasy. Susanne is an expert on the subject of zombies, and is affectionately known by many of her fans as "The Zombie Lady."

She lives in Kansas with her family and two dogs. To contact Susanne and to learn more about her current and upcoming projects, visit www.SusanneLambdin.com.